Praise for Dragon • P

"A dark madcap quest filled with educational (and often bloody) identity crises. The tragicomedy is never deep, but it's plenty of fun." —*Publishers Weekly*

"Swann piles on some inventive mishaps with a lavish hand....Add a nicely unconventional 'happy' ending, and it's a fun romp for fans of funny fantasy." —*Locus*

"An amusing lighthearted quest fantasy ... uses the concept of movies like *Freaky Friday* to tell a fun tale, through the filter of a mediocre thief."

—Genre Go Round

"A plot twist that you really don't see coming.... You can connect with the characters and ultimately understand the decisions they make. *Dragon Princess* is a good story for those who like an adventurous fantasy to enjoy." —Fresh Fiction

"Fun without being fluffy, and entertaining without being inane. It straddles the line between humorous fantasy and some of the darker stuff and does so with style. *Dragon Princess* has wit, action, and hilarity in equal measures and should prove an enjoyable read for those looking for something fast-paced and fun."

—Owlcat Mountain

"The best part of this series—and what makes a truly good humorous story rise above all others—is that there *is* some seriousness behind all of the tongue-in-cheek fun." —Joshua Palmatier, author of *Shattering the Ley*, at SFReader.com

"*Dragon Princess* is full of witty banter, comical situations, irreverent humor, and loads of twisted irony."

—That's What I'm Talking About

Dragon • Wizard

S. Andrew Swann

DAW BOOKS, INC.

DONALD A. WOLLHEIM, FOUNDER

375 Hudson Street, New York, NY 10014

ELIZABETH R. WOLLHEIM
SHEILA E. GILBERT
PUBLISHERS
www.dawbooks.com

For Hazel, because you can be the
princess *and* the dragon.

CHAPTER 1

My name is Frank Blackthorne, and I'm going to tell you a story.

By this point in the chronicle of my ill-advised adventures, I should be able to dispense with the introductory preliminaries aside from the brief necessities of scene-setting.

We begin this chapter of my tale within the Kingdom of Lendowyn, of late slightly less impoverished and much less insignificant from a diplomatic perspective. Being the nominal victor in a multi-front war will do that. More precisely, we begin within the halls of the Northern Palace, recently reclaimed from the Grünwald diplomatic mission while a small army of workers repaired the damage done to Lendowyn Castle from battle, fire, and dragon collision.

We begin exactly three hundred sixty-five days after the end of my first tale—my first wedding anniversary. Which also happens to be the day that everything I'd done to reach that point would finally catch up with me. But, like all the plotting and conspiracy that had dogged me ever since I had first set foot into Princess Lucille's painful royal shoes, it would be a while before I realized it.

And, as an aside, I still inhabited the body of Princess Lucille, despite spending the past six months in an intermittent effort to dislodge myself from it. But no wizard we'd found could offer a solution—at least no wizard the Lendowyn court could afford. Lendowyn might not be completely broke anymore, but King Alfred prioritized the castle repairs before my own issues.

I couldn't really blame him, since I was in large part responsible for the damage.

Even within my budget, some wizards wouldn't take Lendowyn's money when they heard that the Dark Lord Nâtlac had a hand in the enchantment. Others came up with increasingly colorful metaphors as to why it wasn't possible.

I came up with increasingly colorful language in response.

Apparently it was extremely dangerous to move a soul from point A to point B. We had the recent coup and proxy war with Grünwald to show for it. However, it gets worse when there's effectively no point B. Over the past year, my original body had crumbled to dust wrapped around the shriveled soul of Elhared the Unwise.

The kind of magic needed to physically resurrect my body was not something you could buy with gold. It was the kind of thing that usually cost souls to do. And even if we found a way around that, it would still leave the princess's body soulless and probably dead. That was a problem, as no one could tell me what that would do to the "temporary" enchantment that had swapped me and Lucille this last time.

So after a few months I had begun looking into a Plan B. In theory, the physical transformation of the body should be safer and more straightforward. I had talked to a few mages, and had been given a few options. But I'd been hesitating a bit on that option, waiting for a good time to talk to Lucille about it. There were a couple reasons for that. First, you could probably trace the last war's root cause down to my failure to communicate with my draconic spouse. Second, even though she had voluntarily given up this body to me, I still felt as if she had a stake in what happened to it.

However, for some reason, that "good time to talk" hadn't happened yet.

I might be married to her, but the fact she was currently a fifty-foot fire-breathing lizard could still be somewhat intimidating, especially because she enjoyed the role so much. Though, in some sense, I think I may have been intimidated for different reasons than most people around her.

When she said how well she thought I was adjusting . . . I didn't know if that made the discussion more difficult because I'd be disappointing a dragon, or because I'd be disappointing my wife.

Husband.

Fortunately, over the past month or so, I had to put the matter aside because I had a party to plan.

Don't laugh.

Being Princess Frank of Lendowyn meant I had a role to play and duties to perform. This was not something I had any right to complain about, given that one of my main objections after being princessified had been the lack of any substantive responsibilities aside from decorating the court. As a result, I had received an object lesson in being careful what I wish for.

After Lendowyn's last major conflict, King Alfred had seemed to take great pleasure in overworking his "daughter" as punishment for becoming uppity. I had to travel every fortnight or so; diplomatic missions to every kingdom, duchy, principality, and city-state in the surrounding area. I had the dubious pleasure of meeting one-on-one with a fairly representative cross-section of nobility; though such "one-on-one" meetings were usually six-on-ten or ten-on-a-dozen meetings when you counted the retainers and servants, which as a member of the nobility I wasn't supposed to count.

Meeting with these men, and they were *invariably* men, did nothing to moderate my opinion of the upper classes. It also did some serious injury to my opinion of my former gender.

This role had fallen to the prince before the king and his accountants discovered a new income stream. Once peace had fallen, Lendowyn suddenly had an influx of tourists coming across the border in hopes of seeing the Dragon Prince. Keeping the dragon at home encouraged more of these curiosity-seekers—and more importantly, their gold—to cross the border. I represented a bit of extraneous backstory that the king could send on a recurring diplomatic roadshow.

Even while I was on the road, I had been working toward the anniversary festival: a week-long exploitation of my marriage to Lucille designed to transfer a year's worth of taxes, tariffs, and license fees into the Lendowyn treasury all at once. As a one-time professional thief, I couldn't help but find it impressive.

And scary.

Sadistically, King Alfred had decided that as princess it had fallen on my shoulders to plan the anniversary celebration. It went beyond how much ale to import and the proper juggler quota for the influx of celebrants who would mob the capital. That was actually the least of it, since those issues, at least, I could pass off to people who had more of a talent for the organization of such things than I.

My nemesis was the grand banquet, the part of the festival for those of "noble" blood; the same class of individuals who had spent the past five months making my meetings uncomfortable.

Mixing the lot of them together had proven to be a nightmare.

By now I'd been involved in court intrigue long enough to realize that these galas were not just an excuse for the high and mighty to eat and drink themselves into a stupor at the expense of the people they ruled. At least not exclusively.

The festival for the "common" folk was simple enough: the consequences for mixing too much ale with the wrong people would not extend much farther than the distance someone could throw a punch.

However, when a celebration involves the inebriation of the noble caste, it comes with layers of diplomatic intrigue and conspiratorial machinations to go along with it. Organizing that level of entertaining requires awareness of dozens of different parties and their interrelationships. Making the mistake of seating the wrong two counts together could, once alcohol was added, result in a border war to prove some lord's virility that would cost the "common" people a lot more than the price of keeping their rulers inebriated.

While my prior life as a thief gave me some comfort level with the part of diplomacy that involved bald-faced lying to people's faces, it didn't prepare me for the kind of detailed plotting that was required for a kingdom-level function like this to actually, so to speak, function.

Some of the invitees were such a perfect mix of loathsome and tedious that I strongly considered suggesting Lucille add them to the menu as a means to cement Lendowyn's position as a kingdom not to be messed with. I only decided against it because, if our Dragon Prince were to broil and eat the Baron Weslyess of Delarin, it would not quite send the message of peace and amity I was supposed to be aiming for.

When the grand banquet actually arrived I felt a sense of relief. I've always been better at dealing with disasters as they occurred than I've been at anticipating them.

The first half of the day was dominated by the royal couple in the palace courtyard, officially receiving the near-endless stream of "important" visitors. For all my worry, that part went a lot better than I had anticipated. As much as they had underwhelmed me when I'd been abroad, today they seemed to be on their best behavior.

Of course that might have had something to do with my husband, the dragon, curled up next to me.

But even though Lucille seemed to curb their worst impulses, the Baron Weslyess still managed to give me a look that made me want to bathe for a week, then catapult the tub at our enemies.

Lucille may have been the main attraction for the masses, but for some reason, the higher the tourist's status, the more interested they were in *me*. In some cases— such as the Baron Weslyess—the interest was decidedly unsettling.

Whichever of the local royal curiosities had been the main attraction, I could draw some satisfaction from the fact that just the banquet celebrating the one-year anniversary of the marriage of Frank the Princess to Lucille the Dragon beat the record held by King Alfred's coronation ball by a factor of five, something I suspect he was grumpy about. It served him right for sending his "daughter" through a diplomatic gauntlet of grabby counts, dukes, and earls.

The size of the event was the main reason for the venue. Lendowyn Castle couldn't handle this crowd, even when it wasn't under repair.

The reception ceremony took an inordinately long time. As the last of them stepped up to my throne, spent an overlong time kissing my hand, and bowed to the dragon curled behind me, the sun had already passed midday.

I had enough of a sense of diplomacy now that I waited until he had backed the requisite five paces into the courtyard and turned away from us before I wiped the back of my hand on my skirts.

"I need a drink," I whispered through clenched teeth and a fake smile that I had held so long that it felt branded into my face.

"You promised me, and Father, no alcohol." The low dry voice of dragon Lucille was something I felt rather than heard.

Whispering, in that draconic body, had been a skill she had struggled long and hard for. It's an impressive feat if you've ever heard a dragon's normal voice before. The tone ranges typically from teeth-rattling, through bowel-melting, to literal ear-bleeding.

A pair of heralds had stepped out before the assembled crowd to give dramatic readings of the evening's scheduled festivities, so no one else was in a position to understand her.

She was right. I *had* promised. That didn't make me any less crabby about it. "After that line of pompous cretins? I deserve one."

Lucille's voice rumbled deep in her throat, never making it up to her massive toothy skull. I felt it in the back of the throne where her neck wrapped around behind me. *"You talk as if I don't know what that's like."*

I sighed and looked up at her. She cut a majestic profile against the afternoon sky. I might have the throne, but she dominated the courtyard.

"I'm talking like you're the only one who does know what it's like."

The heralds continued with their litany, making up in volume what they sacrificed in comprehensibility.

"I understand how you feel. But getting drunk before the main event is not a great idea."

"Yeah, I know." I'd be the first to admit that I didn't make the best decisions while drunk, but sticking me in a ball gown and a tiara and forcing me to receive every single emissary, diplomat, ambassador, baron, knight, and two-bit lord while completely sober was a punishment disproportionate to any crime I might have committed under the influence ...

Well, maybe aside from accidently triggering a coup and a war with our neighbors Dermonica and Grünwald, but that turned out all right in the end. Sort of.

Maybe I did deserve it.

CHAPTER 2

The grand banquet was lavish by Lendowyn standards, far in excess of our original wedding, which had been a somewhat hurried affair. An army of guests swarmed the great hall, gathering at long tables that had been arranged to focus attention at the end of the hall opposite the main entrance. Normally the massive floor-to-ceiling stained-glass windows were the dominating feature, especially as light from the low evening sun filtered through them.

However, today Lucille dominated that end of the hall. The evening sunset through the glass backlit her ebon scales in a flaming rainbow, casting her shadow across the attendees. For such a large crowd, our guests were atypically quiet.

The effect was worth the effort I'd taken to actually have the Dragon Prince attend the banquet. Back when it was clear that the size of this event would require a change in venue, I had stolen a squad of dwarven engineers from the repair work at Lendowyn Castle to make sure that the massive windows at that end of the hall—the only openings into the keep itself that were large enough to admit my husband—were able to open.

Like we had in the courtyard, I held court next to her, seated on a throne, completely upstaged by her mere existence. I felt gratified being overshadowed. I'd never liked being the center of attention.

Lucille, on the other hand, seemed to bask in it. More than making a full hall's worth of the alleged nobility somewhat nervous, what made my efforts worth it was the obvious pleasure Lucille took from being the focus of terrified fascination.

For what it was worth, the staging of this banquet, beyond the pedestrian diplomacy involved, had been my anniversary present to her. And if the shocked stares upon seeing her inside the palace weren't enough for her, the pyrotechnics as she roasted a half-dozen spits' worth of boar were quite the attention grabber.

When she returned to my side, after her demonstration of apocalyptic cookery, she whispered, *"Reminds you of the first time we ate dinner together, doesn't it?"*

After Elhared's spell had placed us in our current bodies, and as we tried to figure out what to do about it, we'd been stuck camping in the wilderness. Her presence had made up for my own lack of supplies and preparation. It was useful having a campmate who could not only capture a wild boar with ease, but cook it for you.

"Yes, it does," I told her.

She settled back in, curling around my throne to watch our guests. I reached out and placed a hand against her neck, the scales not nearly as hard as they looked, still warm from her display of culinary pyromania. She grumbled deep in her throat and leaned in so I didn't have to reach as far.

About six months ago another magical mishap— entirely my fault that time, I had decided to play with one of the Dark Lord Nâtlac's evil artifacts while drunk—had rendered a brief moment when we had both been human. That might have resulted in something, if it hadn't been for that brink-of-war thing that had occupied our attention at the time.

That's what I told myself.

I wondered what Lucille told herself.

I know she loved being the dragon, as much as anything. Perhaps she didn't need to tell herself stories justifying her actions. Maybe she had no regrets.

Must be nice.

Now that our official welcome was over, as servants moved dragon-fired carcasses from spits to table, the most interminable part of the evening began. Every delegation had the chance to toast the host couple and offer some form of gift.

I have nothing against gifts, in theory. But each presentation was accompanied by the drone of some count or baron talking as if they were the initiate of some monastic cult that, rather than taking vows of silence, chose instead to say nothing using as many words as possible.

As an example, the Baron Weslyess presented a gown incorporating a corset so tortuous in appearance that I suspected that if some unsuspecting woman actually wore it, the event might constitute an act of war. He presented it with a flourish and praised my virtue with a speech so filled with double meanings that it was remarkable that the gods of language did not appear to strike him dumb on the spot.

"I really need that drink," I whispered as he vacated the floor to the next presenter.

"I know."

After a long procession of increasingly inebriated well-wishers, we were finally greeted by someone whose bearing approximated his title. Prince Daemonlas strode forward wearing an outfit with more lace and ruffles than I wore at the moment. As he bowed to us he swept the ground with a heavy fur-lined cape that was anchored across his shoulders by an elaborately embossed gold brooch the size of a dinner plate.

If he wasn't a member of the elf-king's court I would have thought him overdressed.

"Your Highness, Prince and Princess, greetings from the Winter Court. To honor this occasion, I bear words from the court of His Majesty Timoras, lord of all realms under the hill."

"At least he isn't drunk," I muttered.

I felt Lucille's claw flick the back of the throne. *"Shh!"*

"I am here to honor a bond, a pledge between two persons, however different, that must be respected. A bond that must be cherished. A bond that, if broken, must be avenged."

Something about the way he said that made me uneasy. Prince Daemonlas pulled a scroll from within his sleeve and the unease I felt became an overwhelming sense of wrongness.

"Lucille—"

This time her claw flicked the throne hard enough to

move it forward about six inches. The prince looked up at the sound of wood scraping against stone, and I forced my most innocent smile. "Please continue," I told him.

My unease continued unabated as he finished withdrawing the scroll from his sleeve. For a royal communication, the parchment had not traveled well. Dirt and rusty spots dotted the surface and the edges were worn and ragged. For a moment or two the elf-prince stared at the scroll. I couldn't help thinking of the way I tended to hesitate just before I did something stupid and irrevocable.

He sucked in a breath. Then with a deliberate, almost mechanical, motion he broke the wax seal holding the parchment shut. Fragments of ebony-black sealing wax fell to the stone floor at his feet. As the pieces hit the floor, they melted, bubbled, and hissed, boiling into curls of black smoke the way sealing wax never does.

I stood up.

"That's not right." This time I didn't whisper and Lucille didn't prod the throne.

Prince Daemonlas bent over the ragged scroll as it unrolled in his hands. His manner had changed, and something in his crooked body language sent an unpleasant wave of déjà vu through me. He opened his mouth to read the elf-king's message, but the syllables that came from his lips belonged to no elven language. The words came from some language that was not designed for a fleshy throat.

I was pretty sure that I had heard those inhuman syllables before.

"Stop him!" I yelled out as a cracking blue-black glow wrapped the elf. "Lucille!"

Next to me, Lucille reached for Daemonlas, and kept reaching. The movements of her body slowed, and one taloned hand froze in midair, the same blue-black glow cracking along the tips of her claws.

Then Lucille started screaming.

Remember earlier, when I mentioned the upper register of a dragon's voice causing bleeding from the ears? I wasn't exaggerating.

The elf raised a shaking hand in our direction, and I did the only thing I could think of. I rushed him, fist raised, screaming something that may have been, "Not again!"

Everything slowed around me. Daemonlas's lips moved, the unclean syllables somehow an audible drone despite the dragon's agonized screams. I moved between his upraised hand and Lucille, and it felt as if a million little spider knives burrowed through my body. Daemonlas's face shimmered and blurred and I saw glimpses of things that were the visual embodiment of Lucille's scream; eyes and teeth and tongues and tentacles and sights that wanted to slice my eyes and make them bleed. I heard something, a voice or a memory.

"You have made an enemy."

Oh cra—

Before I could even complete the thought, a human avalanche swept me away from Daemonlas, tackling me to the ground. I yelled at the oversize breastplate that pinned me to the ground. "No! Brock! Get! The! Elf!"

I'm certain that my large retainer meant well. He was probably one of the smartest men in the royal court, knew too many languages to list, knew more herbal lore than most people who plied it as a trade, and had the unfortunate fate of looking like a terrifying barbarian warrior. Unfortunate because, smart or not, he didn't have much tactical know-how or martial ability, and in a fight tended to carry himself like a large, confused, near-sighted puppy.

I stopped yelling, because Brock's weight pushed the breath out of me, and there was no way I could make myself audible over the cacophony of dragon screams and demonic chants. I pushed against him, and at least got enough of my meaning across to get him to roll off me.

When my view wasn't blocked by clumsy barbarian, I saw my other retainers converge on Daemonlas, for all the good it did.

The princess's personal guard had good and bad points. They were capable, loyal, and somewhat blood-thirsty. They all shared with me histories as outlaws. They were also, by happenstance, members of a warrior reli-gious order devoted to their martial training—though it was a warrior order devoted to the Goddess Lysea, pa-tron of love, beauty, art, poetry, storytelling, and so on—an order where they were the only members.

They also were all teenage girls.

To be fair to them, Daemonlas cheated by having that evil black-blue aura do his fighting for him while he chanted, hand raised toward an agonized Lucille. I saw Mary, the largest of the girls, charge the elf, aiming for the kidneys. About a foot short of reaching him, she slammed into an invisible wall and an explosion of black lightning threw her back fifteen or twenty feet. Laya hung back and loosed a sling bullet, but the projectile never con-nected with Daemonlas's skull, evaporating in a lightless crackle and a puff of toxic black smoke. Grace swung a sword and came back with a smoldering hilt. The others were just as ineffective in their attacks.

The only person not attacking was arguably the most capable member of the royal guard, Sir Forsythe the Good. By all rights, he should have been the first one into battle. Quite often I've known him to charge in before anyone knew there was a battle. Instead, he knelt down before the possessed elf, his parade armor reflecting the twisted black glow around Daemonlas, leaning on his sword, head bowed.

Praying?

"Forsythe! You idiot! What are you doing!?" I screamed, even though I knew exactly what was happening.

Like my girls, Sir Forsythe had a long and twisted story behind him. It involved both the Goddess Lysea *and* the Dark Lord Nâtlac. The Goddess, somewhat upset about the semisecret Nâtlac cult in the Grünwald royal court desecrating her temple, showed the children of the cult members the full glory of truth, beauty, and goodness, and then cursed them to serve the Dark Lord with a full self-awareness of what they were doing. It was a pretty effective revenge. The cursed children found endlessly creative ways to engage in self-destruction. Sir Forsythe had only survived the internal contradiction by going a little insane. His nickname, "The Good," had been originally meant as an insult by his peers. After a rocky introduction, he had pledged fealty to me after I had defeated the Dark Queen Fiona of Grünwald, largely because I had inadvertently become the High Priestess of the Nâtlac cult.

A role I had given up in such a way that the Dark Lord personally told me, "You have made an enemy." Not a message you ever want to hear from a deity of evil darkness. And what I had seen in Daemonlas, and what I heard from the elf's throat, was clearly Nâtlac.

Whatever earthly pledge had been made by Sir Forsythe to me, his soul was still damned to serve the Dark Lord.

Black lightning crackled across Sir Forsythe's armor. I think I heard his voice say, "Let me serve you."

"What are you doing?" I screamed at him.

The blackness tore at his armor, as if looking for an opening. "Let me serve you!" Sir Forsythe's voice tore through everything. Even Daemonlas's incantation seemed to miss a beat. The dark swirled from the elf to twist around Sir Forsythe like a whirlwind made of torn scraps of the void.

"Let! Me! Serve! You!" Sir Forsythe slowly stood. I heard the creak of his armor and I realized that Lucille had stopped screaming. Under his feet, cracks appeared in the stone floor, leaking the same blackness that swirled around him. His sword rose unsteadily upward.

"Let! Me! Serve! You!"

He's not praying to Nâtlac.

The great windows exploded behind Lucille, scattering shimmering rainbow fragments of glass through the air. Sunlight streamed in from outside, striking Sir Forsythe's sword. The blade reflected with a glow a hundred times brighter than the late sunset light striking it. The shadows tearing at Sir Forsythe vanished before that light.

For the briefest moment I saw a ghost of a woman standing in place of Sir Forsythe. She stood eight feet tall, unbound hair flowing around her otherwise naked body. In both hands she held a golden sword engraved with the images of flowers in such detailed relief they appeared to sprout from the blade.

Then it was Sir Forsythe again, thrusting his own glowing blade. It cut through the air like a goddess laughing, penetrating the elf's black aura to bury itself into Daemonlas's torso.

For a moment the hall was silent except for the sound of stained glass tinkling to the ground.

Then I heard laughing; this time less like a goddess, and more like those glass fragments burrowing into my ears.

The elf lowered his arms and sagged onto the sword, the tattered scroll slipping through his fingers. Daemonlas shook his head and smiled. "Too late."

Daemonlas slid off the sword to collapse on the ground at Sir Forsythe's feet. Sir Forsythe echoed my own thoughts, "Too late?"

A geyser of black and blue lightning erupted from the wound in Daemonlas's chest, throwing Sir Forsythe aside. The twisted spray of lightning shot at Lucille, splintering my throne. When it hit her, I felt it, as if something huge and invisible slammed inside my skull.

I spiraled into darkness as Lucille screamed again.

CHAPTER 3

As I came to, my first coherent thought was, *Not fair . . . I didn't drink anything this time!*

From somewhere, I heard someone yelling.

"What did you do? *What did you do?*"

For a few moments I thought the shouting was directed at me. Given my history, my own inclination was to blame myself for any disaster even though it was difficult to imagine exactly how I could be responsible for this one. As my mind emerged from the painful black fog, I tried to answer the angry person . . .

. . . and realized *I* was the one shouting.

Huh?

Sensation returned to me, and I could feel and hear myself shouting the words. The right side of my rib cage ached where Brock had tackled me, and the ache turned into a dagger in my side when I sucked in the breath to shout again. I smelled smoke and felt dirt in my eyes, and my eyes blinked all by themselves. I stood above the body of Prince Daemonlas, my hands balled into fists in his cape to either side of the bloodstained brooch. I had lifted him up to shout in his unmoving face, and I shook him to emphasize each word.

Fine, I just blacked out and went insane there for a moment.

I tried to remember what had pushed me over the edge like this, and suddenly everything in me screamed, *Lucille!*

That was the cue for me to spin around and look for her and see what happened.

But I couldn't move.

That wasn't exactly right.

I still looked down at the dead elf, I still shook him, and I still demanded to know what it was he'd done.

And that *still* wasn't right.

It wasn't *me* doing any of these things, even though I stared into the elf's dead eyes, felt the blood-tacky fur of his cape sticking to my fists, and felt the hoarse tickle in the back of my throat as I screamed ...

I had no control over *any* of it.

Worse, I smelled smoke and heard pained groans all around me. The dead Prince Daemonlas was the last thing I wanted to focus my attention on.

"He's dead, Your Highness." I felt a gentle hand on my shoulder and someone else turned my head to look up at Mary, the first of my handmaids-slash-bodyguards to have attacked Daemonlas. She had her other arm in a makeshift sling, clutched against her scorched leather armor. Bruised swelling marred the left side of her face. Past her, in the peripheral vision of eyes that refused to move for me, I could see signs of chaos, broken tables, wounded diplomats, and the great windows open on a purple twilight sky ...

And no sign of Lucille.

"Can we track the dragon?" I heard myself say.

"Sir Forsythe dived out the window after her—him—"

"Is Brock . . ."

The way I heard my voice trail off frightened me. *What happened to Brock?*

"Bad, but looks worse than it is."

Someone shook my head without me and my voice lowered to be near inaudible. "Why did he have to . . ."

"Your Highness?" Mary said, "If he didn't, you'd be dead right now."

I watched as my hand rubbed my lowered face by its own volition. "How many people have to hurt themselves saving me?" I heard my voice whisper.

My own brain still spun, disoriented, recovering from the blackout. It sank in. I felt myself breathe, I could see and hear and smell . . .

But it wasn't my body anymore.

I felt my foot kick something that felt suspiciously like an elf corpse. My mouth snapped, "Why?"

Then I spun around, looking at the wreckage of the banquet, *our* banquet, and understood what had happened.

Lucille was home.

Then what am I doing here?

I heard my voice ask Mary, "Why would Frank do this?"

Why would I . . .

"It wasn't Frank, your Highness." Mary pointed at the ex-elf. "It was this guy. Wasn't it?"

"Yes, yes." My head turned to look at the wreckage

and my arm swung out in a gesture encompassing the broken and charred tables and a distressing number of bodies. "His spell pushed me out of my body. But the dragon did all this."

"You don't know *that* was Frank."

No, you don't, I thought.

"Who was it then? And, more importantly, if it wasn't him, where is he?" Lucille turned our body away from Mary and started shouting orders at the ambulatory servants.

I realized I might be in a bit of trouble.

I had to catch up on what had happened based only on snippets of conversation and glimpses of the aftermath as Lucille tried to take control of the situation.

Right after Prince Daemonlas had died, and I'd blacked out, whoever resided in the dragon's body attempted to reprise the boar-roasting scene from earlier with Lucille as the main course; the Lucille resident in my—her—*our* body. Fortunately for us, Brock's combat effectiveness was increased fivefold whenever protecting his princess was involved. Unfortunately for Brock, that still didn't amount to much. He shielded us from a blast of dragon fire using an overturned table. He just didn't manage to do so while on the same side of the table as we were.

He had survived only because he hadn't been the focus of the dragon's fury, and because Sir Forsythe intervened to grab the dragon's attention.

Brock had been bandaged and left seated at the edge of the wreckage. Between the tears in our eyes and

Lucille's tendency to avoid looking directly at him, I didn't get a good look at the extent of his injuries.

She took his unbandaged hand and I heard Brock groan. "Who's there?"

"It's me. It's Lucille."

He groaned again and I don't know if he heard her. "Did Brock save the princess?"

Lucille sniffed and nodded. "Yes. Brock saved the princess." She wiped our eyes and bent over to kiss Brock on the forehead. When I caught a glimpse of his face I wanted to cry myself. The side of his head was scorched and he was missing a good part of his left ear. He looked past us, staring out at nothing. Someone had stripped the armor from his upper body and had bound his left arm completely in bandages that were already becoming discolored.

"Brock is tired."

"The battle's over," she whispered to him. "The princess is safe."

"Brock saved the princess."

"Yes, he did. Rest now."

"Brock needs to rest now."

His groans subsided and his breathing became more regular as he closed his eyes.

Lucille stood and yelled commands at the nearest servants. "You! You! And you! Get this man to a room with a bed. No one leaves him alone!"

A quartet of men responded with "Yes, Your Highness!" and carried Brock off the battlefield.

Oaths may be cheap for someone who had lost the ability to affect the physical world, but as I watched them carry Brock away, I vowed that whoever or whatever bore responsibility for this would suffer dearly for it.

As the nightmare progressed I couldn't imagine feeling more powerless. And it was no consolation to realize Lucille didn't feel any better.

I could only imagine what she was going through, being left solely in charge of this diplomatic disaster. In fact, "diplomatic disaster" understated exactly how badly things had gone. Prince Daemonlas may have triggered the catastrophe, but as far as the attendees knew, Lucille the Dragon had been the one to terrorize the ceremony.

Despite everything, Lucille took command of the situation better than I could have.

She ran around organizing our small staff of retainers to bring some semblance of order to the disaster our anniversary had become. In the space of an hour the wounded were all being tended to and the unhurt ushered into guest rooms far away from the great hall.

Unfortunately, by the time things seemed under control, there were already several delegations that had slipped away to spread the bad news to their home kingdoms. Given the number of dead still littering the hall where they had fallen, this was a very bad thing.

As the depth of the situation sank in, she pulled together my personal retainers. I guess they were *her* personal retainers now. I felt a great wave of relief when I saw that no one else had been injured as severely as Brock.

Although the verdict was still out on Sir Forsythe. No one had seen him after he'd leaped out the great windows after the dragon.

Lucille gathered them all around the splintered throne as the night air blew in through the shattered grand windows, a half-dozen handmaid-warriors; Grace, Mary, Laya, Thea, Krys, and Rabbit. Lucille looked out the window at the horizon, as if she was searching for the dragon.

For me.

The wind bit our face as she said, "You're here because, after Brock and Sir Forsythe, you're the people Frank trusts most."

"Your Highness?" I heard Krys's voice from behind us. "Why are you talking like Brock?"

Lucille sighed, and Mary said, "It isn't Princess Frank anymore."

"*What?*" said several voices at once.

Lucille turned around to face Mary. "You didn't tell them?"

"Too much to explain," Mary said. "And people could have overheard."

Lucille nodded.

Grace, the nominal leader of the six, stepped forward hobbling as she leaned on a crutch that was made for someone about two inches taller. "What happened here?"

"Beyond what you saw?" Lucille gestured at the corpse of Prince Daemonlas, which still lay where it had fallen nearly two hours ago. "The spell he cast threw me out of my body and back into this one."

Grace waved at the remains of the great hall and said, "So you didn't do all this?"

"No."

"Then who did?" Laya asked.

Lucille hesitated and Mary filled the silence by quietly saying, "You don't *know*."

"Don't know what?" Grace asked.

"Frank," Lucille whispered.

Most everyone else responded by saying, *"What?"* except Mary, who looked disappointed, and Rabbit who made up for being mute by providing a you-must-be-crazy expression.

"It's the only thing that makes sense. We swapped bodies. Again."

Krys shook her head. "No, it doesn't make sense. That would mean he tried to kill you, that he almost killed Brock."

"That's better than the alternative."

"What alternative?" Grace said.

"That he's gone."

The only sound in the hall was the wind blowing from outside and the distant sound of chirping insects. I saw the girls' faces through Lucille's eyes and realized they all thought I was dead.

"No! I'm here! I haven't gone anywhere!" I tried to shout through whatever barrier separated me and Lucille. We were in the same skull, she *had* to sense I was here on some level.

Or not.

For all my mental screaming, Lucille went on talking to the girls as if I wasn't there. So much that it became hard for *me* to believe I was still there.

"I'm going to need your help," Lucille said to them.

Grace nodded. "If we can help Frank—"

"Whatever happened to him," Krys interjected.

"We're at your service, Your Highness," Grace finished.

"Good. Thank you."

"What do you need from us?" Grace said.

"First I need all of you sworn to secrecy. No one outside this room is to know Frank is missing."

I am not missing! I'm still here!

The response was three "What"s, two "Why"s, and a puzzled expression from Rabbit.

Lucille sighed, and she explained, "First off, we don't know if the spell misfired when Sir Forsythe killed the elf. If this was an attack directed at me specifically, and the body-swapping is unintentional, we don't want the attacker to know what happened. It could invite another attack."

"With all due respect, Your Highness," Grace said, "that seems kind of weak."

"Uh," Krys added, "and I think the attacker's dead." She waved at the unmoving elf-corpse.

"That spell the prince used," Lucille said, "I don't think it came from the Winter Court. Until we know why Prince Daemonlas did this, and where the spell came from, we can't just assume he was on his own here." Lucille sighed and turned around to look back out at the night sky. "And there's a more important reason."

"Which is?"

"If my father thinks I'm still in the dragon's body, he is much less likely to order something irrevocable."

She turned away from the night and started explaining her plans in earnest, and gave me even more cause for objections. "I will need to go back to Lendowyn Castle with news of what has happened, and to retrieve *Dracheslayer* and the Tear of Nâtlac."

A dragon-slaying sword made sense, but the Tear was another story. *That's crazy! Mix that with some unknown spell and even the Dark Lord himself can't predict what will happen!*

My pleas were still inaudible, and only one of the girls seemed to realize how insane bringing the Tear of Nâtlac into this mess actually was. The mute girl Rabbit tilted her head and looked at Lucille as if she had just suggested ritual suicide.

I wished she was able to voice her objections.

"Four of you will come with me," Lucille said.

"Four of us?" Grace said.

"Someone has to stay here and help manage the chaos."

Grace nodded and patted the side of her crutch. "I guess we know who's staying, Mary?"

Mary sighed, looked down at her sling, and nodded.

"You stay, heal, keep an eye on Brock, and wait to see if Sir Forsythe comes back. The rest of us will return to my father, and hope this doesn't spiral further out of control."

CHAPTER 4

Lucille spent most of the night assigning jobs, and trying to convince delegates from various kingdoms that this wasn't the prelude to a war of conquest directed at their nations. I actually would have found that amusing, the idea of Lendowyn—of all nations—launching a war of conquest, except I'd spent too long playing at the leadership role and I knew the implications. The fear of war was too easily self-fulfilling.

Lucille managed much better than I could have. She even managed to reassure a terrified Baron Weslyess who was on the verge of defecting from Delarin and pledging loyalty to the Lendowyn Crown in return for keeping his land holdings and servants. If I was in charge, I probably would have accepted his surrender just on general principles.

In the hours just before dawn, Lucille took her first actual break since I had awakened behind her eyes. She knelt next to Brock's bedside, holding the large barbarian's uninjured hand, watching his fitful sleep.

"I'm sorry," she whispered to him. "I wish you hadn't been hurt because of me."

Because of me, Lucille. Because of me. I knew our own history well enough that, knowingly or unknowingly, the probability was that any major disaster rested on my shoulders, not hers. That probability approached certainty once the Dark Lord Nâtlac became involved.

Beyond my own sense of responsibility, I wished he wasn't the one on this sickbed if only because, had it been anyone else, we'd have Brock around to help treat the wounded.

"I promise you, we'll find out what happened, and why."

She looked at his wounded face, then looked away.

"Frank," she whispered, "what happened to you?"

I didn't do this. Lucille? Don't you know that?

She closed her eyes and squeezed Brock's hand. Brock groaned weakly and squeezed back.

"You better be alive somewhere," Lucille whispered. "Or someone's going to pay."

She stood and wiped her eyes with the back of her hand.

"Who am I kidding?" She looked down at Brock, this time without averting her eyes. No longer whispering, I could hear the dragon in her voice. "Someone's going to pay, regardless."

I agreed with that sentiment. Not that it was worth much coming from a disembodied consciousness that couldn't even communicate with the rest of the world, much less extract a fitting vengeance on the architect of the current catastrophe.

Though, for all of Lucille's worry about conspiracies, the probability was that the conspiracy began and ended with the late elf-prince. Not that I'd say that to Lucille right now, even if I could. Sometimes self-deception is the only way we keep going.

She left Brock's side and said to herself, "Be alive, Frank."

I'm doing my best.

Lucille left Brock's side to join the small caravan back to Lendowyn Castle. Four mounted guardsmen accompanied the royal carriage out into the pre-dawn light. Krys and Rabbit rode inside with Lucille while Thea and Laya drove the team pulling the carriage at a speed that stopped short of shaking everything apart.

I felt every inch of Lucille's fatigue. Our fatigue. Both our minds, and the body we shared, had been awake for nearly twenty-four hours now, and I had enjoyed precious little sleep the night before the ill-fated festivities.

Once she removed us from the immediate crisis, unable to do anything but sit and watch the gradually lightening forest slide by the carriage, the weariness swelled around us, pulling us down like heavy mud sucking at our boots.

"What's going to happen?" Krys asked.

"I don't know." Lucille shook her head, watching the forest, distorted through the wavy glass of the carriage's small window. "It's bad. We had representatives from just about every royal house for two hundred miles— except for Grünwald." She laughed to herself.

"Your Highness?"

Lucille rested her temple against the thick glass of the small window. "In a fortnight Grünwald may be the only kingdom we *aren't* at war with."

"But it was the elf-prince, wasn't it?"

"Yes," Lucille said quietly. "But it was the tooth, claw,

and fire of Lendowyn royalty that tore and burned their flesh. Where will they direct their swords?"

Krys was silent and Lucille closed her eyes.

After a time Krys asked, "Do you really want to let King Alfred believe you're still Frank?"

"If there's any chance it is Frank inside that dragon," Lucille said without opening her eyes.

"But your father—"

"I won't have him order Frank's death out of convenience."

Damn it, Lucille! That is not a good idea. Even if it was me, that's not a good idea.

"But—"

"That's enough!" Lucille snapped, the dragon taking her voice again.

Krys shut up.

All things considered, I should have been panicking, but the last twelve hours had drained the emotion from me, and I felt the full force of Lucille's exhaustion. At this point I even found the occasional mental scream at Lucille too tiring. She kept her eyes closed and may have exchanged another few words with Krys, but I managed to fall into something that might have been sleep.

My awareness drifted away into vivid imaginings that were half memory and half dream.

Maybe half hallucination . . .

I wore Lucille's body in my dream, and I stumbled across a familiar battlefield, the muddy ground strewn with Grünwald's dead. The killing ground spread out, away from a stone circle that had been recently reconsecrated in Nâtlac's name.

I knew that, because I'm the one who had done that consecration when I'd ritually sacrificed the high priestess of the Nâtlac cult, the last queen of Grünwald.

She hadn't left me much choice in the matter.

Ravens picked at the bodies as I stumbled past the carnage, and I felt a sharp burst of anger. Not at the queen and Grünwald, but at the Elf-King Timoras. He had been the one to drop me here with Lucille. I had bargained with him—never a great idea with an elf—to free the Dragon Lucille in return for a ring I had stolen from the queen. Among a list of other promises, I had extorted free passage back to the mortal world for both of us.

Unfortunately, I hadn't specified passage back to somewhere that wasn't inhabited by the Dark Queen Fiona and her army.

That's the thing about elves. They'll keep their promises to the letter, but they can be very creative about interpreting those letters.

Something crunched under my feet. I looked down and saw a small hand mirror, its broken shards ground to silver powder under my feet. I remembered that, too; a "gift" from the elf-king that had never seen any use. My anger flared because that seemed another way Timoras had passively betrayed me. Who sends someone into a battle with a magic mirror? Someone who expected it to break and relieve them of the burden of holding to the last part of their agreement.

And Prince Daemonlas was Timoras's son. How is the elf-king going to react now?

I looked up, and thoughts about the elf-king fled from me.

I stood at the base of a familiar hillside. The bodies at the base of the hill had been burned, and the source of the fire rested unmoving at the top of the hill.

I *knew* the dragon—Lucille—had survived this battle.

Still, I had fallen completely into this dream. I saw her giant body, peppered with arrow shafts blacker than her scales, and she appeared as inanimate as the burned corpses at my feet.

I screamed her name as I ran up the hillside. Carrion birds erupted into flight as I stumbled and slid up a slope slick with a dragon's life's blood. I reached the crest, hoarse from screaming, and everything fell suddenly quiet. Even the ravens' calls had faded to nothing, leaving only my breathing . . .

. . . and, from behind the dragon's body, the sound of metal scraping across stone.

I ran to see what made the sound.

Digging a hole in the earth on the other side of Lucille's half-severed neck was the wizard Elhared the Unwise.

"What the . . ."

"The gang's all here," said the wizard.

"What are you doing?"

"Digging up a wedding present," Elhared said.

Not Elhared, I thought with the sluggishness of dream-memory. The mind in Elhared's body belonged to the dragon, displaced at the same time as Lucille and I had been. The mind of the wizard had—

"Oh darn," said faux-Elhared, dropping his shovel with a clatter.

"What?"

"I don't think this is going to work." He reached into the hole and pulled out a severed head that was little more than hide covering a skull. It seemed remarkable that enough hair remained for the pseudo-wizard to maintain a grip. "I'm afraid it's broken."

He tossed it at me, and I caught it by reflex. It felt lighter than it should have been. As decayed as it was, I could still see recognizable traces of my own face in it.

It had been my body, but Elhared had been living in it when he had died. When I had killed him.

I dropped the skull.

"Never goes wrong in the way you expect, eh?"

I looked up and stared dully at the dragon wearing Elhared's skin. He should be in an elf prison somewhere, where I had left him. Some knowledge this was a dream leaked back into my awareness.

He continued. "But it's not just you, is it? No one's plans go the right way, in the end."

"What are you trying to do?"

He laughed and said, "Be careful what you wish for, Frank." The false Elhared faded as I became aware of the reality wrapping Lucille's body.

I felt a throbbing headache that I couldn't decide was mine or hers. She had been awake longer than I had been, and the sun was disorientingly low in the sky. I watched in mute confusion as she ordered a bunch of stable hands around, without knowing what time of day it was, or where we were.

By the time I figured that it was late evening, and we had stopped by a town to swap our exhausted mounts for fresh horses, we were back on the road to Lendowyn

Castle. Lucille was awake now, and shared the carriage with Laya and Thea, both in exhausted sleep from driving the horses all day.

We rode hard another six hours to reach the walls of Lendowyn Castle sometime after midnight. Lucille dismounted the carriage under a waxing moon and looked up at the castle walls wrapped in wooden scaffolding.

Now the fun begins, I thought.

Alfred the Strident, my father-in-law and king of Lendowyn, met us in the throne room. Even here wasn't completely free of signs of the work being done to the castle. The tapestries, along with every horizontal surface, were coated by a veneer of fine gray stone dust. Stacked against one wall were long, freshly hewn timbers. The room smelled as if a kingdom's worth of stonemasons and carpenters had decided to air out their aprons simultaneously.

When Lucille entered, our four handmaids trailing her, King Alfred the Strident, Monarch of Lendowyn, was already waiting for her. He leaned against the throne rather than sitting on it, right hand massaging his temple under the band of a somewhat canted circlet. He stared, eyes unfocused, into the middle distance. I'd never seen him look so old.

I dislike the nobility on general principles, and I save the largest portion of my distaste for kings and their ilk, but for once I felt sorry for the man. Lucille brought herself up short when she saw him, and I knew that his pained appearance affected her as well. For a moment I thought seeing him like this might just dissuade her from her ill-advised plan to impersonate me.

However, she had inherited a stubborn streak from her father. No one else heard her subvocalize, "*Remember, you're Frank.*"

A heavy silence followed us in, and made itself at home as uncomfortably as an unwanted relative. King Alfred left the quiet unbroken for a full minute at least before he turned his head toward us. His eyes smoldered at us, ringed with red, sunk into wrinkles that the dim torchlight made into crevasses.

"So, Frank, since when do you lean so heavily on formality? We're family here." I think I heard him choke a little on the "f" in family. "Don't wait on a doddering old man to give you leave to speak."

I felt Lucille wince at the words. She opened her mouth, and I felt her almost say, "father." She caught herself and began, "Your Majesty, I come with dire news."

"Of course you do, Frank." He rubbed his temple again. "What disaster have you plunged my kingdom into this time?"

Krys took a step forward and said, "Your Majesty, this was not Princess Frank's faul—"

The king stiffened as if his spine was a cable suddenly drawn tight. I almost heard the crack of the air as his finger snapped up to point at Krys. "Silence! Do not presume to speak here. My daughter's wife might coddle your insolence, but speak out of turn in my presence again, young man, and I'll have you in irons!"

Lucille looked back and forth between her father and Krys as she took a step protectively between the two. She raised a hand, but it seemed to take her a moment to unravel the gender confusion packed in King Alfred's outburst. It wasn't completely his fault. Krys didn't dress the part of a handmaid—warrior order or not—but it did make it a little easier not to sympathize with him.

In the end Lucille just ignored it and pressed on. "Lucille was attacked!"

That got his attention. "What?"

"One of the guests, Prince Daemonlas, cast some form of magical—"

"My daughter, is she all right?" All emotion leaked out of his voice, and he enunciated every word as if each one threatened to spin out of control.

"She's alive."

I could see in his eyes that he understood the magnitude of what remained unsaid between those two words. He lowered his hand, which he still had raised in Krys's general direction. I could hear his knuckles pop as he made a fist.

"What happened?" He left a space between the two words with room enough for even more left unsaid.

"A magical attack from Prince Daemonlas," Lucille said. "He rose to present his toast and read from a scroll that held some form of enchantment. The magic was aimed at Lucille."

Lucille described what happened in detail beyond what I could have seen. I realized that, unlike me, she had suffered no blackout. She had witnessed the rampage as the dragon prince had torn apart the banquet—starting with trying to roast her and/or me. An attack that would have been fatal if not for Brock's timely but ill-advised intervention. The king stood in stony silence as Lucille related the disaster; the scion of Lendowyn royalty laying waste to counts, barons, and diplomats before crashing through the remaining stained glass to fly off into the night, Sir Forsythe in pursuit.

When she was done, he asked, "The elf is dead?"

"Run through by Sir Forsythe."

"And the knight was the only one to pursue my daughter?"

"Yes."

He nodded and walked slowly around to collapse into his throne.

"Your Majest—"

King Alfred silenced her by raising his hand. "No more," he whispered. "You've said enough."

He glared at nothing for a few moments before clapping his hands sharply. A servant came out of nowhere and the king snapped, "I want all my ministers in here, now."

The servant clicked his heels and withdrew before I was aware of him as much more than a shadow against a dusty tapestry behind the throne.

King Alfred said, "You can go."

"What?"

"I have a war to plan."

"Your Majesty?"

He sighed. "Go."

"But what about your daughter?"

"Do not . . ." His voice snapped violently, but trailed off as he stared into Lucille's face. He shook his head. "You don't understand, do you, Frank?"

"Understand what?"

"You can't unswing a sword."

"But she's under some kind of geas. A magical compulsion—"

"That matters to no one outside this room. To everyone else, Lendowyn has begun a war. And once in a war, your only options are win or surrender."

I felt Lucille freeze and I wished I knew what she was thinking. I felt certain that she had not anticipated her father's reaction. I didn't blame her. She may have grown up noble, and may have a much greater talent for leadership than I had ever shown, but she was still young. Friction with reality hadn't managed to smooth off all the rough edges of idealism in her. I don't know if her experience as a dragon accelerated or retarded the natural growth of cynicism, I just knew that, from where she stood on that journey, her father had traveled beyond the horizon ages ago.

She gathered herself and said, "Your Majesty, let me take an expedition to Fell Green. If we have a wizard examine Prince Daemonlas's scroll, we might find out how to reverse what happened to Lucille."

"Frank, I don't want you anywhere near any wizards right now."

"But, Lucille—"

"Frank, I don't say that plan lacks merit." He held out his hand. "Give me the scroll. I will have it examined. You will remain in Lendowyn Castle, safe and out of mischief."

Lucille froze again. I imagined that she ran a series of arguments through her head, and they all ended the same way. She had been so used to winning arguments with her father that she hadn't thought through the implications of having such an argument as Princess Frank. Not that she was wrong in her reasons for the deception. I'm quite sure that if King Alfred thought that the one in dragon skin was yours truly, he'd at the very least write me off completely to concentrate on his new war—if not go out of his way to find the resources to hunt me down.

"Uh," she said, "I will have it brought up as soon as everything's unloaded."

The king frowned and closed his hand. "Make sure you do. And no magic, understand? We do not need things becoming more complicated."

"Yes, Your Majesty." She bowed her head and backed out of the throne room.

She left the king to have his emergency war council with his ministers, the elf-prince's scroll still tucked into her belt, where she had stashed it when we had left the Northern Palace.

CHAPTER 5

Lucille threw herself down on the mattress in my—our—bedchamber and groaned.

"Your Highness?" Krys had followed us into the room. Rabbit and the others hung by the still-open door. "I'm sorry for speaking out of turn."

"What?"

"To the king, interrupting—"

"Oh, that?" Lucille sighed, rolling onto her back to stare into the shadowed canopy above us. "Don't worry about it."

"If I hadn't angered him . . ."

"You think that had anything to do with—" Lucille laughed. "You don't know my father. This was my own doing, outsmarting myself."

"Outsmarting yourself?"

"By posing as Frank. Sure, I've kept Father from ordering the head of the dragon. I just overlooked the fact that Frank doesn't have much chance of convincing him to do anything."

"You could tell him the truth."

Lucille shook her head. "Except he'd just see it as Frank attempting to manipulate him. No, we're going to leave him be, for the moment. At least he doesn't seem more ill-disposed toward Frank than he usually is."

"There's nothing we can do now?" Krys asked.

Lucille looked back at Krys and the three others. I felt the hint of a smile on her face. "Now what would Frank do in my position?"

The girls looked at each other, but didn't say anything.

"Honestly," Lucille asked them.

"Honestly?" Krys asked.

"Yes."

"Don't you know?" Laya asked from the doorway.

Lucille swung her legs down so she sat on the edge of the bed and nodded. "We'll need five horses prepared, provisions to get at least as far as Fell Green."

Rabbit grinned.

Laya patted Rabbit on the shoulder. "I don't think that will be a problem."

"It wouldn't be the first time we had to slip out of this castle in a hurry," Krys said. "It'll be even easier with all the workmen and supplies going in and out."

"We'll need a few other things," Lucille added.

"The scroll," Krys said.

Lucille pulled the parchment from her belt. "We have that."

"You didn't give . . ." Laya started to say, trailing off. Next to her, Thea giggled.

"You were already planning this," Kris said, a hint of admiration in her voice.

"Frank has been a bad influence on me." Lucille tucked the scroll back in her belt. "However, we'll need two other things."

"What?"

"First off, *Dracheslayer*—"

"That black sword with the glowing red writing?" Laya asked.

"The one that protects against dragon fire," Krys said.

"Yes. It's locked up in the armory but—"

Krys nodded. "If we hunt down the dragon—Frank or not—having that makes sense."

"I can get into the armory," Thea said, still giggling excitedly.

Laya tilted her head at the young girl. "She's good with locks."

"I'm sure," Lucille said. "Just take someone who can carry the sword, it's rather large."

"I can carry it." Thea's lower lip came perilously close to a pout.

"I'll go with her," Laya said. "You said two more things."

"The other thing we'll need is the Tear of Nâtlac."

NO! By all that is holy, unholy, or ignored by the gods! BAD IDEA!

I screamed at the top of my mental voice. No way should we be anywhere near that thing. Even if the spell that the elf-prince cast hadn't been obviously of a piece with Nâtlac's evilness, there was no predicting how that jewel would react to whatever had happened to Lucille, much less myself or whoever the dragon was now.

Right then, I might have started thinking about who now currently inhabited the dragon's skin, if I hadn't been overwhelmed by the effort to make Lucille hear me.

Listen! I'm here! Don't touch that thing! Think of how badly things went last time!

Of course, Lucille didn't hear me. Worse, of the four girls, the only one who even looked as if she might realize how bad an idea it was happened to be Rabbit. She looked at Lucille with her head cocked like she couldn't quite understand the crazy words coming from her mouth.

I kept screaming in our skull to no effect as they solidified the plan to slip away from Lendowyn Castle.

"The horses will be the easy part," Krys said. "The stable hands pasture them early in the morning when they clean the stables. If five of them are led off, it will be hours before they're noticed missing."

"They won't be pastured with saddles on," Lucille said.

"No," Krys answered. "But we have the rest of the night to grab those, saddlebags, provisions, and stash them in the woods out by the royal pasture. With Rabbit, I think we'd be ready to meet you off the main northern road about an hour after dawn."

Lucille looked at Laya and Thea, "Is that enough time for you two?" The girls looked at each other and Thea nodded enthusiastically.

"I think we can manage," Laya said.

"Good." She looked at Krys. "We'll meet up with you and Rabbit an hour after dawn."

"We'll have the horses ready." She turned to go with the others.

"Krys?" Lucille asked.

"Your Highness?" She paused.

Lucille looked at the girls by the doorway and said, "Give us a moment alone."

Laya and Thea looked at each other while Rabbit reached out and closed the door. Krys turned around uncertainly, a worried look on her face. "Is there a problem? Did I do something wrong?"

"No. Nothing like that. I just wanted to apologize for my father."

"Really? I did speak out of turn."

"Not that. I wanted to apologize about him calling you 'young man.' He's older, and his vision isn't . . . are you laughing?"

Krys snorted and shook her head. "No, Your Highness." She spoke through a very tight-lipped expression that tried not to be a smile.

"You *are* laughing."

Krys sucked in a breath and said, "You don't have to apologize for him."

"Am I missing something?"

You just haven't spent much time with Krys.

"You do notice how I look?" Krys said.

"A lot of girls look boyish."

"And dress? And cut my hair?"

"Well . . . You're *trying* to look like a boy?"

Krys suppressed another laugh.

"I'm sorry," Lucille said after a moment. "I didn't realize."

"It's fine," Krys said. "Sometimes I think Frank's the only one who understands me." The mention of my name drained all the levity out of Krys's voice and her expression went slack and pale.

Lucille grabbed her shoulder. "We'll get him back."

You don't have to. I'm still here!

Krys nodded and gave an unconvinced, "Yes."

"You go and get things ready so we can help him."

Krys took a step back and nodded. "Yes, Your Highness." Her grim smile contrasted with eyes that were shiny and red. She turned on her heel and left us to go with the others.

Lucille paced around alone in the bedchamber lost in her own thoughts. I wished there was some way I could comfort her, hold her hand, or at least tell her I was still around.

She stopped at the window and looked out at the northern night sky. "I wish you were here, Frank."

I wish you knew I was here.

"You know more about this thieving outlaw stuff than I do."

The girls know what they're doing.

"You could tell me what I'm doing wrong."

Like taking evil magical artifacts?

She sighed and threw herself back on the bed without disrobing.

"We'll figure this out, Frank. I promise."

Get some sleep. You're still exhausted and it's only a few hours till dawn.

She didn't need my encouragement. Her eyes were already closed and I had the strange sensation of being able to hear myself snore before following her into slumber.

We didn't have time to dream. I heard shouting and commotion and shot up from bed, blinking sleep from my eyes. I ran to the window where I heard shouting and galloping hooves. Looking out past the construction below my window, I could see the front gate open to admit a small crowd of disheveled riders who shouted at the guardsmen with some urgency.

I couldn't make out all they said, but I could hear the word "dragon" quite clearly.

Oh crap.

It was about this time I realized that I had done all this under my own power. At least, I thought I had. Once I came fully awake and tried to move consciously, my body remained where it was.

Lucille's body.

She blinked a few times and shook her head. Then she glanced at the purple sky. "Too early," she whispered.

She turned around and headed out of our bedchamber.

I decided that our dash to the window was so obvious and reflexive an action that I had just convinced myself that I'd been in control. That realization unleashed a crushing wave of self-pity. The illusion of autonomy, however brief, made it much much worse when I couldn't so much as blink an eye on my own.

I barely paid attention until Lucille met the newcomers at the entrance to the inner keep of the castle. Once I focused on where we were and what we were doing, Lucille was in the midst of a ragged rabble of wounded guardsmen and commoners from one of the border towns near the Northern Palace.

Apparently the Dragon Prince hadn't exhausted his hostility on our banquet. He had taken his aggression out on at least one village.

Lucille kept questioning the victims, as if trying to poke

some hole in their story. I tried not to listen. I had seen the kind of destruction they talked about, the last time a truly evil soul inhabited that dragon's body. I understood Lucille's panicked attempts at denial. I'd felt similarly back then because I'd thought the dragon had been her.

By the Seven Hells, it's not me!

While Lucille stood in the courtyard with the refugees, a guard came out of the keep and called for the spokesman of the "latest group" for an audience with the royal war ministers.

"Latest group?" Lucille repeated.

Another nearby guard overheard her. "Yes, Your Highness. This is the third."

"From the same town?"

The guard shook his head. "No. Three different towns. They all arrived in the past hour or so. From the north, east, and west."

"What about the other two? What happened?" I know Lucille had the same worry I did. Had troops already begun to move against Lendowyn? But if it was in response to the attack at the banquet, that reaction would have been impossibly swift. If the refugees were reaching Lendowyn Castle now, the attacks would need to have been within hours of the incident at the Northern Palace. Other kingdoms wouldn't have had time to receive the news, much less rally an armed response.

The guard's explanation was only slightly more plausible. "Dragon attacks," he said.

"Three towns? He attacked three separate towns in one night?" Lucille's voice came uncomfortably close to hysteria. "How is that even possible?"

She had a point. Leveling a village takes some time. I had some trouble imagining how our dragon could pull off a trio of attacks at once.

Before the guard had a chance to elaborate, someone screamed. Everyone turned in that direction, toward a commotion by the main gates. Next to us, the guard drew his sword.

By the closed gate, the crowd backed away. One man was being half led, half dragged away. He still screamed, weakly now, cradling his right arm. That arm was blue-white below the elbow, and glittered slightly in the growing dawn light.

Frozen? What the—

Lucille turned from the injured man to look at the main gate. Wisps of unnatural fog seeped through, between and beneath the timbers of the gate. As she watched, fans of frost spread across the wood, wrapping it in the same glittery blue-white that had coated the screaming man's arm. In moments, the gate seemed frozen solid behind a wall of icy fog. Fog that seemed oddly localized and refused to burn off in the dawn sunshine.

In another few moments, the fog became dense enough to completely hide the gate itself from view. The swirling mists now seemed to be lit from within, the cold blue light source appearing from some place much farther away than the gates immediately behind the fog.

There was something strangely familiar about it all.

Lucille stepped forward.

CHAPTER 6

Please, Lucille, this isn't a good idea.

She didn't listen to me.

Lucille walked toward the edge of the fog, quickly flanked by every armed guardsman stationed in the courtyard. I still yelled in her head not to step out into the open toward this—whatever it was. However, Lucille's time as a dragon had made her more assertive—even when it might not have been appropriate.

Fortunately, while something moved in the fog, we weren't about to face the evil hordes of the Dark Lord Nâtlac. Not unless the Dark Lord had recently suffered from the same budget constraints that had plagued Lendowyn's treasury since the kingdom's inception.

The fog swirled, wrapping a tunnel leading off to somewhere else. A single shadow slowly appeared through the mists, walking toward us from someplace beyond where the castle gates still stood. As the figure moved toward us, one of the guardsmen stepped in front of Lucille and called out, "Halt! Who approaches? What is your business?"

The figure stepped out of the fog, and as if cued, the fog itself broke apart and blew away into wisps of nothing. He stood tall, a stride or two in front of the still-closed gate to Lendowyn Castle. He wore spiked armor of the coldest blue. The dawn light shone off it and through its rippling surface, like ice from the purest lake. The wind blew past him, carrying a chill that fogged our breath and burned the skin.

I knew him instantly. I don't think Lucille, or anyone else here, had ever seen him to recognize his face—though the armor made of ice should have been a big clue that he had stepped straight out of the Winter Court.

"I am Timoras, and I am here to speak with the Crown of Lendowyn."

Given the elvish penchant for grand gestures, titles, and ceremony, I decided the elf-king's laconic introduction was not a good sign.

Lucille pushed the blocking guardsman aside and stepped out into the courtyard to face Timoras. "Speak then."

Lucille? Maybe you should let your father handle this?

"My son is dead." Timoras spoke, and the air itself appeared to freeze, his breath sending twirling crystals to glitter in the dawn light to drift down to the now frost-covered cobblestones.

"My condolences, Your Majesty, but—"

"Do *not* presume!" Timoras snapped. His anger was stripped of any remotely human element, as if an avalanche could speak. I decided that I'd rather see the dragon angry, or the Dark Lord Nâtlac for that matter.

"Prince Daemonlas attacked the court—"

"Silence!" Timoras snapped, waving his hand in a dismissive gesture.

"No!" Lucille snapped. "I will not be silent!"

Uh, Lucille, is this a good idea? Remember, all that diplomacy stuff we're supposed to pay attention to?

"You dare?" Timoras said, the words so cold the sound left frost in our ears.

Lucille strode forward and glared at the elf-king. "You dare? You stand inside *my* threshold, in *my* kingdom. You are not my king, and you have no leave to command here. Your prince came to our land to engage in an act of war, Timoras. If you are not here to answer for it, you'd best return under the hill."

I felt our heart pounding in our chest, and sensed the copper taste of fear in our mouth. None of that made it into her words. I didn't know whether to be impressed or terrified.

Timoras stood unmoving, apparently struck dumb by her outburst.

"Have you no words, King Timoras?"

In response, the elf-king did something truly terrifying. He smiled.

"Oh, Frank, you have come a long way. And you still remain ... *interesting.*"

Wait a minute ...

Lucille was impersonating me, but the fact Timoras called us "Frank" meant that he didn't know what the prince had done.

Or he was playing along with Lucille's deception. I wouldn't have put it past him.

"Why are you here?" Lucille asked.

The Elf-King Timoras smiled wider. "I am here to declare war on the world of men."

"What?"

"Were my words unclear, Frank?"

"Make war on the world of men?"

"Was it not men who took the life from my son?"

"If you have a quarrel it is with the nation of Lendowyn," Lucille said.

"I see," said the elf-king in a breath of frost. "You admit to my quarrel, then?"

"Your son provoked—"

"Yes, yes." He dismissed Lucille with a wave of his hand. "But your protests are *boring!*" At his shout, what seemed like a thousand ravens erupted, cawing, from trees beyond the castle walls.

I wondered if the elf-king brought them along strictly for the dramatic impact.

Lucille stepped forward despite my every effort to move our legs backward. "Are you *insane*?"

Please, Lucille, shut up!

"I am disappointed, Frank. You've argued with gods, yet all you offer *me* are base insults." He waved his hand, and the fog reappeared, shrouding the elf-king.

Lucille yelled, "No" and took another step, and the fog shrouded us as well.

"No?" His voice came from behind us. Lucille spun, but we only saw gray-white mists. "You wish me not to raise an immortal army and cleave the world of men in two?"

She kept spinning, trying to find the source of his voice.

She only stopped when we felt an icy hand on our shoulder.

"Then give me something," he whispered into our ear from behind.

"Give you what?"

He sighed and I felt the breath on the back of our neck. He muttered something that sounded like, "Sure, make me do all the work."

"What do you want?" Lucille repeated.

"What else would I want? The person responsible for my son's death. And an equivalent exchange."

Lucille turned around to face him, little more than a spectral shadow in the fog. "Exchange?"

He sighed again. "Lendowyn took my child. Give me Lendowyn's child." He paused a moment. "Alfred, the king? His child. Remember?"

"Me?"

"Frank, you're starting to annoy me—you were better at this once. No, not *you*. I want the scaly one." He let go of her shoulder.

"The dragon," Lucille repeated.

"Yes, yes." He tossed something at us, and Lucille reflexively grabbed it, a spherical pendant on a chain. "You have a day to give me the dragon, along with whomever bears responsibility for my son's murder. If you don't, we rain destruction on the world of men. Everything clear now? Good."

The shadow that was the Elf-King Timoras spun on its heel and stomped briskly away through the space where the gates still stood, trailing the foggy shroud like a cloak behind him. Before the shadow and fog vanished completely, I thought I heard his voice in the distance.

"Don't be so obtuse next time we meet."

Lucille held up the chain so she could look at the pendant. Carved inside a crystal sphere were two teardrop-shaped champers connected by their narrow ends. Black sand filled one chamber, and as we watched, sand slowly leaked into the other.

In other words, exactly like an hourglass—except, at the moment, the sand fell sideways.

"That was not the smartest thing I could have done," Lucille whispered to herself as she clutched Timoras's pendant in her fist.

Welcome to my world.

She spun at the sound of commotion by the front of the inner keep. "What is happening out there?" King Alfred's voice carried across the courtyard while someone else yelled, "Make way! Make way! Make way for the king!"

Lucille sidestepped until we were shadowed by a doorway next to the gates. As we backed into the shadows inside the outer wall, Lucille watched the keep's entrance. A crowd massed by the keep's wall and a trio of royal guardsmen sliced into its heart like an arrow through pudding. An obviously cranky and sleep-deprived King Alfred followed the guards. He reached out and grabbed the collar of one of the nearest guards who'd been on duty in the courtyard. Even though the man was twice his size, the king moved him easily, as if the difference in status actually translated into physical strength. Before the guard's back faced us, I could see the white mask of fear slide over his face.

Never pleasant to be in proximity of an angry monarch.

King Alfred's voice sliced across the courtyard, silencing the crowd noise around us. "What happened here?"

The guard's voice stammered and wasn't really audible. I made out the words "elf" and "princess."

King Alfred unleashed a string of profanity so vile that it might have made the Dark Lord Nâtlac blush. He released the guard and faced the courtyard. "Frank!" He called out. "I want you here right now!"

Lucille swallowed and backed away from the open doorway, deeper into the shadows. She shook her head. "No talking to him like this," she whispered.

She gasped when she backed into someone.

"Your Highness?"

She half jumped and half spun to face another guardsman, one of the men who manned the main gates. "The king is requesting you."

"Ah y-yes," Lucille said with an uncharacteristic stammer. She clutched the pendant so tightly that it cut into our palm.

The guard reached for us. "Perhaps you should—"

Lucille recovered quickly. Looking directly in the guard's eyes, she said, "You did not see me. I was not here."

His hand stopped. "But, Your Highness?"

Even though her volume had dropped to a whisper, her tone, and the hardness in her voice, dropped to registers that could rival the dragon's. "Do you *really* want to step into a dispute between me and the king?"

The guard, being sane, did not. He took a step backward.

"Good," Lucille said. "Go back to your post and forget you ever saw me."

He nodded.

As Lucille slipped away, I couldn't help thinking that she was still—for all intents and purposes—standing in for me as far as everyone in Lendowyn was concerned. That meant the guard was backing down from a threat by Princess Frank.

I wasn't sure how I felt about that.

"Only a day," she muttered as she reached the stables on the other side of the castle wall. "The dragon? The person who killed the prince? Does he think I'll just give him Sir Forsythe?"

She paused by the entrance.

"As if I *have* him. Or Fr—the dragon."

After a moment catching her breath, she whispered, "He didn't say 'killed,' did he?"

She echoed my own thoughts. Timoras had said, *"You have a day to give me the dragon, along with whomever bears responsibility for my son's murder."*

"Is this some sort of game to him?"

Of course it is.

She slipped inside the stables, and almost immediately collided with Krys, who'd stepped out into our path just as we entered. Lucille fell one way down the aisle, the saddle the other.

"Your Highness!"

"Ack," Lucille responded in the closest imitation of myself she had managed up till now.

"What are you doing here? You're at least an hour before—"

"Change of plans. We need to leave now!"

"But Rabbit hasn't had time—"

"How many horses?"

"Two, maybe three?"

"That will have to do. Saddles, tack?"

"Enough bridles, and provisions, but I only have one saddle—"

"Including that one?" Lucile pointed as she dusted herself off.

"Two, then," Krys said.

Lucille threw the pendant's chain over her neck to free her hands. She gestured toward the door Krys had emerged from. "The saddles are in there?"

"Yes, what are you—"

Lucille ran into the dim storeroom and pulled a saddle off of the rack closest to the doorway. She grunted with the effort. "Just in case Rabbit had time to free that third horse. Let's move!"

She pushed past Krys and turned left at the end of the aisleway.

"No," Krys called, "Other direction!"

Lucille spun around and ended up following Krys past a series of empty stalls. Rushing with our loads meant we had no pretense at stealth, but the stable hands who glanced up from their chores to look at us saw our clothing and quickly looked back down at their work.

One of the many perks of nobility. Look the part and none of the folks shoveling manure will see fit to challenge you, even if you run full tilt into a pasture with a saddle and no horse.

CHAPTER 7

Lucille ran with Krys toward the woods at the edge of the royal pastures. Between gasps for breath, Lucille brought Krys up to date on the situation.

"You said *what* to the elf-king?" Krys shouted over her shoulder.

"He came. Into my kingdom. To make. Ultimatums."

"You're right. Frank has been a bad influence on you."

Lucille followed Krys into a clearing where a pair of horses stood bridled and tied to a large fallen tree. One horse had a saddle and saddlebags ready. Nearby, a pile of extra bridles and saddlebags waited. Lucille stopped and dropped her saddle by the pile of extra equipment. "Where's Rabbit?"

"Getting a third horse, I presume." Krys walked over and started positioning her saddle on the second horse.

"We can't wait long," Lucille said, lifting the pendant to look into it. "Getting to Fell Green—even at full gallop—might take most of the time he gave us."

"And then we hand over Frank and Sir Forsythe?"

Lucille shook her head. "I'm hoping that knowing what happened with the prince and his spell might show some way out of this."

"Do you really think Frank is out there attacking border towns?"

"I don't know—"

Lucille was interrupted by a neigh and the sound of hoofbeats. Rabbit came into the clearing, leading horse number three. She looked at Lucille with an expression that conveyed awareness that something had gone very wrong.

"Change of plan," Krys said as she finished strapping the bags and saddle on the second horse. "We're leaving now. Get that horse ready."

Rabbit looked from Krys to Lucille.

"We have an ultimatum from the elf-king. And my father may be angry enough to send a team of guardsmen after us if he figures out where we've gone."

Rabbit's eyes widened and she got to work putting a bridle on the new horse. Lucille looked over at Krys, who had finished with the second horse and was busy now with a knife, carving a series of cryptic symbols on the trunk of the dead tree.

"What are you doing?" Lucille asked.

Thieves in any given area, especially those who belong to a guild, all have a native code to pass messages back and forth. Most thieves are illiterate, but most learn a series of symbols that can communicate things like "guard dog" and "clients at this inn aren't worth the trouble." They aren't as arcane or elaborate as the glyphs used by wizards, but they're just as impenetrable to the uninitiated. Of course Lucille had no idea about any of that.

Krys just explained, "I'm leaving a message for Laya and Thea that we went on ahead. So they can meet us at Fell Green."

Lucille shook her head. "No, don't send them there without us. Going to Fell Green is dangerous enough when I don't have to worry about my father sending guardsmen after us. And they'll probably have two artifacts I don't want falling into anyone else's hands."

Krys stopped carving. "What then? They should go back to the castle?"

"No. Tell them we'll meet at the Northern Palace. It's closer. We have to go back that way anyway, to go after the dragon."

Krys nodded and resumed carving her message.

We rode north largely in silence. Krys asked a question or two, but Lucille's monosyllabic answers must have discouraged any further conversation. I knew the impossible time pressure ate at her, because every few minutes she would fondle the pendant around her neck. This left me with nothing to do, even as a spectator. As the same woods rolled by us for the third hour, I discovered that I didn't need Lucille's body to tell me to sleep.

Apparently I could do that on my own.

I realized that when I noticed I walked an overgrown path toward an overgrown temple, a temple I knew was on the wrong side of the Grünwald border. Behind me a woman's voice asked, "Miss me yet?"

I spun around and faced the Goddess Lysea.

She wore a literally statuesque body, the same animated carving of personified sex and beauty that she had first greeted me with. This moving idol was normally a larger-than-life marble sculpture stationed behind the altar in the half-ruined temple on the hill behind me.

Right now she towered over me, the perfect curves of divinely fleshy marble reminding me painfully that my dream-self wore my original male body. She reached down and trailed fingers too warm to be stone across my trembling cheek.

Did I mention that all she wore was a carved garland of flowers in her hair?

"Is this a dream?" I asked. "Or another vision?"

She gave a dazzling smile and whispered in my ear, "Are you thinking of the consequences of acting on what you're feeling right now?"

"Uh—" Between the warring feelings of lust and fear I wasn't able to find any coherent words.

She placed her finger on my lips and whispered, "If what I say is important, does it matter what I am?"

She lowered her finger and kissed me on the lips. I probably would have blacked out if I hadn't already been unconscious.

"You do know you aren't mine to claim, don't you?"

I shook my head and looked around at the changed landscape. We stood on a ridge now, looking over a vast plain. An army gathered below us, thousands of men and horses preparing a tent city. I saw the banners of a dozen kingdoms.

"Is this happening now?" I asked.

"Is that the important question, Frank?"

I looked toward the horizon and saw, in the distance, the new dragon-bearing banners of Lendowyn over a much, much smaller force. No, this wasn't happening now, the logistics of massing a force this size required weeks . . .

"But why?"

"Are you understanding now?"

This went far beyond the provocation caused by events at the banquet. I'm sure, in a few cases right now, angry kings, counts, and dukes were starting to organize their forces. But I knew the noble mind well enough to know that the death of one or two diplomats or members of the court would, in almost all cases, be a simple pretext for some campaign that had already been planned. An excuse to seize some land or treasure that had been coveted beforehand.

That's not what Lysea showed me. Below us was a response to a genuine military threat.

"The dragon," I whispered. "He's attacking our neighbors, and it's a direct attack by the Lendowyn Crown." I looked down and studied all the banners and saw colors from the north, west, and east. "But how could one creature . . ."

"Do you understand what you presume?"

"It's not the dragon?"

She took my hands. When I looked away from her I saw another army moving through a city of spun-sugar spires. When I turned away from the tall forms in too-elaborate, too-shiny armor to see where they were going, I saw darker siblings wearing leather armor, weaving through the gnarled trunks of an ancient wood.

"Oh crap," I whispered, as two armies' worth of elves converged on the hillside that demarked the border between the bright city and the dark woods.

"What is more dangerous than a love denied?" Lysea asked.

"Is this happening now?"

"Does time mean what you think it does here?"

"Why are you—" I was about to ask why she insisted on answering my questions with more questions, when I realized what she meant. Time traveled slower in elf-land, under the hill. The time I'd been there, weeks had sped by for the mortal world while I had only been there for a few hours.

The hourglass.

"We may just have time!" I shouted as I turned to Lysea. "And that would suit the elf-king's sense of humor, wouldn't it?"

She smiled at me and I realized things had gotten way too cold. I looked around, and we stood on a ledge on a barren mountainside. "Where is this?"

"Don't you see?"

In dim twilight I saw a crumpled, broken body half hidden in a niche in the rocks. I turned away.

"You know now?"

I nodded, because I knew with the certainty of dreams that the corpse I looked at was my own. "How do I stop this?"

She reached down and lifted my chin so I looked up into her face.

"Above all else, what does any god want?"

I woke and for a moment, a mane of black hair dominated my vision.

Lucille jerked upright and I saw that was a literal mane,

belonging to the horse she rode upon. Lucille shook her head and blinked as if she had just snapped awake herself.

A shout cut through my sleep-induced disorientation.

"Your Highness!" Krys's voice came from somewhere to our right.

"I'm fine," Lucille snapped without looking in her direction.

"No, you're not." Krys rode up so that she was even with us. I saw her just out of the corner of Lucille's eye. "You almost fell off."

"You're exaggerating."

"Look down. Your right foot isn't even in the stirrup anymore. And where are your reins?"

Lucille blinked and looked down at her empty hands. "What?"

Krys walked her horse in front of ours and I realized that we weren't moving. Lucille looked down and we saw Rabbit standing next to our horse, holding the dropped reins and patting the animal on the neck. She looked up at us with a half-smile and shook her head.

Krys sighed. "You're lucky he's well trained."

"Yeah . . ."

"We have to make camp. You're in no condition to continue."

"We can't stop. Running out of time."

Look at the pendant, I thought at her. If my dream-vision meant anything straightforward, it would be that.

"I know, we only have a day," Krys said. "But you still need rest." She yawned. "We all do."

Lucille lifted the elf-king's pendant up from where it hung around her neck. *Yes.* She squinted at the small hourglass and said, "By this we only have . . ." She trailed off, staring at the slow-moving sand.

"Your Highness?"

"That elf bastard!" she snapped so viciously that Rabbit winced.

The implications of my dream were right. The black sand had barely begun to coat the bottom of the empty chamber, only very slightly more than had been there when she had first looked at it. Judging by the angle of the sun it was evening, nearly a half day gone since the elf-king's appearance at dawn . . .

A half day in the mortal realm.

Time flowed a bit more leisurely under the hill, where Timoras held court. A day in the Winter Court could be a week, a fortnight, a month . . .

The elf-king had declined to specify *whose* day his ultimatum entailed.

Typical.

Lucille leaped off her horse.

"If it wasn't an act of war I'd strangle that smug inhuman ass."

"What is it?"

Lucille yanked the pendant over her head and threw it, chain and all, at Krys. Krys caught it out of the air.

"We have time. He's having a joke at our expense."

Krys peered into the pendant. "It's falling up?"

Lucille shook her head and rubbed her eyes. "No, it's just falling under the hill."

"Huh?"

"His day. Not ours." Lucille sighed. "Let's make camp. I'm about to drop."

*   *   *

After tying the horses at the edge of a clearing where they could graze, Lucille spread her bedroll under a sheltering tree and flopped down. She hadn't so much as removed her boots, but just the act of lying down made our muscles melt as if we had returned to my featherbed at the castle. She let out a long sigh.

A grunt came from a few feet away, and Lucille turned our head so we could see what it was.

Krys had slid down to sit, leaning her head back against the same tree. Despite her closed eyes, she noticed Lucille's attention. "Rabbit has the first watch, Your Highness."

Lucille glanced back toward the clearing. Rabbit sat on a fallen log, honing a knife with a whetstone. I don't know how Lucille saw her, but I thought her time with the court over the past few months had done her some good. She was still wiry, but it seemed more muscle than bone. Her black hair had filled out and now hung in a single thick braid between her shoulder blades. Her almond eyes sparkled in an impish face that no longer seemed gaunt. The only things marring her appearance were the small ugly scars on the corners of her mouth, left there by the thugs who had taken her tongue.

Lucille leaned back and closed her eyes.

Someone sniffled next to us. Lucille turned to look at Krys again. Krys had changed, too, over the past few months. Like Rabbit, she had lost the gaunt look all the girls had suffered from in midwinter. Also, she was at least a year older than Rabbit, and a decent food supply had fueled a growth spurt that had gained her at least a couple of inches in height. That meant she was taller than Lucille now, though that didn't say much. She had allowed her hair to grow in, and now wore it in a style reminiscent of the Lendowyn guard—still very short in front, and no longer than a couple fingers' width around the rest of her head. That, combined with the armor she chose to wear, made her appear much more the young squire than royal handmaid. Not that she ever looked the part of handmaid, or played the part, for that matter.

She had grown too much to be called boyish.

At the moment the only thing that detracted from her appearance as a handsome young man was the shiny smears on her cheeks.

"Krys?"

Her hand went up to wipe her eyes and she turned half away from us. "I'm fine."

"What's the—"

"I'm not crying."

Lucille sat up. "Krys, it's all right to be upset."

"I'm not upset!"

"Krys?"

"I'm angry!"

"I understand."

Krys sniffed into her hand and nodded. "I know you do."

"We'll find out what this scroll was meant to do and where it came from. Then we will find Frank."

"He's gone," Krys whispered.

I'm right here!

"Sir Forsythe may have caught up with him by now."

Krys turned her head to glare at Lucille. "You *know* that wasn't Frank."

"No, we don't—"

"Yes, we do." Krys snapped. "You really think it's Frank out there torching villages?"

Lucille opened her mouth and closed it. She shook her head. As she blinked I felt a wet heat in the corners of her eyes.

No, please, I'm still around! Lucille! Can't you hear me?

"Yes," Lucille whispered.

"I'm sorry, but you know that couldn't have been him."

"It has to be, otherwise . . ."

"He's gone," Krys said, her tone so flat and final it left Lucille speechless.

Krys's voice softened a little. "I know hope. I know how much we seem to need it. I felt it when they took my dad. I hoped for nearly ten years, before I gave up. And the thing is, the longer you hold on to it, the worse it gets when you have to let go."

Lucille!

Lucille cried silently as she nodded. "And we don't have that kind of time."

"But we'll find out what happened," Krys said quietly.

They were quiet for a long time before Krys asked, "Why?"

"What?"

"Why would the prince do this?"

That's a damn good question.

Lucille closed her eyes and sighed. "I don't know."

"Get some sleep," Krys said.

We're in the same skull! Why don't you hear me?

Lucille didn't respond to my cries. She just lay down.

Before she shut her eyes again, I thought I saw Rabbit standing and staring at us, but it happened too quickly for me to be certain what we saw.

After several minutes it was clear that Lucille was sound asleep. After a while in darkness, I joined her.

CHAPTER 8

Lucille woke up before dawn, sometime before I did. I came to awareness realizing that she was holding up the elven pendant, staring into its depths. The sky above was dark and overcast, and the light came mostly from a fire that the girls must have made while we slept. I saw it dimly refracted in the depths of the pendant. The fire was weak, but enough to see the very slight movement of sand within the hourglass.

I wondered what Lucille was thinking.

Probably wondering how to meet Timoras's demands, as impossible as they are . . .

What?

If I could move, I would have jumped out of my skin at the unfamiliar voice. It didn't sound so much a whisper as someone—a woman's voice—very far away.

Who?

I wanted to turn my neck and look, but Lucille kept her attention annoyingly on the very boring hourglass.

Is there someone there?

Frank?

Lucille was lucky that she was in control of all our bodily functions, or we would have had to clean some

sheer terror out of our leather. I had no voice, but somehow I was talking to someone . . .

More to the point, they were talking back.

This did not bode well for my sanity.

Who's there? Who's talking?

I'm not imagining . . .

The tiny voice faded into inaudibility.

Lucille? I screamed in my mental voice. *Can you hear
me? Is that you?*

. . . no, it's me . . .

Who?

The tiny voice was gone.

"Me" who? Please, answer me.

Something caught Lucille's eye and she lowered
the pendant. She turned her head to look next to us.
Krys and Rabbit had traded positions during the
night, and Rabbit had been sleeping on her own bedroll next to us.

She wasn't sleeping now.

Rabbit had turned to face us, eyes wide and mouth
half open. She appeared to pale in the dying firelight.

"Is something wrong?"

. . . Frank? . . .

The sound was a very distant mental scream. But I
saw Rabbit's lips move very slightly as I heard it.

Rabbit? You can hear me? You can hear me?! I tried
to imagine the dragon screaming the words.

In response Rabbit raised a hand to her mouth and
nodded.

That was all the confirmation I needed.

I tried yelling at her to let them know I was still alive, trapped in here with Lucille. But I didn't hear any response. The tiny voice was gone, and I might have believed it was my imagination if it wasn't for the frustrated expression on Rabbit's face.

She had lost my voice, too.

I felt badly for Rabbit. She was mute, but she had always been good at communicating with her peers. At least that was how it had always seemed to me. Now as I saw her pacing and gesturing at Lucille and Krys, I realized that the apparent ease of her communication was due almost entirely to the self-imposed limits she had placed on what she attempted to communicate.

In other words, "I'm hungry" is a lot easier to get across nonverbally than, "Frank's alive and I can hear his disembodied voice."

Worse, I wasn't exactly sure she knew I was alive. Remembering odd glances from her, here and there, I suspected she had heard me a few times now, but from her point of view I might just be a ghost.

But I wasn't a ghost.

I was alive.

Wasn't I?

Trapped behind Lucille's eyes, I began to worry that it was a distinction without a difference.

Rabbit paced around the remains of the fire between Krys and Lucille, shaking her head.

"What's the matter?" Lucille asked for what might have been the dozenth time.

Rabbit sighed and pointed at Lucille's forehead, then at her own ear.

"You hear me?"

Rabbit made a gesture of grabbing something and not quite catching it.

"No, but close," Kris said.

Rabbit nodded.

"I said something?" Lucille asked.

Rabbit frowned and stomped her foot.

"You want me to say something?"

Rabbit pointed at herself, then at her ears. Then she pointed at Lucille and covered her ears.

"I said something you didn't want to hear?"

Rabbit gave a frustrated look at the heavens, spun around facing Krys, and repeated the sequence; pointing at herself, then at her ears, then pointing at Krys and covering her ears.

"Krys said something—"

Lucille was interrupted by a frustrated grunt from Rabbit.

"I'm sorry," Lucille said. "I'm trying. Why don't you just write it down?"

Rabbit turned and glared at us.

"What?" Lucille said.

"Your Highness," Krys said, "we never had much chance for tutoring."

"What do—oh."

Rabbit gave Lucille a withering stare that I thought was a little unfair. Yes, it was a bit much to assume that a homeless teenage girl, an outlaw who had spent at least one year living a feral life in the woods, might have picked up some skills in reading and writing. But in all fairness, it was a bit much to assume a pampered aristocrat had any idea what such a life might be like.

But then Rabbit's eyes widened and she smiled.

She pulled out her dagger and cleared a space on the ground. Literate or not, she still knew the same thieves' symbols that Krys had used earlier. It might be a limited vocabulary, but it would probably be better getting the idea across.

That's what I thought, anyway.

Rabbit sketched a circle with a dot followed by a pair of triangles joined at the tip.

"Ah," Krys said.

"What does that mean?" Lucille asked.

"A friend was here before?" Krys said.

Rabbit underlined the triangles.

"A short time before?"

Rabbit underlined the triangles again.

"Very short time before?"

Underlined violently.

"Now?"

Rabbit dropped the knife and clapped her hands.

"A friend is here now?" Krys asked.

"What does this have to do with what I said?" Lucille asked.

Rabbit pointed at herself and her own ears again. Then she got up and pointed at Lucille, her finger poking the hollow between our breasts just above the hanging pendant. Then she reached over and covered our ears with her cupped hands.

"I don't —"

Krys interrupted, "You're hearing something we don't!"

Rabbit spun around and clapped her hands again.

"What are you hearing?" Lucille asked.

Rabbit turned and pointed at Lucille.

"You're hearing me?"

Rabbit sighed and put her face in her hands.

"You're not making sense."

Rabbit glared at us, then pointed at her ear and slowly again at our chest.

"But not me?" Lucille asked, puzzled.

Rabbit slowly nodded.

"I got it!" Lucille said.

"What?" Krys asked.

Lucille grabbed the elf-pendant that had been hanging from her neck. She held it up in triumph. "You're hearing this thing!"

Rabbit stared at the thing, then stared at Lucille.

"No," Lucille said, "that's the only thing that makes any sense." She dropped the pendant. "Why are you pointing at me when you don't mean *me*?"

Rabbit spread her hands in a gesture that said, "And?" Her face looked expectant.

"How can it be me and not me?"

Come on, Lucille, what else could she mean?

Rabbit waved her hands, "Go on."

"Me and not me," Lucille repeated.

Rabbit turned and pointed down at the symbols she'd written in the dirt. *A friend is here now.*

Krys clapped her hands. "I got it! She's talking about *Frank!*"

Rabbit grinned, made a joyous grunt and ran to embrace Krys so hard that she lifted the taller girl's feet off the ground.

"Frank?" Lucille whispered.

Rabbit turned around and nodded. The goofy grin on her face froze the moment she locked eyes with Lucille.

"Frank?" Lucille's voice sounded low and hoarse, clawing its way through muscles that were taut enough to strangle them. I felt her clenched fists, and felt her pulse throb in our neck. "You heard *Frank*?"

Rabbit nodded slowly, her smile boiling away like a snowdrift before an angry dragon.

Krys's face showed a growing alarm. I didn't blame her. Lucille's anger was not to be trifled with, and that was only partly because she recently played the role of a dragon. Krys took a half step forward and said, "Your Highness—"

Lucille silenced her by raising one hand and glancing in her direction. She didn't even move her head.

Why doesn't that ever work for me?

"You're telling me that you've heard my wife . . . husband . . . Frank?"

Rabbit nodded.

"How?" Lucille said.

Rabbit stared a couple of moments before slowly shaking her head and giving the barest of shrugs.

"You don't know how."

Rabbit spread her hands helplessly. I felt sorry for her.

"You don't—" Lucille bit off her own words. "When? *When* did you hear him?"

Rabbit immediately pointed up, and then lowered her arm to point below the horizon.

"What in the Seven Hells does that mean?" Lucille snapped.

"Your Highness—"

Lucille spun around to Krys. "What!"

"She's pointing at the sun . . ."

"And that . . . oh."

"She's saying that she heard him about the time you both woke up. Sun just below the horizon, through the trees there."

Rabbit nodded at Krys.

"When we woke . . ." Lucille sighed, and I felt all the tension drain from our body. I suddenly realized where her thoughts were leading her.

No! Lucille! I'm really here!

"I'm sorry I yelled at you," Lucille said to Rabbit. "This wasn't your fault."

Rabbit cocked her head and furrowed her brow in confusion.

"We're all under a lot of stress," Lucille said. "But we should get back on the road to Fell Green. Time's still slipping away."

As she turned away from them to gather her horse, I caught Krys and Rabbit exchanging a confused glance out of the corner of our eye.

"Lucille?"

She looked back over her shoulder at Krys.

"What about Frank?"

Yes. What about me?

"Krys? You know."

"No. I don't."

Lucille turned back around to face Rabbit and spoke in a voice that was little above a whisper. "You don't hear him now, do you?"

You hear me! I mentally screamed at her. *Here I am! You hear me! Of course you hear me!*

Rabbit shook her head "no."

"No," Krys said. "No. You're wrong. He's still here." She grabbed Rabbit's shoulders and said, "He's still here!"

"It was a dream, Krys," Lucille said. "She just dreamed what she wanted to hear. What we all wanted to hear."

Rabbit! Tell her she's wrong!

Instead Rabbit reached up and hugged Krys. She shook her own head, but I could tell that she was just as convinced as Lucille was.

I'm here damn it!

But if I was, why couldn't Rabbit hear me now?

Lucille's trio rode on most of the morning in silence, leaving me alone with my thoughts. I didn't *feel* dead. Not that I would have any clue what that would feel like. I had just assumed that death was such a disruptive change that you couldn't help but realize when it happened.

I don't know why I had expected it to conform to my expectations, no other aspect of my existence ever had.

Still, despite my inability to act or move under my own volition, I wasn't some disembodied spirit. I was very bodied. I could feel Lucille's armor chafing the inside of our thighs as we rode. I felt the fancy braided hairdo, left over from the banquet, tugging against our scalp. I felt trails of sweat dripping down the center of our chest, spreading to make the underside of our boobs itch.

I felt us breathe. I felt us sigh. I felt the corners of our eyes burn as we blinked our tears away.

I found the atmosphere so depressing that I almost felt relieved when an arrow shaft sprouted from the path ahead of us.

CHAPTER 9

The horses half-reared and backed as a huge jet-black stallion stepped out into the path. A tall gentleman with a close-trimmed beard rode the beast, his hair—as much of it as was visible beneath his broad hat—as black as his horse, his leather as black as his hair. I didn't get the greatest look at the guy, as Lucille turned her head to look at the path behind us for an escape route. Of course, a pair of mounted highwaymen were already behind us, long swords drawn and at the ready. They had picked a good place for an ambush, where the trail hit a long blind curve between two steep hillsides covered in deadfalls impossible for a horse to navigate and dense enough to hide an archer or five.

"I am afraid this is a robbery." Lucille turned back around as the black-clad man spoke. I felt an itching familiarity when she focused our attention on him. His skin was nearly translucently pale, in ghostlike contrast to a cascade of black that the Dark Lord Nâtlac would probably think was a bit much.

Lucille drew her horse up and straightened our spine. "You have the gall to prey on travelers on the king's highway in broad daylight?"

"My apologies, but my archers are not very good.

They need to see the target, or they have a habit of damaging things I want." He dropped the reins and bent over to whisper something in his mount's ear. Then he vaulted off as if his horse was an ebony statue. His landing would have done Sir Forsythe proud, lightly on both feet, facing us so he didn't even need to turn his head to continue talking to Lucille. "But please, do not let my bowmen's incompetence prompt any of you to act rashly. A shower of arrows would end badly for you all, no matter how poorly they are placed."

"What do you want?" Krys snapped.

He spread his hands. "What does anyone want? Good food, strong wine, hale companions, a warm place to lay my weary head, someone to comfort me through the long dark night. Alas I must satisfy myself with your gold, weapons, and jewelry. Please be so kind as to dismount."

Why did he seem so familiar?

Lucille exchanged a glace with Krys.

"Oh dear, you aren't going to resist, are you? There's no reason for this to be unpleasant."

"Do you know who I am?" Lucille asked.

Lucille, bad plan. Royalty won't intimidate him. He'll just see it as an opportunity for ransom.

She dismounted, and I caught a glimpse of Krys's face which showed the same reservations I had. When our feet touched the ground the height differential between us and the black-clad highwayman became very apparent. She only took a half step toward him, since any closer would require her to painfully bend her neck to look him in the eye.

"Will you care to enlighten me, fair lady?"

"My name is Frank Blackthorne," she said.

Uh, what are you doing?

The highwayman arched an eyebrow. "You are?"

"You know me?"

"In my experience, very few women call themselves Frank."

"Then you know that I carry the whole weight of the Lendowyn Crown behind me."

"Are you trying to impress me, Your Highness?"

Steel crept into her voice, a tone of authority I had only managed to emulate once or twice myself. "Then maybe you know my history. I've stolen the rings off Grünwald's Dark Queen while her whole court looked on. I cast her into darkness while the armies of the Dark Lord Nâtlac were torn apart before me. I have *been* that Dark Queen. I've married dragons and have been kissed by gods. I have torn nations apart and reassembled them. The road I travel leads to war with the elf-king himself. Do you imagine you hold any terror for me?"

Okay, when you put it that way, it sounds a little impressive.

The highwayman clapped slowly, and suddenly the familiarity made sense. The subtle combination of boredom, arrogance, and bemusement must run in the family.

Lucille apparently didn't notice. "I suggest you allow us to go unmolested."

He shook his head and said, "War with the elf-king, you say? That is very interesting. How is Uncle Timoras these days?"

"U-Uncle?" Krys sputtered.

"You're an elf?" Lucille said, only slightly less startled than Krys.

"Not by my uncle's account—and I would count him an expert on such matters."

What was it about royal bastards that made them want to muscle in on my profession?

Lucille stared at him. I guess she was trying to see his elvish heritage. To me, it was obvious in his bearing, his posture, the body language and mannerisms, the pale skin—but I was used to looking through disguises. Most people, including Lucille, would focus on the externalities like the fact that no elf would be caught dead with facial hair or such a drab monochrome outfit.

He clapped his hands sharply. "Focus, My Lady!"

Lucille blinked. "Huh?"

"You mentioned war. That's no trivial statement. Timoras's kingdom has not borne arms against an enemy for over a thousand years. Were you inflating your own importance? Or has my dear demented uncle become bored enough to play general? Are there armies moving? Tell me!"

He kept edging forward until he towered over us.

"King Timoras has threatened war—" Lucile began.

"Against Lendowyn? To what end? This kingdom is less than irrelevant to him. You must be mistaken. Or lying."

"Not Lendowyn."

"Of course not. Against whom then? What great foe has moved my uncle to arms? Tell me! Who does he move against?"

"Everyone," Krys said quietly.

Our highwayman paused, closed his mouth, and took a step back, looking in Krys's direction. "Everyone? What do you mean? *Everyone?*"

"In his own words," Lucille said, "he intends to 'declare war on the world of men.'"

He laughed.

"I fail to see the humor," Lucille said.

He shook his head and wiped his eyes. "No. You obviously mistook some rhetorical flourish of his. He can be prone to hyperbole."

"He seemed deadly earnest to me."

"I know that humans can find elf humor somewhat dry. Even with my heritage, I often find some idioms inscrutable—"

"I think he was upset about Prince Daemonlas."

"Did my cousin become involved with some mischief?" He glanced back at Lucille with a knowing grin. "Or . . . *a woman?* Of course! That is that what all of this is about. Daemonlas always had a weakness for mortal women. He's found yet another royal strumpet to seduce, hasn't he?"

"Prince Daemonlas is dead," Lucille answered.

The grin froze on his face and he almost ceased to breathe. "What?"

"Prince Daemonlas is dead," Lucille repeated.

"Dead? How?"

"He attacked our anniversary celebration and my . . . spouse . . . with hostile magic."

He grabbed our shoulders. "*No!* Answer my question! How did the prince die?"

Krys said, "I think it was the broadsword through the chest that did it."

That stopped our highwayman so sharply that you'd almost think the same broadsword had pierced him. He let our shoulders go, took a step back, and bowed slightly. "I apologize for my rudeness, but I am afraid I have become aware of a prior commitment that requires my immediate attention."

He turned and started striding quickly back toward his mount. I heard a tramp of hooves behind us and suddenly Rabbit's horse was cutting off Mr. Highwayman's retreat. As he backed away from her, Lucille echoed my own thoughts, "What are you doing? Hello? Archers?"

Krys drew her sword and dismounted, taking a step to be in line with our man's retreat. "Check behind us, Your Highness."

Lucille looked back to where our retreat had been cut off. The two mounted men were gone. "What?"

"You seem to be left on your own," Krys said to the man. "Have anything to say now?"

He sighed and held up his hands. "Perhaps my choice of compatriots was unfortunate."

Lucille faced him again. "Why did they leave you?"

"Struck by that same prior commitment I mentioned to you, I suspect. Without so much as a good-bye. I suppose I am at your mercy."

"What prior commitment?"

He sighed and rolled his eyes. "Does all wit escape you, Princess Frank? That is what is generally referred to as a joke. A small bit of levity to lighten a hasty exit."

"Very small," Krys said.

"You'll notice," Lucille said, "I'm not laughing."

"You should learn to. It makes inevitable doom much less depressing."

Lucille drew a dagger from her belt. "You have not caught me on the best of days."

He backed up a step, stopping when Krys's sword prodded his side.

Lucille approached him with the dagger. "Do you understand the gravity of your situation?"

"You just told me that the king of the Winter Court has lost his only heir to human hands. The fact that you are not fleeing for your lives tells me that it is you who underestimate the gravity of the situation."

Lucille brought her dagger up between his legs to press against his inner thigh.

Given the height differential between us, it was the easiest vital spot for Lucille to threaten. Still I mentally winced a little in sympathy for our half-elven highwayman.

He sucked in a breath and said, "That isn't necessary."

"Your answer is to run?"

"I doubt that my silver tongue and winning personality would sway the fury of an army of immortals who have not tasted blood in a thousand years."

"You have not swayed me." Lucille pressed upward with the blade and said through clenched teeth. "Shut. Up."

For several moments the only sounds surrounding us were the wind through the branches, distant birds, and the horses shifting their weight. After an extended period, Lucille said, "I have dead. I have wounded. I have villages being attacked under the guise of royal authority.

I have a missing spouse and dragon. I have the elf-king threatening war. I have very little patience. Nod if you understand what I am saying."

He nodded.

"Answer me in as few words as possible."

He nodded again.

"Your people ran—"

"They weren't really my people you under—" His words ended with an intake of breath and a tensing of muscles as Lucille increased the pressure on the dagger. "Your Highness?" he said in a breathless whisper.

"Fewer. Words." Her own words came out in a snarl. "Are they more elves?"

"What?"

"Was I unclear?" She leaned into him, the dagger's blade pressing into the gap between his groin and his inner thigh, our hand so close that I felt his pulse through her glove.

Lucille?

"No. Just a band of human brigands I—"

"Words." Lucille snapped.

He stopped talking.

"*Uncle* Timoras?"

There was a long pause before he asked, "Was that a question?"

Lucille ground her teeth in a manner I found intensely uncomfortable. "He is your *uncle?*"

"Well, he—" He sucked in a sudden breath and said, "Yes! Yes! Please lower your hand, Your Highness."

"Why are you in our path?"

"Robbery?" He sounded unsure of himself.

"*Why* are you in our path?"

"My deepest apologies. There's been a misunderstanding."

"Yes?" Lucille's hissing voice came very close to that of the dragon. "Just a coincidence? One day after the elf-king makes his threats, his *nephew* shows up?"

"Just lucky, I guess?"

"Enough of this!" she snapped and moved her hand. The would-be highwayman jumped back and stumbled, barely avoiding impaling himself on Krys's sword as he fell backward against Rabbit's horse, knocking his broad hat askew as he landed flat on his back.

While he was prone, Lucille leaped on him, landing with her knees on his chest and her free hand on his throat. I felt the fury coursing through her. Not the emotion, but I felt the throbbing temples, the thudding pulse, and the burning copper taste of her breath in her throat. She raised the dagger and a shining long sword blade interposed itself between her dagger and the man's throat.

Lucille's head snapped to face Krys. "What are you doing?"

"Calm down. Please."

Lucille may have been too furious to notice, but Krys's sword blade trembled and her skin was deathly pale.

"What?" Lucille snarled at her through clenched teeth.

"Please. Take a breath. Think."

Beneath us a tentative voice spoke up, "Listen to the young lad."

She stabbed the dagger down, stopping short just before cleaving the bridge of his nose. "You, *shut up.*"

To Krys, she asked, "Why in the wide world should I calm down? I've lost my . . . too much. I've lost too much. And this, this worm? He tries to take even more? And listening to him? Gods, it is like chewing on gravel."

"He's not a threat now."

"Really? Timoras's *nephew?* How convenient is that? Would you put it past the elf-king to place one of his agents specifically to prevent us from reaching Fell Green?"

"Maybe?" Krys said. "But so ineffectively?"

"See," he added. "I make a horrible spy."

"Silence!" Lucille snapped at him. I felt the pulse recede and her breaths came longer, deeper, and cooler. After another moment, her tone was almost conversational. "Why shouldn't I just put him out of our misery?"

"If he is Timoras's nephew, he might have some useful information."

Lucille nodded and lifted the dagger from the man's face. "That, at least, makes sense."

Krys added, "And if you parley with the elf-king again, having a hostage might offer some leverage."

I felt him shaking under Lucille and she turned to look at him. "Why are you laughing?"

He shook his head. "I'd make a poorer hostage than I do a spy."

"Why?"

"You think he cares what you do to me?"

"He'd go to war over the prince."

"His full-blooded heir. That means he's also the *queen's* son. What do I matter?"

Lucille climbed off him and stepped back, sheathing her dagger.

He looked from her to Krys and asked tentatively, "So you are not going to kill me?"

"Not at the moment."

He sat up and felt around behind him, finding his hat and replacing it at a rakish angle. "You have my gratitude, Princess."

"Wonderful. Get up."

He did so and Lucille asked, "So, nephew of Timoras, what name do you go by?"

He swung his hat around in a deep bow and said, "May I introduce myself as Robin Longfellow." He straightened up, beating dust from his trousers with the brim of his hat. "I am in your debt for leaving intact this skin, of which I am so fond." He replaced his hat and smiled, and I swear that I saw his eyes twinkle.

Despite living a year in the body of a young woman, I had gained no particularly deep insights into the subtleties of male beauty. To this day my classification of my fellow males tends to fall into the same three categories they've always had, handsome, average, and ugly as an ogre's afterbirth.

To me, Robin's features tread the line between the first two, possibly just edging into handsome. But that smile, the twinkling eyes, and the tilt of his broad hat seemed to have an effect on Lucille. I felt her pulse and the catch in her breath, and I had lived in this body long enough to know the meaning of the warmth we felt in certain places.

She finds this incompetent half-breed wannabe thief attractive?

Whatever she thought of him did not make it into her

voice. "In return, perhaps you can explain the astounding coincidence of your presence here."

"Certainly," he said. There was such self-assured confidence in that one easy word that I knew that he saw through the tone of Lucille's words as surely as I had.

And I felt jealous.

Things never go wrong in quite the way I expect.

CHAPTER 10

Our ne'er-do-well highwayman Robin Longfellow had a plausible, if somewhat facile, explanation for his presence on the road to Fell Green. Fell Green was a wizard town, and it existed not quite in the world of men. In fact, Fell Green was as far away from our world as it was close to the elven lands under the hill. That made it a crossroads for traffic from there to here, one of the easier, more well-traveled pathways.

"The reason I felt mirth at the young lad's suggestion you hold me hostage to my uncle—well, my plans had been to raid my cousin and his entourage."

"That makes no sense!" Krys snapped incredulously.

"I assure you that Prince Daemonlas, in addition to being narcissistic and given over to unseemly passions, is—pardon me—*was* a frightfully lazy creature. He would have been quite unwilling to extend the effort to walk through the wilds like his father. He would have certainly traveled the easy route home."

"No," Krys said. "You pretty much said it's the end of the world because the prince got himself killed. And you were going to rob him?"

"Robbing is a different business than killing."

Krys shook her head in disbelief. She turned her head in our direction. "Now what?"

"Bind him," Lucille said.

"Your Highness?" Robin objected.

"I don't trust you, Robin Longfellow."

"You have my word that I will work no ill against you."

"That's good," Lucille said. To Krys she said, "Relieve him of his weapons, and anything else on his person."

"But—"

"Robin Longfellow," Lucille said, "you will stay with us until we reach Fell Green. Please don't make this any more unpleasant than it already is."

The rest of the day we rode with the would-be robber, Robin Longfellow, tied at the wrists and slung over the saddle of his own horse like a sack of grain. Rabbit led the animal by the reins from her own mount. As the day wore on, Lucille would steal glances at the elf-king's pendant. The sand flowed slowly in the tiny glass.

I felt in the way she bit her lip that even the little that had filled the bottom was too much.

However, between the time lost at Robin's hands, the exhausted horses, and the fact that the road to Fell Green seemed to have a habit of moving about, we did not reach our destination by sunset. No one said anything, but I knew Lucille felt keenly the fact that, had we been given only the one mortal day, we never would have made it in time.

Once the sun set, we made camp again under the open sky.

Robin looked relieved to be seated in front of the fire, even if Lucille left him bound. Supper consisted of a few dried sausages heated on a rock nestled in the midst of the fire.

The leathery meat was spicy as all hell, and stank of garlic and mustard and a dozen other things. I would have preferred hunger, but Lucille didn't consult me.

Robin looked across the fire at us and asked, "Is this necessary?" He held up his bound wrists.

"Yes," Lucille said. "You're connected by blood to the elf-king. I want you to tell me what he's planning."

Robin arched an eyebrow. "My Lady?"

"You heard me."

"Well, if that's *all*. Just untie me and I'm sure I will bring you a report the next time I attend the Winter Court's council of advisors."

"I'm not joking," she told him.

"If you aren't, then you seem to be aware of a promotion in my status no one has seen fit to share with me. Then again, since I've spent the last few decades traipsing across the mortal realms with outlaws, actors, and storytellers, I may have been hard to reach."

"You know his mind, Robin Longfellow. I would see you share that knowledge."

Robin sighed and looked into the fire. "That is not a merry subject."

"If you wanted that, you should have favored the actors over the outlaws."

Robin chuckled. "You seem to know the theater as well as the elf-king."

"And you seem to know Prince Daemonlas."

Robin gave a shrug and a slight nod of the head in acknowledgment. "*Of* him," he said. "Perhaps I know of other things you might find of use. But I suspect not. So much of courtly gossip is trivial, and boring. And you, Princess Frank, are *not* boring."

I did not like the way he said that.

Lucille pointed her dagger at him. "You are edging close to boring *me*."

"Please, as I am your guest, perhaps you might indulge me this tiny bit? Pretend that we aren't adversaries, just fellow travelers chance met, making our acquaintance."

"Why?"

"Because it costs you nothing and may make this journey more pleasant."

Lucille sheathed her dagger and I felt her frown. "I'm not forgetting you attempted to rob us."

"Which led to no lasting harm but to my own pride. I make my apologies."

Lucille sighed.

"Is civil discourse such a burden?" he asked.

Lucille shook her head, but I felt her grit our teeth.

While Lucille and Robin spoke, I noticed Rabbit out of the corner of Lucille's eye. She set a small iron teapot on the hot stone next to the meat. While that heated up, she pulled a small dry green bundle out of her pouch and placed it in the bottom of a battered tin cup. The package looked familiar.

What Brock the barbarian may have lacked in martial prowess, he made up for in herbal lore. He supplied the court with any number of preparations for any number of ailments, and when he packaged his work he often

folded his creations up in a single broad leaf of some
plant or other. I only saw Rabbit's little bundle briefly,
but the way the dried leaf had been folded was definitely
Brock's work.

The reminder of my burned friend made me a little
sick to my stomach. Or it would have if my emotions had
any connection to the body I resided in.

If I could only *do* something.

Waves of self-pity broke over me again, and I lost focus in the depths of my own despair. Words were spoken
around me, words I heard but didn't listen to. Lucille
talked to Robin, but I didn't really see him anymore.

Why should I give the world any attention anymore?
I was powerless to affect it.

Somewhere, mixed with the words around the campfire, I heard a voice that didn't belong. A long, distant
sigh of relief.

Ahhh.

My attention suddenly focused on the distant sound.
What?

Ahhh!

The relief turned into a startled exclamation. From
the edge of Lucille's field of vision I saw Rabbit sit bolt
upright, nearly spilling her foul-smelling tea in her lap.

Rabbit? I called in my mental voice.

Frank?

You can hear me?

How can I hear you? Am I dreaming again?

It's no dream. It wasn't the first time either.

You almost sound closer.

You, too.

She stared at Lucille, but Lucille kept grilling Robin the half-elf.

They don't believe me, Rabbit thought at me as she sipped from the cup. Her voice had surged until it was a near-normal volume.

I have trouble believing it myself, I agreed. *I've been stuck in Lucille's body since . . . since it all happened.*

I heard something like a sigh.

What?

I probably am imagining this.

No, please, I really am here.

You're a voice in my head that claims to be Frank Blackthorne. You know how much I want it to be you?

I—

About as much as I want to be able to talk to people again.

Her nonexistent voice echoed in my nonexistent ears.

She was right. It did sound too good to be true. If I didn't know I was me, I'd have some trouble with it.

It's me, I thought at her.

Why then? Why can I hear you and Lucille can't?

Good question. I had repeatedly screamed at Lucille and hadn't managed to prompt so much as a twitch. Why would Rabbit be more sensitive to my voice than the woman I shared skull-space with?

Frank?

I'm still here.

Why?

I wish I knew. I don't even know what happened to me.

Rabbit sighed, both in my head, and in the real world.

Maybe, I thought, *we can ask a wizard in Fell Green.*

Who will talk to them? Rabbit followed the thought with a silent, sad little laugh. *You or me?*

In my head she sounded a lot older than her years.

I'm sorry.

You don't need to apologize to me. It isn't your fault I've gone nuts. I guess after all these years I needed someone other than myself to talk to.

I'm not a hallucination, I told her.

Any hallucination worth the crazy would say that. She lifted her cup in a vague toast in Lucille's direction. Lucille didn't notice, and kept talking to Robin. *I hope we find you Frank, wherever you really are.*

Hallucinations . . .

The word reverberated in my head as I strained my attention at her through Lucille's wrongly pointed eyes. I watched her take another sip of the cup.

The cup made of an herbal mixture prepared by our barbarian herbalist, Brock.

What are you drinking?

What? Rabbit seemed startled by the question.

In the cup, what is it?

What does that have to do— She bent her head, and looked down into the liquid.

Yes?

The scars in my mouth, they still hurt. I winced a little inside, hearing that from her. *Brock made me these herbs, they help with the pain. The tea, leaves I can chew . . .*

Sometimes Brock's preparations had some side effects—the kind of side effects that can send shamans on unscheduled vision quests.

I'm not going crazy, she thought to me.

No you're not, I agreed.

You're just the tea talking. I heard her sigh of relief in my head as well as the real world.

I'm not the tea!

I only hear you when I've taken it, or chewed the leaves. What else could you be?

I sighed. I wanted to argue with her but I couldn't think of a convincing line of reasoning.

I felt the universe laughing at my expense.

F-Frank? Her voice was suddenly small and scared.

I'm still here.

I didn't mean to insult you—

Don't worry about it . . . Hey, why you worried about my feelings? I'm just a hallucination, right?

Doesn't mean I want you to leave.

I'm not going anywhere.

Good.

You know, just because the medicine lets you see or hear something doesn't mean it's not really there.

Doesn't mean it is.

I mentally grumbled in frustration.

Frank? I'm happy you're here, even if you aren't really here.

Thanks. But it's frustrating not to be able to talk to anyone else.

Tell me about it.

Sorry.

Don't worry about it. She echoed my earlier thought.

You've been mute all the time Grace and the other girls have known you?

I saw her head nod out of the corner of Lucille's eye.

They named you Rabbit.

Yes.

So, what's your real name?

What?

What name were you born with?

It's been so long . . . She paused a long time, as if she didn't quite remember. Then her mind snapped excitedly, *Rose. My name used to be Rose. I haven't thought about it for years.*

Rose is your real name? It's pretty.

No.

It isn't pretty?

No. It's not my real name. My real name is Rabbit. That's the name I earned. Rose is someone else.

She sipped the last of her tea and looked into the empty cup.

I wonder how long it will last, she thought at me.

So did I. *Rabbit, will you help me?*

Help a voice in my head?

Yes.

I can't convince anyone I really hear you. I don't believe it myself.

I know.

What then?

Do you think you can convince Krys to have some of your tea?

CHAPTER 11

Lucille wasn't in a position to see what happened between Rabbit and Krys. I desperately wanted some form of muscular control so I could pace, or at least fidget a little while I waited for the outcome of the discussion between the two girls. Lucille continued ignoring them, focusing on Robin, our half-elven prisoner. That offered a small bit of distraction, so I settled in—mentally speaking—and returned my attention to that conversation.

"May I ask you something, Princess Frank?"

"What?"

"Why are you traveling to Fell Green? If you truly wish to halt the oncoming storm, would it not make more sense to accede to my uncle's demands? He would be bound by his words—"

Lucille snorted.

"And now you find me amusing?"

"Only a fool would place their faith in an elven promise."

"Oh? You know that he does not lie."

"Truth is not the same thing as honesty," Lucille said.

"Wise words," Robin said. "But wisdom is not the same thing as intelligence."

"Now let me ask you something."

"You haven't answered my question."

"Tell me why. Why would Timoras go to war over something the prince himself instigated?"

Robin chuckled. "You have little dealing with elves, I presume."

"As little as possible."

"They take hospitality very seriously. They grant some leeway to the mortal realms, being uncivilized as they are—"

"Hey—"

"But murdering a guest is beyond the pale, even for a liberal interpretation of your obligations."

"It wasn't murder. He was—"

"Is the prince dead?"

"Yes."

"At someone's hand?"

"That isn't—"

"In your house?"

"He attacked m—the prince." Robin arched an eyebrow, noticing the shift in the middle of Lucille's statement. "And why," she continued, "declare war on everyone?"

"Who was present?"

"What does that have to do with anything?"

"They share culpability."

"They . . ." She shook her head slowly. "I see."

If the elf-king thought all the attendees shared responsibility, he probably did want to go to war with literally everyone. At least the majority of this continent. The fact that Robin talked about "an immortal army that hasn't tasted blood in millennia" did not make me feel any better about the situation.

"What's the point of this then?" Lucille held up the pendant. "If he wants war, why bother to give us an ultimatum at all?"

Robin chuckled. "Who said anything about what my dear uncle *wants*?"

"Pardon?"

"If King Timoras does not extract a full measure of compensation for the death of his only heir, he is likely to join him." At this point I couldn't count that outcome as a bad thing. "The intrigue of the Winter and Summer Courts . . . it makes mortal battles of succession look like toddlers squabbling over a plate of sweets." Actually I had always thought it was the nature of aristocracy that gave that appearance. "His position is incalculably weakened by the loss of the prince."

"Really?"

"A potential survivor with the means and the patience to plot a revenge has long been a deterrent to any direct act against the king. And relations between the courts are ever strained at best."

Lucille spoke my thought as I was thinking it. "If that's the case, why wouldn't a plotter kill the prince first? In fact, maybe that is what this is. Maybe he was under some sort of geas?"

Robin chuckled again, and I began to realize that I really didn't like him.

"What?" Lucille asked.

"Poor planning indeed."

"Why?"

"What fate do you think awaits the king's rivals?"

"I suppose he won't kill them all like a sensible tyrant."

"Direct, but prone to ally his enemies together. Not to mention many serve the queen, who might object. No, I suspect that his chief rivals will have the honor of leading the troops in their first battle in a thousand years."

"What do you—"

It may have felt as if my own mouth spoke the words, but I missed what Lucille said because my whole mind was suddenly hammered with the sound of a young man's voice saying, *BLECH!*

In the real world I heard coughing from somewhere outside Lucille's field of vision, followed by Krys's voice, "Why? Why would you have me drink—" The words broke off with more spitting and coughing.

Horrid . . . Ick . . . To the Seven Hells with her practical jokes!

Krys? I thought at the vaguely familiar voice.

The coughing, spitting, and cursing halted abruptly.

In my head I heard the new voice say tentatively, *Frank?*

I gave a mental cheer.

Rabbit heard you . . .

Yes! Yes! You can hear me! I mentally screamed at the heavens. *I'm here, Krys! I'm still here!*

I hear you all right. I heard a mental shush.

Sorry, I thought quietly. *I'm just excited.*

I'm sure, Krys thought. *But, Frank?*

What?

Why do you have to taste so nasty?

I didn't realize exactly how frayed my sanity had been until I was able to communicate. It did untold good for my state of mind, despite still being trapped as a passenger in Lucille's body. When Rabbit had questioned my existence, I had come pretty close to doubting it myself. But now that I could communicate with Krys, I had external confirmation that I wasn't a figment of anyone's imagination.

What laid all the doubts to rest was telling Krys Rabbit's given name. It was something no one else was in a position to know. The joyous yelp Rabbit gave at the news was enough to interrupt Lucille's conversation with our guest to glance over at the two girls hugging and crying just at the edge of the light from the campfire.

"What's going on over there?" Lucille asked them.

Krys and Rabbit disentangled themselves and faced us as if they'd been caught raiding the royal pantry. "Nothing, Your Highness," Krys said, with a subtle glance at Robin the Highwayman.

I felt Lucille arch an eyebrow. "Really?"

"Please forgive the interruption," Krys said, bowing slightly.

"Uh-huh." Lucille turned back to face Robin.

"They make a handsome couple," Robin volunteered.

"Uh, sure. Let's get back to the elf-king's court . . ."

I let Lucille continue the conversation without me while I consulted with my personal retainers. I found Robin's assumption about Krys and Rabbit amusing, not because of Krys's rather impressive attempt at crafting a male persona—I'd be the last one to look askance at anyone's gender issues—but because I knew the two girls could annoy each other as much as any two blood siblings I'd ever seen.

What now? Krys's voice spoke in my head.

First things first, I thought back. *How many of those herb packets does Rabbit still have with her?*

Krys whispered at Rabbit since the other girl's presence in my mind had faded. I guessed that our communications had lasted maybe half an hour. Not very long in the scheme of things.

Three more packets.

I thought something unkind. *All right. One has to be for Lucille—hopefully that will last longer since I'm in her head. You're going to have to talk to her after she's done with tall, dark, and elvish here.*

Sure. We should get some more of this stuff.

Do either of you know what's in it?

Even though she wasn't in Lucille's field of vision, I could sense her shrug. *No clue.*

And Brock's in no shape for sharing recipes, even if he was here.

It was one more thing we were going to have to track down in Fell Green.

"You're kidding," Lucille said when they finally freed her from her elf interrogation. Krys walked her away from the campfire while Rabbit watched the prisoner.

"No," Krys told her, her voice barely above a whisper. "Rabbit did hear Frank. This stuff Brock gave her for pain allowed us to talk."

"Uh-huh," Lucille said slowly.

"He said he's still in your head." Krys tapped a finger on her own forehead for emphasis.

Lucille shuddered, and I felt a little insulted by her reaction.

"Rabbit was trying to tell us earlier," Krys said.

Lucille closed her eyes and shook her head. "How is that possible?"

"I guess when you left the dragon, he didn't have anywhere else to go?"

"I guess not." She swallowed and opened her eyes. "Tea, you said?"

Krys nodded.

"I suppose I need to have some then." I heard the doubt in her voice. If Krys noticed it, she gave no sign.

Krys already had a tin cup of the concoction prepared and handed it to Lucille. Lucille glanced back at the campfire, where our prisoner was busy chatting up Rabbit. They were out of earshot, so we didn't hear exactly what the elf was saying. However, the occasional syllable made its way to us, ringing a little higher than I expected.

He's singing?

I was occupied with the incongruity of it, so I was caught off guard by one of the foulest-tasting liquids to ever pass my lips, in my mouth or anyone else's. The sensation was nearly indescribable, combining the worst elements of pond scum, swamp gas, and the kind of fungus that grew on dead things. Fermented slime mold came to mind.

Then I smelled it.

Once it was slithering down our throat, the odor of the stuff struck us from the inside. Once that hit, I realized that I had unfairly disparaged slime molds and fungus. The smell clawed its way through our sinuses like a rabid goblin tearing its way through a burlap sack filled with carrion and feces.

The only reason Lucille wasn't choking against the

assault on our senses was the anesthetic properties of the unwholesome concoction. The brew had completely paralyzed our gag reflex. Our mouth and throat had gone largely numb, but that did little to reduce the awful tastes and smells tearing through our skull.

Oh gods!

Holy Crap!

Frank?

Her mental voice tore through my thoughts like dragon fire through a scribe convention. *Ahhhh. Too loud.*

Frank? Her stentorian internal monologue lowered from the apocalyptic to the merely catastrophic.

Yes. I'm here. I gave a mental sigh.

You sound different. A puzzled note leaked into the demonic chorus of her thoughts.

I wasn't born with a princess's contralto, you know.

It's strange . . .

Stranger than your *mental voice? You couldn't scream "dragon" louder if you spit brimstone at me.*

I am a dragon!

The thought came reflexively quick at me and I doubted she knew what she said/thought until after we had both heard it.

I . . . I . . . Frank?

I'm sorry. It makes perfect sense. I didn't want to upset you.

I suddenly found out what uncontrolled draconic laughter sounded like inside the dragon's head. I had a brief worry about Lucille's sanity.

Lucille?

Upset me? You're worried that you upset me?

Well. . .

You're alive! she screamed in my mental ears. **You're alive! You're alive!**

My entire consciousness vibrated with the words, my soul ringing like church bells on a high holy day. I was stunned, and from more than the sound. My natural attitude, especially as things go wrong around me, tended to float somewhere between a critical remorse for my own bad decisions and a reflexive self-pity over those things for which I couldn't claim responsibility. I knew that it was a bad habit of mine, and I usually made sure to include it on the list of things I berated myself for.

Having my skull—our skull—shaking from a dragon leaping and shouting for joy at the mere fact of my existence, it didn't quite track with the kind of depressive nihilism I was comfortable with. It made me consider that, just maybe, something good *had* happened to me.

Yes, I'm alive. I said to myself as much as Lucille.

Good thing, because my mental companion still danced around me singing, **You're alive!**

Lucille . . .

You're alive!

We've established that . . .

You're alive!

Lucille! I snapped.

She finally stopped. After half a beat she said **Yay,** very quietly.

I couldn't keep from a mental chuckle.

I thought you were gone, really gone.

I gathered that. But I've been here since that debacle at the banquet.

Here?

I'm still in your head—my head—

Our head?

I don't think there was anywhere for me to go when you left the dragon.

I felt our head nod, and she froze a moment, hand halfway to her chin. **And I was planning to use the Tear—**

Yeah, I'm pretty sure that would be a bad idea.

"Damn it!" she said aloud and in my mind at the same time. Next to us, Krys winced as if she heard the dragon's voice speaking through Lucille.

I'm sorry; it made sense if you didn't know—

That was my backup plan. It was all I had in reserve. Damn!

It was the only way we knew to return her to the dragon. The nature of the artifact was to swap the wearer's identity to the nearest compatible body—for definitions of "compatible" forged within Nâtlac's evil jewel. However, we knew from experience that if Lucille wore it, she would end up in the dragon's skull. It made sense. If I had been in the dragon, however demented, it would return me to the princess's body. If it wasn't me, it would be easier to detain a hostile princess than a hostile dragon.

But, since I was in Lucille's skull, not the dragon's, there was no telling how the Tear of Nâtlac might react.

I understood how that must feel, having that one option close for her. I felt more than heard the tumble of random confused thoughts that followed her outburst, rage and guilt the primary emotions.

Oh Frank, I don't mean . . . I'm so happy you're . . . but . . .

You don't have to explain.
We need to get you a body.
Both of us.
And the elves . . .
We need to deal with the elves, I agreed.

We talked, and I think the conversation—just being able to communicate—was as much a relief for her as it was for me. I also discovered something else.

I realized, as she sought some measure of approval from me, that she was scared, way more scared than I had given her credit for. I had been riding along and watching her as she took command of a horrible situation, as she faced the elf-king one-on-one as if he was just another Baron Weslyess . . .

And the fear she felt wasn't for her life and limb. Her life as a dragon among humans seemed to have dulled her sense of that to—it seemed to me—an unhealthy degree. Her fear was that she would make a mistake and more people would get hurt.

A year ago, had you suggested to me that an aristocrat, someone of allegedly noble blood, might care about something other than their own skin and their own grasp on power, I would have patted you on the head, made some condescending comment about your optimistic and trusting nature, and would have immediately begun planning how to use such an absurd belief to separate you from your purse, since you were obviously too weak-minded to be trusted with any gold.

A year of knowing Lucille—and to an extent I'm still not willing to admit, her father—had slowly forced me to

amend my belief that all aristocracy was inherently populated by parasitic narcissists who thought way too
highly of themselves.

Not *all* aristocrats. Just *almost* all.

That was the kind of epiphany that had allowed me to
remain the princess of Lendowyn this long without hat-
ing myself.

Or Lucille.

I knew that her near-misstep with the Tear of Nâtlac
had rattled her, but I had no idea how much she had
been second-guessing herself until she started asking my
opinion on what was happening. I think she asked me
about every decision she had made since I had lost consciousness at the banquet.

Especially about impersonating me.

I didn't know what to do.

*No, you're right. You don't want your father having the
dragon killed out of hand. Even if it's not me in there, it's
your body—*

It was another mistake. Like the Tear.

Lucille?

**Look at the damage it's already done. The dragon's
alive, attacking villages now—**

You made a judgment call.

The wrong one.

*Maybe. But you weren't in any position to attack the
dragon anyway. Neither was your father.*

Hmm.

What was in your power to do?

This is all just so frustrating.

Believe me, I know.

I'm sorry, I didn't mean—

I know what you meant.

Trying to figure out what to do . . . I should have just turned myself over to him. "Equivalent exchange" and all . . .

Three problems with that—

You're along for the ride, too. And I wouldn't turn Sir Forsythe over to him, even if he'd stayed around. And . . . what?

He actually specified the dragon.

Because he thinks the dragon is still royal.

Does he?

What do you mean?

His exact words, "You have a day to give me the dragon and whomever bears responsibility for my son's murder."

Slip of the tongue?

How many elven agreements have you heard of where they were fuzzy and imprecise about language? That's how they manage to screw people over so effectively. They rely on their victims to make assumptions and misunderstand the wording. Is Timoras going to make that kind of mistake unintentionally?

And he said, "whomever bears responsibility for my son's murder . . ."

Not, "the person who killed him."

He thinks his son was set up?

Suspects it, at least. If your elvish boyfriend back there's right, Timoras has to threaten war because he can't point at who did it—

My elvish what?

—and he has to retaliate somehow or his rivals will

move against him, no matter who was behind the original attack.

What did you mean by that?

You're awfully interested in Robin Half-Elf.

Are you kidding?

I honestly thought I had been. But I realized that something about our mental connection made it harder to mask certain things. I realized that my tone had cut a bit deeper than good-natured teasing warranted.

I'm sorry, forget it.

You think I was . . . Are you insane? Some bastard highwayman?

Not that far from what I was when we first met. I hadn't intended to think that. I really didn't want to think that at her, but it leaked out before I could stop it.

I don't believe you. All that's happening, and you're jealous?

It's not the right time for this—

You're the one who brought it up.

I wasn't thinking.

Isn't that all we're doing here?

You know what I mean.

No, Frank, I don't.

I froze, guarding my tumbling thoughts from more embarrassing leakage. What *did* I mean? Why did I have to throw in that dig at Robin? It had slipped out before I even thought about it, so to speak. I know that I didn't trust him. He seemed a little too convenient. And a little too handsome . . .

What in Nâtlac's Hell?

I *was* jealous.

I steeled myself and thought at Lucille, *I'm sorry.
Sometimes I just get stupid.*

She didn't respond, and I could almost sense her fuming.

*I can't help but envy the man who monopolized your
attention like that. It doesn't make a lot of sense, especially
given the nature of our relationship . . .*

I trailed off because I felt as if I was venturing into
dangerous territory again.

*You see, I never told you how I've regretted—the one
time that we were both human again—I didn't . . .*

She should have interrupted me again.

Lucille? I'm floundering here.

Nothing.

Lucille? Are you there? Did the tea wear off?

Still nothing.

"*Lucille?*"

Krys spun and turned to face us in response to my last
call. I met her gaze before I fully understood what had
happened.

"Your Highness?" she asked in a concerned tone.

"I think we have another problem," I whispered with
Lucille's mouth.

CHAPTER 12

I stumbled over to a tree and glanced back over Lucille's shoulder to check on Robin Elf-Boy and Rabbit. Neither seemed to be paying any attention to me.

Good, things were complicated enough.

Krys stepped up and placed a hand on Lucille's arm. "What's the matter?"

"Give me a moment." The sound and feel of my own thoughts emerging from Lucille's throat felt surreal and disorienting.

Lucille? Can you hear me?

Lucille?

No response.

I felt very alone.

"Are you all right?" Krys asked.

I shook my head. "She's gone," I whispered.

"She's . . . *Frank?*"

"Yeah." I leaned my back against a tree and rubbed my temples, closing my eyes. My head didn't throb, not like the agony that had accompanied my prior bouts of body shifting. However, every fiber in my being still expected the pain trolls to come with their pickaxes to mine the ore from the back of my eyeballs.

"Frank? How . . ."

I shook my head slowly. "Brock's tea," I said. "It must have had a more intense effect on us. I didn't think this through." I sighed. "What else is new?"

"What are you talking about?"

"If that stuff is powerful enough to let you hear my thoughts when you're over there," I gestured at Krys. "I should have considered what it would do to someone I shared a skull with."

"Is Lucille . . . ?" She couldn't finish the thought.

"I think she's still here, just like I was."

Krys nodded and took a step back toward the campfire. "We just need to make some more—"

I grabbed her arm and she jerked her head back toward me.

"No."

"No? What?"

"Two problems. First, we only have two of those packets left."

"We'll get more."

I nodded. "At Fell Green. But that's why we should wait. There we can have an expert tell us what's happening to me and Lucille. What if there's more going on? Other side effects?"

"But Lucille . . ."

"If we just swapped, she'll be okay. I survived it. But if I have learned anything by diving in and using magic without bothering to find out the consequences, it's that it doesn't end well."

"Uh . . ." Krys had personal experience with my bad decisions. My drunken use of the Tear of Nâtlac literally triggered a war involving most of the major powers on the continent. It was my own bad example that had kept Krys from making a similar mistake the short time she had possession of the Tear. She stepped back and looked at me. "You're right . . . Are you sure Lucille's all right?"

I grimaced. "No, I'm not. But if this did some harm to her, I'm not confident that more of the same wouldn't just make things worse."

"So we find an expert."

"Yeah."

She pointed at Robin. "What about him?"

What about him?

I sighed. "I don't trust him, but I'd trust him less out of sight. And Lucille already told him we were Princess Frank. That simplifies things."

Actually it didn't simplify anything.

"So we're taking him?"

"We're taking him." I winced at my own words, thinking about the last exchange before I lost contact with Lucille. Why was it I always seemed to find ways to make a bad situation worse? Nope, good old Frank Blackthorne couldn't just leave Lucille happy that he wasn't dead or playing crazy dragon . . .

I reached between my breasts, lifted the elf-king's pendant, and stared at it.

Who *was* the dragon?

It was a question that I'd been a bit too preoccupied to consider. We had all been too preoccupied to consider. Lucille had thought—hoped, really—that it had been *me* inside the dragon skin. I'd known better, but I think my focus had been distorted by being little more than a rider following Lucille around. She had been avoiding the subject, so I'd only paid attention to the problems she had been addressing. There were enough of those to keep anyone busy.

But it was the obvious question. I think the only reason Lucille, Krys, or Rabbit had yet to bring it up is they were distracted by the fact I was still alive. As touching as that was, it overlooked a major issue.

Once the prince's spell fired, Lucille was no longer in residence. So someone or something else had replaced her in the dragon's head. Knowing who or what would probably be a big clue to who was behind all this.

"Are you sure you're all right?" Krys asked.

I dropped the pendant and looked up at her. "No."

Again we slept on bedrolls around the remains of the fire. Even with his hands still tied, Robin didn't seem particularly perturbed and fell asleep immediately.

Of course he snored.

Almost as bad as Rabbit.

Despite my royal status, I insisted on taking at least part of the watch so Rabbit and Krys could get some rest. They objected, but for better or worse, I was in charge regardless of who was driving my skull at the moment. Besides, there was little chance of me sleeping now.

Also, I knew myself well enough to know that I wanted some time alone to brood. I wasn't done wallowing in self-pity.

"Ah," I whispered to myself, "and I bet you didn't pack any alcohol."

I shook my head and stared into the fire.

"Lucille, I'm sorry."

Of course no one responded.

"You know sometimes I talk without thinking. I didn't mean . . ."

I shook my head.

"I don't know what I meant. I know I didn't want this—" I placed my hand on my face, her hand on her face. "Not at your expense. I'm really hoping you're still there, watching like I was. We're going to figure out something. There'll be someone at Fell Green . . ."

My voice trailed off as I watched the embers flicker. I tried to sense Lucille, but, if anything, my skull felt emptier than usual.

Our skull.

I kept flexing my hands in a half-conscious confirmation that I was still in control of Lucille's body. For about the tenth time I second-guessed my decision not to accept Krys's suggestion that I quaff another draught of the evil herb tea. The uncertainty of Lucille's presence ate at me.

So did my sudden responsibility.

Say what you wanted about my period of limbo behind the princess's eyes, it had relieved me of my apparently unlimited potential to make things worse.

"Did I do the right thing?" I asked Lucille. "I don't know. I want to take that tea. I want you back. But that has all the hallmarks of the hasty decisions that have worked so well for me in the past."

The night surrounded me in suffocating silence. Even the snores of Robin and Rabbit seemed muted.

"It just seems a bad idea before consulting someone who knows better. I don't want to make things worse again."

I stared at the embers until their red light seemed to be the only thing left in the universe. The forest around me retreated into impenetrable darkness. Slowly the silence became complete.

I was proud of myself for realizing something was wrong before I began hearing the distant screams of millions of tormented souls. My head snapped up as I jumped to my feet. Around me, the trees had been replaced by fleshy pillars, ropy with veins, that climbed out of the ruddy light to vanish into complete blackness above. The forest floor was now made from an infinite plain of irregularly shaped flagstones that all bore some remnants of the beings who had been shaped to form them; eyes, noses, teeth, fingers, tongues. The flagstones pulsed and breathed, eyes looking at me, fingers making weak gestures, tongues licking their lips.

"Oh no," I whispered. "You're kidding me."

"Having a happy anniversary, Frank?" The voice burrowed into my ears like a hornet attempting to lay its eggs in my brain.

I spun around to face the Dark Lord Nâtlac.

In the long list of entities I never wanted to see or hear from again, the Dark Lord was at the head of it by a large margin. As deities go, he was probably the one most likely to drive his worshippers into gibbering insanity. Even if he granted you a favor, you could count on it causing countless deaths, destroying empires, and bringing the recipient to the brink of hopeless despair—not like I'm talking from direct experience or anything.

Worse, we had not parted on good terms. There's nothing quite as corrosive to one's optimistic view of the future as the realization that one of the seven nastiest lords of the Underworld is annoyed with you.

The Dark Lord Nâtlac looked much as I remembered him. He appeared as a tall, handsome man wearing a long robe of black leather formed from the remnants of tanned faces—human and otherwise. If you looked too closely at it you might see the expressions on them grimace, eyes move under stitched eyelids, and tongues press against sewn lips.

I looked too closely and thought I recognized one of the faces as the late Queen Fiona.

"What are you doing here?" I blurted without thinking. It probably wasn't the most diplomatic greeting.

"What do you think?" His voice burrowed in, laid its eggs, hatched, and burrowed out the other side.

"Gloating?"

"Do I need to gloat?" He walked up to me and glided a finger down the side of Lucille's face. His touch felt as if it left a sticky trail from some half-rotten fruit, to be consumed by a trail of tiny carnivorous ants.

"I . . . uh . . ." Strangely enough, confronting the evil lord of absolute darkness left me a few syllables shy of my normal eloquence.

"Did you doubt me?"

I sputtered and tried to shrink away from his corrosive touch. "W—Wh—Wh—"

"Why am I here? What do I want?" He stepped away from me and I exhaled in relief. He spun to look up into the unfathomable upper reaches of his realm. "Frank, do you truly seek answers to questions you already have the answers to?"

I had a brief flash of memory, the dream-vision of the Goddess Lysea. *Above all else, what does any god want?*

I looked at his profile, staring up into the darkness, and something felt . . . off.

It's hard to articulate what exactly it was. After all, it was the nature of the Dark Lord Nâtlac to be either subtly or grandly *wrong* along every possible axis one might measure "right." His conversational tone sounded normal while still having a chitinous undertone that burrowed into my brain. His profile appeared like a handsome man while still suggesting that, just around the corner on the side I couldn't see, writhed an abomination that might make the gaping abyss of absolute madness appear perfectly reasonable. Just his touch on Lucille's cheek had left behind a sense of slivers of glass wriggling very slightly under the surface of our skin.

Every time he'd ever shown up, things had been "off."

But what I felt now wasn't that.

"You caused this?"

"Was there any doubt?"

I realized that I still stood in Lucille's body. Maybe that was it? I decided that it was probably a good sign. The times I had actually been "in" the Dark Lord's realm, I had worn my original body, the one that had been worm food for over a year now. Whatever I saw of the environment around me, the fact that I wore Lucille's body meant that I hadn't gone to him, he had come to me.

Wait a minute. Why is that a good *sign?*

"What do you want?" I asked.

"So that is the question you want to ask me?" The

Dark Lord gave a smile that reminded me of maggots swarming carrion.

I realized what was wrong—aside from everything else.

I took a deep, steadying breath and straightened my spine, and I stared directly at the Dark Lord Nâtlac despite the effort making my eyes want to rebel and crawl back into my skull to escape.

"Up to now," I said quietly, "you've been a lot more direct."

"You think you know me?"

"Yes," I whispered. "I don't want to. But I do." I glanced around at the pulsing, ruddy landscape and added, "Or, I should say, I know the Dark Lord Nâtlac."

I looked back at the disturbing eidolon before me and said, "You? Not so much."

He laughed and it was like a thousand undead kittens digging gangrenous needle-claws into the flesh of my ears. "You don't know me?"

"Who are you?"

The agonizing laugh continued.

"*What* are you?"

He wheezed and shook his head. "You believe who or what I am matters at the moment? You think that is the question?"

"What's the right question?"

"Don't you already know?"

I shook my head in frustration. "What's the point of this if you don't tell me anything?"

"Why don't you tell me? Isn't this *your* conversation?"

"You came to me."

Whoever, whatever it was, stepped up uncomfortably close and whispered into my ear, lips brushing my cheek so lightly that I could feel something squirming that wasn't anything close to human flesh. "Wasn't I already here?"

I woke up screaming.

Krys and Rabbit ran to my side instantly as I sat up on my bedroll hyperventilating. I felt my own face reddening, half in terror, half in embarrassment.

"Frank?" Krys asked, kneeling next to me. "Are you all right?"

I nodded involuntarily and said, "Nightmare."

I reached up to rub my eyes and my head jerked away from my own touch.

What?

I stared at my own right hand and I had an uneasy feeling that I wasn't doing the staring.

"Frank?" Krys asked.

My head shook by itself, eyes never leaving my hand, frozen in place before my face. "No," Lucille's mouth whispered without me.

At least you're still here. I mentally sighed in relief.

From beyond Krys, I heard Robin's voice. "Is something the matter?"

"No! Nothing!" Lucille snapped at him, shifting so our body faced away from the half-elf. She looked over at Krys.

"What?" Krys whispered.

"I can't move my right arm," Lucille whispered back.

What?

Her right hand still hung where it had stopped while I'd tried to rub our eyes.

While *I* had tried to rub our eyes.

I experimentally tried to wriggle our fingers.

Lucille jumped back as if her own hand was a broadsword swinging at her face.

"I didn't do that." Her words came out in a strangled gasp, a shout she only managed to restrain at the last minute. "What's going on? I didn't move—"

I felt the tide of panic rise in our voice, in our heartbeat, in the copper taste of our breath. I did the only thing I could think of. I raised my finger and gently pressed it against our lips.

"Wha—" came Lucille's half-hidden voice.

Krys stared at us with wide eyes. She glanced back at Robin, who was getting to his feet. Krys leaned in with a conspiratorial whisper. "Your Highness? Could that be Frank?"

"I don't . . ." Lucille trailed off, because I had swung her hand up between us and Krys and gave them both an enthusiastic thumbs-up gesture.

"I guess so," Lucille finished.

I reached up and patted her gently on our cheek.

CHAPTER 13

It was a good thing I only had control of an arm. While she tried to get up from the bedroll I unconsciously reached over and "helped" to push her upright. Apparently my timing was off, because I sent her off balance and almost toppled her back over.

If I had been controlling a leg, we'd have had some mobility issues.

Even walking around a couple of paces felt strange. Our arm fell into a natural swinging motion — which was fine, I guess — but it was *my* natural swinging motion, which seemed slightly out of phase with hers. I felt it as a weird jerking sensation in our shoulders. I know she felt it, too, same body and all, and she'd simply come to a halt every dozen steps or so, and shake her head.

When we got to her horse she put her left hand up on the saddle and stood there a moment.

"Frank?" she whispered in a voice so low that only we heard us.

Oh, right . . .

I lifted our right arm so I could grip next to her left and briefly distracted myself by pondering how the current situation had made the pronoun confusion around my life even worse.

She cleared her throat, and I realized that she actually wanted both hands to help pull herself into the saddle.

Sorry, I thought at her, even though she still apparently couldn't hear me.

We vaulted, somewhat unsteadily, into the saddle.

Our hands fumbled at cross-purposes, taking up the reins before we managed to coordinate our grip left and right.

Oh, this is going to be fun.

Lucille must have had similar thoughts, because she subvocalized, "*Please don't get us killed.*"

I rotated our right hand slightly, careful not to jerk the reins, so I could give her a thumbs-up.

She let out an exasperated sigh.

What do you want? My communication skills are somewhat limited at the moment.

The five of us rode the final few miles to Fell Green without any incident. Rabbit led Robin's horse from her own, but Robin got to ride upright this time. Lucille rode up front with Krys, mostly I think to avoid interacting with Robin. It was clear that the half-elf sensed something strange was going on, and Lucille probably didn't want to damage the fiction that she was Princess Frank.

Along the way Krys found a dozen ways to quietly ask what was happening and Lucille found an equal number of ways to say she didn't know. For myself, I would have thought that having a small measure of physical control, a means to confirm my presence and interact with the world, would have been a good thing.

But it didn't feel like it. If anything, my random control of Lucille's right hand and arm felt ominous, as if the rules were changing before we knew what they actually were.

We managed to reach the Fell River and the bridge to Fell Green without me inadvertently asking the horse beneath us to do anything inconvenient.

The entrance to the wizard town wasn't much to look at. Literally.

As we approached, all that was visible was an old stone bridge arcing over the Fell River connecting Lendowyn to its neighbor Dermonica. Despite a relationship that had thawed a bit over the past year—largely due to a war I accidentally started—this particular crossing appeared ill-traveled. Any town of any significance was, pointedly, inconveniently far away.

The bridge also had a reputation for moving around so that, unless you had our particular destination in mind at the outset, you would never find this particular bridge regardless of what any maps might tell you.

Of course finding the lonely old bridge was only halfway to Fell Green.

"*Heads up, Frank.*" Lucille whispered.

She placed her left hand, tensed her leg muscles, and hesitated a moment for me to catch up to the dismount. I was just a hair's breadth behind her, and the only sign of uncoordination was a slightly unbalanced landing that caused her to take an extra step to the right. I don't even think the horse noticed.

She took a step forward, toward the bridge. She stopped suddenly and looked over her right shoulder. Then she took a backward step and cleared her throat, tilting her head slightly where the horse stood.

Oh, yeah.

I reached out and took the reins where they arced under the horse's neck so Lucille could lead the animal on foot. I marveled at how the universe had found something more annoying than locking me powerless and silent in Lucille's skull.

We walked up to where the stone bridge met the shore and a familiar old beggar stepped out from behind one of the pillars flanking the entrance to the bridge proper. He was bald, as ancient as any man I had ever seen, and wore a ragged robe the same shade of milky gray as his clouded eyes. In one hand he leaned on a staff, and in the other hand he held a cracked wooden bowl. He held out the bowl and started to say, "Alms."

Then, as he fully rounded the pillar, he stopped, straightened his spine, and a sour expression crossed his face.

"You two again?" He harrumphed and held out the bowl.

Lucille reached into her pouch one-handed and took out a gold crown for each of us. Four coins rattled into the bowl, and he tilted his head slightly, bowl still held out.

I could feel a puzzled expression cross our face, and the not-so-blind gatekeeper looked annoyed. Slowly, enunciating each word as if speaking to someone who didn't quite grasp the language, he said, "Both. Of. You."

After a moment, Lucille said, "Oh," and tossed one more coin into the bowl. Only then did the wizard city of Fell Green deign to show itself.

The moment the last coin clattered into the bowl, the opposite shore suddenly appeared much closer. That was because a dagger-shaped island had appeared in the middle of a suddenly much wider Fell River. The bridge before us now led to a stone-cobbled highway that bisected the island before continuing on to another bridge that continued the passage to Dermonica. To one side of the highway, a great walled city rose up, claiming half the island until no crag or stray stone was left unworked. It seemed quite possible that there might be no actual island beneath the stones on that side of the highway, only the city itself plunging deep beneath the rapids of the Fell River.

On the opposite side of the highway was a wood, deep green and primeval. The greenery was a bit too lush and a bit too vibrant, as innocent of any artifice as the city side was innocent of any sign of nature.

I thought of the dream-vision Lysea again, where I stood between the elf city and the elf woods, with armored fae emerging from both.

Lucille grunted, disrupting my thoughts. I realized that we had started walking forward, and our right arm trailed behind us, still limply holding the horse's reins.

Yeah, right.

I gently pulled our arm forward, leading the horse to walk up next to us. We led our small party over the bridge and between the city walls on one side, and the dense forest on the other. We walked between worlds now, elven and mortal as well as city and forest. It wasn't the only way between, but it was the easiest. I suspected

that our half-elf highwayman was right when he specu-
lated that the prince had come this way. Had trod upon
the same road we walked now.

I realized that it wasn't coincidence that this place resembled my vision with Lysea. I suspected that, if we
could see beyond the veil between this place and elfland,
I might see the same city and the same wood, and the
same army of fae massing at the mound between city
and wood.

That was not reassuring.

I felt better when we passed through the city gates
and left the road and the brooding forest behind us.

Once inside the city proper, Lucille paused a moment
to check the bauble around her neck to assure herself that
the apocalypse wasn't imminent. It didn't seem to be.

She put the pendant back, paused, then picked it up
again.

"Oh crap," she whispered, sounding almost like me.
She stared into the depths of the hourglass and I tried to
see what she saw.

Oh crap.

"What's the matter?" Krys asked.

"The sand's moving faster now."

Of course it was. We had just taken a journey halfway
under the hill by entering this city. If the pendant ran on
the elves' time, we were much closer to it here.

"What do we do?" Krys asked.

"Act quickly and leave," Lucille said. "That's all we
can do."

From behind us, Robin spoke up, "Is there a problem,
Your Highness? Perhaps I can be of some assistance."

She let the pendant drop and said, "It's none of your concern."

Lucille had a better memory for the city layout than I did. She navigated us through the streets without pausing.

The city we walked through wasn't particularly different from any other large city full of shops, merchants, and travelers. If it weren't for three things, we may have been in any other comparably sized town.

The first, and most obvious difference between here and, say, the capital of Lendowyn—other than appearing less threadbare and poverty-stricken—was the large numbers of folks that would have counted as tiny minorities elsewhere. The streets were filled with all manner of inhuman creatures: dwarves, trolls, goblins, pixies, ogres, and beings less familiar to me, all mixing with a humanity that bore more than its share of rich robes bearing arcane symbols. All these different populations mixed freely in a crowd remarkably absent of sounds of terror or breaking bones. Everyone carried on with their business with a notable lack of violence and bloodshed.

Less violence and bloodshed than on a typical street in Lendowyn's capital, now that I thought about it.

The second difference was in the *kind* of wares and services being provided. Elsewhere practitioners of the wizardly arts, black, white, and gray, tended to carry on their business well out of sight of the general public. There was a good reason for this. Wizards and such tended to use supplies that just weren't pleasant. The objects that weren't horrifying to look at tended to have an odor that threatened to turn your sinus cavity inside out. Here those wares were spread out on blankets, or filled carts, in full view of the nauseated passerby.

The remaining difference was the fact that no one showed any particular interest in the bound prisoner we led along with us. There were few enough places where anyone would intervene with an armed trio on behalf of a tall dark stranger—maybe in a capital city one of the city guard might stop us and inquire what was going on—but almost *anywhere* the public would have at least eyed our group warily, if only to avoid us.

Here in Fell Green, no one spared us a second glance.

Before I realized it, Lucille stopped us in front of an inn called The Talking Eye.

I don't know why I should have been surprised at her choice of lodgings. Our unceremonious departure from Fell Green last time had nothing to do with the inn or its management, and more to do with the armies that had converged on the town. If another war hadn't yet broken out, I supposed we didn't have a problem.

Like the street vendors and the rest of the general public, the innkeep at The Talking Eye was unperturbed at Robin's bound presence. The vaguely goatlike old man didn't spare any words for Robin, and only briefly acknowledged his presence with a glance while quoting a price for lodgings.

Lucille paid it without haggling.

The old goat gave us another serious look and told us, "House rules—no rituals." He glanced at Robin. "Don't like cleaning up blood."

"No problem," Krys said back to him as Lucille led us to our room.

Once in our room Lucille stared at the lone bed and sighed.

"What now, Your Highness?" Robin asked in a slightly amused tone.

"Sit down," Lucille told him. She glanced down at her right arm, then pointed at a chair with her left. She gestured with that hand at Rabbit and Krys and said, "Keep an eye on him."

She turned away and lifted the pendant again. The very slow hourglass was closing on half full now. Were it just from our travel here, that would leave us with only three days. But Lucile watched the sand move, and I knew that she was trying to gauge how much of that had come from our brief time at Fell Green.

She dropped it and reached into her belt and pulled out the scroll that the elven prince had been reading. To my relief, she didn't unroll the parchment to look at the uncomfortable script lining the page. She simply glanced at it as if reassuring herself that it was still there.

"Is it truly necessary for me to remain bound?"

"Yes," Lucille said simply.

"Ahh, ever the gracious hostess."

Lucille swung around, pointing a clumsy accusation at him with the scroll in her left hand. Before any words left her mouth, Robin added, "I don't suppose you noticed?"

"Noticed?" While she spoke I reached up and placed her right hand on her wrist and gently eased her arm downward until the scroll pointed at the floor. I didn't know if the thing was still loaded.

"The streets. The city. You have been here before, have you not?"

"And?"

"Did you notice what is missing?" Robin asked.

Lucille stared at him, and Krys filled the silence. "No elves."

"What?" Lucille turned to her.

"Last time we were here," Krys said, "there were plenty of elves around."

Robin nodded. "Here we are as close to Timoras's realm as one can get without traveling under the hill."

"And the elves?" Lucille asked.

"I suspect they suffered from a prior commitment," he said.

Lucille snorted. "I would have expected at least some of them around laying odds on the outcome."

"I'm sure they are," Robin said, "but a sane book-maker does not take wagers while standing in the middle of the field of honor."

Here?

Lucille echoed the word as I thought it, "Here?"

"Did being princess during the past war teach you nothing about strategy? What would be the first thing the elf-king would do in a war against the mortal world? What would any general do?"

"Protect his flanks," Lucille whispered. "This place and anywhere like it. They'll be the first to fall."

"Ah, Francis, apparently you do make as credible a sovereign as I do a thief."

The name stung me. For the moment I had forgotten that, to Robin, Lucille hadn't ever been anyone else. In response, Lucille said something that, for reasons I couldn't account for, I found horribly disturbing.

"Don't call me Francis," she said. "I hate that."

CHAPTER 14

Lucille tasked Rabbit with babysitting the prisoner while she took Krys to accompany us to a wizard's lair.

Once we were a few dozen paces away from The Talking Eye, Krys asked, "Your Highness?"

"Yes?" Lucille said in a preoccupied tone. Her gaze had been sweeping the streets and markets around us, apparently confirming what Robin had said. Not a single elf in evidence.

"Are you Lucille or Frank right now?"

Her gaze snapped back to Krys. "What?"

"Who am I talking to?"

"Me—I mean, Lucille."

"Okay." Krys nodded and kept walking.

"Wait, why did—What?"

"You just sounded like Frank back there," Krys said.

"That's ridiculous," she responded.

Yeah, as if things weren't confusing enough.

"As if things weren't confusing enough," Lucille continued.

My internal monologue was brought up short like a pixie colliding with a cast-iron frying pan. She hadn't just repeated my thoughts, she had spoken them simultaneously.

ucille stepped up and used the knocker. This time I
ced that, in addition to the knock being muffled by
damp wood, there was also an audible squish that
e my skin crawl. I made an effort to keep my hand
scratching anything. I didn't want to startle Lucille.
never liked this place," Krys said.

understood the sentiment.

ucille reached up for the knocker again, but the
r screeched open on its rusty hinges, leaving her
hanging in empty space.

You two again!?" rasped an elderly man's voice. Lu-
shifted her gaze slightly downward to look at the
ped form of the Wizard Crumley. His long white beard
ned even more green-streaked than last time, and I
ced some rough texture that might have been the start
patch of moss in there.

We've come to—" Lucille began. Crumley inter-
ed her by leaning close to us and taking a deep sniff.
t was uncomfortable enough, but the sensation of his
y exhale brushing against us made our skin crawl
se than the swampy insects and the too-warm mists.
He shook his head.

To hire your services," she finished.

Of course you have. But you know the enchantment
ne. Don't you, my fair dragon?"

ucille nodded and I had a brief episode of confusion
e I realized Crumley referred to our last visit. That
been my long-concluded, Nâtlac artifact–induced
swap with Bartholomew. *That* enchantment was
gone.

at must have been what he was referring to.

What did that mean?

Whatever it was, I didn't think I liked it.

I found myself clenching Lucille's hand into a fist.

"Are we going to Crumley?" Krys asked.

Lucille nodded. The Wizard Crumley was not the
most inviting of wizards—especially to anyone with mil-
dew allergies—but he had been something of a help on
our last trip here. He also had some knowledge of the
Dark Lord Nâtlac and was willing to share it . . .

Willing to *sell* it, anyway.

"You think he can tell us who made that scroll?" Krys
asked.

"At least what it was intended to do," Lucille answered.

As they talked I thought I saw a familiar face in the
crowd near the front of an inn much more lavish than
The Talking Eye.

No, that can't be who I think it is.

Lucille abruptly jerked her head around to stare in
that direction.

"What is it?" Krys asked.

"I thought I saw . . ." she trailed off.

"What?"

Lucille shook her head as she studied the crowd. I
didn't see any sign of our mutual friend anymore. I don't
think she did either. She turned her head back to our
path. "Nothing," she said. "Probably just someone who
looked like him."

"Who?"

"King Dudley of Grünwald."

"King Dudley? Why would he be here?"

"Exactly." Lucille again echoed my thoughts precisely.

I knew that, as a prince, Dudley had frequented Fell Green quite often. I doubt that continued after I had relieved Grünwald of his mother, the queen. Since then his bastard half brother Bartholomew had sparked a multifront war that had decimated Grünwald militarily and—last I had heard—left the Grünwald court in a maelstrom of intrigue and conspiracy that would most likely capture Dudley's complete attention.

Of course, I may have had a hand in the latter as well—having unintentionally swapped bodies with Bartholomew for a while. Though you could argue that the body swap was intentional on my part. It was the "with Bartholomew" part that had been unintentional. That, and the whole plunging all the neighboring kingdoms into war thing.

So, of course, it would be an evil coincidence that our perennial nemesis from Grünwald would be here in Fell Green, especially considering he was—like most of his mother's family—a devotee of Nâtlac, and probably the high priest or something, now that the Dark Lord and I were on the outs.

It would be an impossibly evil coincidence.

If it *was* a coincidence.

If the evil scroll the elf-prince had read at the banquet was a spell from Nâtlac's repertoire, where better for it to have come from? King Dudley had a long list of grievances with me and Frank . . .

Huh? Me and *Lucille*.

My thoughts tumbled and Lucille stopped walking and shook her head, seeming to echo my own confusion.

"Your Highness?" Krys said.

"I'm all right," Lucille said. "I just had a ⟨ ⟩ sation."

"Lucille?" I felt Krys's mailed hand on o⟨ ⟩

"Give me a moment, I'll be fine."

The Wizard Crumley lived in an unpleasant ⟨ ⟩ Fell Green. Regardless of the weather elsewh⟨ ⟩ ley's neighborhood seemed perpetually co⟨ ⟩ blanket of air that was always too warm and ⟨ ⟩ The moisture saturated the air to the point t⟨ ⟩ to condense into something more steam tha⟨ ⟩ stones of the road and the surrounding build⟨ ⟩ slick with algae and moss, and on every bui⟨ ⟩ exposed timber appeared black and spongy w⟨ ⟩ Clouds of buzzing insects hovered over pudd⟨ ⟩ road, puddles that had stood long enough to ⟨ ⟩ own scum of algae.

The winding narrow lane that led to Cru⟨ ⟩ zigzagged as it descended below the nomina⟨ ⟩ the Fell River even as it approached the ⟨ ⟩ though there was no way to visually confir⟨ ⟩ where we stood. Once we stopped befor⟨ ⟩ streaked black door that led to the wiz⟨ ⟩ found ourselves in a virtual canyon made ⟨ ⟩ rounding buildings.

All of which, I noted, faced away from⟨ ⟩ happened in this alley was something th⟨ ⟩ denizens of this foul part of Fell Green h⟨ ⟩ to witness.

Now there's a pleasant thought.

"I have a scroll. I need to know what it did, exactly, and where it might have come from."

Crumley sighed. "This is the Dark Lord again, isn't it?"

"How do you know?" Krys asked.

Crumley turned toward her and wriggled his fingers. "Wizard!" he said. He took a step back and straightened. "Also, his magic is stinking up the place something fierce. You brought money?"

Lucille took out a pouch and handed it to the wizard. He hefted it and grimaced at it in his hand. He muttered, "Of course, too much to turn down." The pouch disappeared into his robes and he waved us forward into the dim corridor beyond the door. "Come in, Madam Dragon, Sir Handmaiden, Princess Thief."

We stepped in and Krys followed, sparing the Wizard Crumley an uncomfortable look.

"Wipe your feet and don't touch anything," Crumley said, slamming the door behind us.

We passed through the same damp corridors as last time, past the same disordered and crumbling bookshelves, down the same narrow algae-stained stairs that descended under the same mineral-crusted vaults.

We ended in the same workshop, deep under the bowels of Fell Green, and probably beneath the bottom of Fell River as well. The vast workshop spilled from the foot of the stone steps, out beyond where torchlight would reach. As before, several long wood tables waited for us, piled high with wizardly clutter; jars, bottles, ceramic crocks; rocks, crystals, and bones; bundles of feathers and others of dried leaves or twigs; and the books, of course. The closest volume was open to an illustration that seemed more recreational than ritualistic, the image of a well-endowed pair, one an elvish woman, the other a creature with a bull's head and an expression that reminded me of Baron Weslyess. Thankfully, Crumley darted forward and slammed the volume shut before I noticed any more details.

"Leftover research," he muttered as he shoved the book into a pile of arcane literature. He kept pushing books out of the way, to the point some slipped over the far edge of the table and thudded on the floor. Crumley didn't seem to notice. He held out his hand and gestured without turning around. "Scroll," he said.

Our hands fumbled with each other as Lucille reached for the evil scroll at the same time I did. We both held the parchment briefly before I let it go. Lucille snorted in frustration.

Crumley took the scroll and muttered almost absently, "Don't worry, that part won't last long."

"What?" Again, Lucille's words and my thoughts were identical.

Crumley didn't elaborate as he pored over the scroll, flattening it on the table. He said "um" a few times, then nodded, "Yes, that explains it. Makes sense."

"What makes sense?" Lucille asked. "What part won't last long?"

"What kind of spell's on that scroll?" Krys asked. For once she, rather than Lucille, echoed my thoughts.

Crumley pointed over to her with a gnarled finger. I noticed that even his nails were stained green. "That, my good fellow, is the question, isn't it?"

He spun around to face Lucille. "Isn't it, though? What spell was cast that caused such . . . inconvenience?"

"What spell?" Lucille asked, annoyance creeping into her voice.

"That's just it. No spell. This is no enchantment, quite the opposite. It is an unmaking, a non-spell, a reversal."

"A reversal of what?" Krys asked.

Lucille sucked in a breath. Quietly she said, "Oh."

Crumley nodded. "Our dragon gets it."

"Gets what?" Krys said.

"Elhared's original spell, the one that made me the dragon, and made Frank the princess. This reversed it."

"But Frank's still—"

"Still in there." Crumley tapped Lucille's forehead with one of his green-stained nails. "No body for him to go back to."

Lucille shook her head. "This isn't . . . I . . ."

"Don't worry," Crumley said. "It won't last."

"*What* won't last?"

"The symptoms will fade as the spirits merge. It will be a little disorienting, but you should be normal after—"

Lucille grabbed Crumley by his robe and yanked him forward. "What do you mean 'merge'?"

"Please," he said. "Unhand me if you want the benefit of my expertise."

She let him go. "Explain," she demanded through clenched teeth.

Crumley sighed. "You are in an unstable situation. Outside of some lycanthropic infections that I only know about theoretically, two souls cannot coexist in the same body for a protracted period. Eventually the identities will merge into a new consciousness."

But I don't want to merge into a new consciousness.
I like my consciousness the way it is.

I think one of those thoughts was mine, and one was Lucille's, but I couldn't tell which one. Crumley kept on talking, but it had turned into an indistinct drone at the edge of my awareness. He had just said Lucille and I both, for all practical purposes, would die. Eventually someone would inhabit this body, but it wouldn't be us.

I guess in some sense it might be our child, but it wouldn't be me. Worse, it wouldn't be Lucille. I might accept giving up what little grip on existence I had left if there was no other choice, I couldn't accept that happening to Lucille.

I couldn't even muster up a comforting denial. I saw the signs of it already even as I was dimly aware of Crumley listing them. The leaking of thoughts and words between us, the body being controlled by both of us now. We probably had a couple of days, at most.

I wasn't surprised that, when Lucille demanded some solution from the wizard, he shrugged in a what-can-I-do gesture. He wasn't able to solve the mess made by the Tear of Nâtlac, why would this problem be any different?

"Any real solution needs to get you or Frank in another body," Crumley told us. "Frank would be easier, since he's the interloper."

"But you can't do it."

"I understand the Dark Lord's magic. Enough to know I'm not going to ever practice it."

Krys spoke up. "Whoever wrote the scroll," she said, "could they do it?"

Crumley chuckled. "Of course they could. Isn't that obvious?"

"Why obvious?" Lucille asked.

"Because," Crumley informed us, "the author of this scroll is the same hand that cast the original spell."

Lucille stared at Crumley blankly.

He had just told us that the author of the scroll the elf-prince used, the source of the magic that had brought us to the brink of war with the elves, the "person responsible" in the elf-king's words, was the late, unlamented Elhared the Unwise.

CHAPTER 15

"Elhared is dead!" Lucille snapped.

Crumley shrugged.

She shook her head and paced in front of the wizard. "No. This can't be Elhared's doing . . ."

"You paid for the expertise of the Wizard Crumley. If you find my insight distressing, maybe you need to hire another student of the dark arts. My best wishes in finding a student of Nâtlac who won't use your own entrails to divine the answer to your questions."

Lucille shook her head. "No, I don't doubt your expertise."

"Good. Lendowyn can ill afford peers so foolish with their own coin."

"So you're saying that this scroll was Elhared's work?"

"I'm saying the author was one who cast the original spell."

Wait a minute, I thought. *The spell he cast on us came from* a book. "Why is this a scroll?" I didn't know when my question made the transition from my thoughts to Lucille's words. I think the shudder came from both of us.

Eventually the identities will merge into a new consciousness.

Our identities.

Already those "couple of days" looked wildly optimistic. A couple of *hours* seemed more likely.

Crumley shook his head. "You both need to learn to listen. I said the hand that *cast* the reversed spell, not the one who *wrote* the original spell."

"Huh?"

Crumley sighed. "This scroll isn't an original work. The author copied passages, inverted them to create an undoing. Based on the additions—in a completely different style—it was written by someone who had experience casting the original spell."

"It *could* have been Elhared. Damn!"

"Your Highness?" Krys asked. "What's wrong?"

"Elhared's still dead!" Lucille snapped. "He probably wrote this scroll a year ago, when he was planning his coup. Or maybe after he took Frank's body and realized his plans had fallen apart."

"Why didn't he use it back then?" Krys asked.

Lucille sighed. "Maybe he liked Frank's body. He was a pretty decrepit old bastard to start with."

"Yes, yes. Is there anything else?" Crumley rolled up the scroll and slapped it into my hand. Then he started shooing us back to the stairs out of the workshop. "I need to get back to my studies."

Yeah right, we thought, imagining the volume with the inappropriate illustrations. She reached up and took the pendant off of her neck. "Can you tell me anything about this?"

Crumley looked at it briefly and snorted. "It's an hourglass—really a day-glass."

"But the sand—"

"Runs slower because it's fae sand. It tracks time under the hill. Nothing particularly strange or magical about that."

"Can we slow it down?"

Crumley shrugged. "I can cast a stasis spell and freeze its movement entirely."

"Yes—"

"But that won't do anything about the elf-king's ultimatum," Crumley said. "Clocks may stop, but time marches on."

"You know about—"

"Of course I do. What of it?"

She looked at the pendant and sighed. "How much time do we have left?"

He looked at the sand and said. "Under the hill, perhaps eight hours. Here in Fell Green, a little less than twenty. In the mortal realm, three days perhaps. Maybe four."

"*Maybe* four?"

"This is not a precise timepiece, and the flow of time can vary. Is there anything else?"

"Your Highness," Krys said, "the tea?"

"The tea?" Crumley asked with a puzzled expression.

Lucille turned around and said, "Yes, the tea."

At least we accomplished one of our goals at the Wizard Crumley's lair. He was able to instantly identify the substantive ingredient in the tea that Brock had made for Rabbit. As expected, the weed had more than simple anesthetic properties. It went by a number of names. The only one Crumley rattled off that I remembered later was "shaman's flower."

I tend to lean more to the descriptive than poetic.

"It's effective in tea, or when chewed. But breathing in the smoke as it burns is most efficient."

I couldn't help but remember a particular den of thieves named The Headless Earl. I had incapacitated the inhabitants by tossing a bundle of herbs into a fire. A bundle that Brock had prepared for me. It had sent the whole population of the great room on an involuntary sprit journey.

"Also, the unadulterated herb is more powerful than the dash that your barbarian herbalist mixed into the mute's tea, so mind the side effects."

"Side effects?" Lucille asked.

"Drowsiness, euphoria, impaired judgment, prophetic visions, dry mouth, and in your case," he pointed to Lucille, "acceleration of the personality assimilation that is already happening."

"What?"

"This herb tears down the walls between your self and reality . . . your self and other selves. That's how you hear a soul that's already half left the world. But those walls are what keep you a separate self."

"Great," whispered Lucille.

Crumley didn't even charge us extra when he gave Krys a large bag of the stuff, adding, "You can buy more anywhere. But remember," he warned as he ushered us out of his lab, "if you do see something, it also sees you."

Apparently he was very eager to get back to his studies.

The door slammed behind us leaving us back in the fetid alley that was half city, half swamp.

Krys hefted her bag of shaman's flower and looked at us. "What do we do now?"

Lucille lifted the pendant that hung around our neck. The sand might have been close to the two-thirds mark in the tiny hourglass. "Back to the inn," Lucille said. "We're running out of time. If Elhared authored that scroll, he isn't the one we want. We need to find who could have found it and given it to the elf-prince."

"What about . . . you and Frank?"

I felt Lucille bite her lip.

"Your Highness?"

"Our priority is stopping a few wars."

"But—"

"No," Lucille snapped. "One thing at a time."

We made our way out of the damper part of Fell Green in silence. For all of Lucille's protests about our priorities, I knew she must be dwelling on the same thing I was.

We were both living on borrowed time. Sure, Crumley said that the author of the scroll could separate us. But the author of that scroll was stone cold dead. Elhared died at my hand, and I had made pretty sure of the fact at the time. Gone along with my old body.

Then something occurred to me . . .

Krys grabbed our arm and shook it, breaking me out of the hopeful thought. Lucille turned at Krys's strained whisper, *"Problem."*

Krys looked down the path ahead. Lucille continued raising her head until we saw the half-dozen large men,

all wearing the spiked, skull-embossed black armor of
the elite Grünwald Royal Guard.

"Never goes wrong in the way we expect," Lucille
muttered, appropriating my own personal motto.

We ran.

That was our only real advantage. The men outnumbered us three to one, outweighed us six to one, and, with
their swords out, bested our reach by Lucille's full height.
But we could outrun them. Lucille darted directly away
from them, Krys on our heels, and they broke into a lumbering run behind us. The surrounding crowd and few
open-air merchants around us all melted away, leaving
the street barren ahead of us. That was a good thing,
since it made the other six Grünwald soldiers stand out
as they rushed us from the other direction.

Lucille took the only escape route we had, a narrow
alley between an inn and a stable. The good news was that
the alley would be too narrow for any of the overlarge
pursuers to engage us at better than one-to-one odds.

Bad news, they were obviously driving us in this direction and a trio of like-armored thugs blocked the opposite end of the alley, forcing us to draw up short. Lucille
spun, but while our pursuit had been slower than us, they
hadn't been slow. That end of the alley was blocked now
as well.

Krys drew her sword and placed her back against
ours. Lucille drew her own weapon, a dagger that would
have seemed substantial if it wasn't for the size of our
potential opposition. I felt a sinking feeling when I realized she held it in her off hand since I still controlled the
other one.

Damn it.

I felt her grit her teeth as our eyes darted all over, looking for some escape. Nothing obvious presented itself.

"Well, well, well," came a smarmy voice from the shadows to our right. Lucille spun around to face the speaker and I felt around her belt for some other weapon. I couldn't find anything.

"If it isn't the Princess of Lendowyn," continued the speaker as he walked out of a shadowed alcove about ten paces away from us. King Dudley had lost some weight. He was still short as one measured such things, but he appeared to have lost the doughy softness that defined the prince I remembered.

"Dudley," Lucille spat.

Dudley smiled humorlessly. "And I'm afraid you have the advantage there, Princess. What should I call you? Who are you this fine day?"

"I am a representative of the Royal Court of Lendowyn," Lucille said, the dragon leaking into her voice. "If you value what is left of your kingdom, you will stand down and retreat with your dogs."

Dudley laughed.

I did not like that at all.

"My kingdom?" he finally said, choking off his laughter before it became something hysterical. "My kingdom, you say?" He wiped tears from his eyes. He stared at us, and I could see the amusement drain away leaving nothing in his eyes but a smoldering hate. "Oh," he whispered. "You don't even know."

"Know what?" Krys said from behind us.

"You brought all of this down upon me and mine," Dudley continued to whisper, voice hardening. "And you don't even know what you've wrought."

"I'm warning you, Dudley," Lucille said, "let us go or—"

"Or what!?" Dudley screamed at us with such force that it gave even Lucille the Dragon pause. "Or your armies again march across Grünwald? Is that it? Is that your threat?" He walked in front of us, stepping in a wide circle around us. He made a couple of gestures with his hand and out of the corner of Lucille's eye I saw black armored men swapping their swords for crossbows.

Not good.

"Why do you think I care?" Dudley asked us. He gestured palm down, and the crossbowmen knelt and braced.

"You'd sacrifice your kingdom for vengeance?"

He had circled until he faced us, his back to the opposite wall. "Thanks to you," he whispered, "I have no kingdom."

His hand dropped, and the crossbows fired.

CHAPTER 16

We should have died there.

However, Dudley was nothing if not predictable. He had this tiresome habit of capturing me with the intent of using me as a sacrifice to his Dark Lord. So I knew what was coming as soon as the first bolt slammed into our midsection, and I saw the tip was blunted. I had only a fraction of a second to contemplate that, before something slammed into the side of our head and we fell forward into blackness.

As awareness leaked back into our senses, I wasn't surprised at the cords binding our wrists or the cold stone of an altar under our naked back. We had been through this twice before.

This was becoming an unhealthy obsession. Dudley needed a hobby.

I blinked and turned my head and realized that *I* was blinking and turning my head.

We were bound spread-eagled across the stone, each limb tightly tied to each corner. The altar formed the focus of some sort of old, disused temple. Long ago it had been some large ceremonial space. Since then, any adornment had long ago decayed and anything of value had been stolen. The stone floor was half hidden under unidentifiable debris, the walls bare stone except for a few traces of crumbling plaster where old frescoes would have overlooked the space. All that remained was carved stone showing worn mottoes in unknown languages, and a pair of crumbling stone statues flanking the entrance.

I could not make out details on the statues because the only light in the room came from a small bonfire occupying the floor between us and the exit.

I groaned and whispered, "Lucille?"

In response, I felt my left hand clench against its bonds by its own volition.

Guess the knock on the head swapped us again.

I felt a strange ominous echo in my thoughts. I also felt a strange sense of my vision doubling without blurring.

None of that boded well.

Something shimmered, past the bonfire, beyond the entrance to the old temple. I squinted in that direction.

I heard a woman's voice, distant and cold. "This is what you found?"

I heard Dudley respond. "Yes, Your Majesty."

That pricked my ears. Aside from his mother, the late Queen Fiona, I couldn't picture any female royalty earning that kind of deference from ex-King, ex-Prince Dudley. I supposed that Dudley might have learned some humility since I'd seen him last, but I thought it unlikely.

Then I saw the royal in question step into view, and I understood. She stood taller than any woman I'd ever seen, aside from the Goddess Lysea when she possessed statuary. She was clad in leather so elaborately tooled with branches and leaves that she seemed to be a moving section of forest. Her face was unquestionably elven, though her skin was as dark as most elves were pale. Flowing green hair spilled down, past her hips, held in place by a circlet made of twisting vines, still green.

The elf-queen herself was talking with Dudley.

"What" was the only word available to me that adequately encapsulated the enormity of seeing her here.

She unrolled a scroll and studied its contents. I knew the scroll. Even if I hadn't recognized the disturbing glyphs that marred its surface, or the stain of black melted sealing wax, there was really only one scroll she'd be looking at that would make sense in this context. She nodded. "This is what my son bore upon his murder?"

"I am certain, Your Majesty."

"Daemonlas, you hot-headed fool," she whispered, crushing the scroll in her hands. After a moment she turned to Dudley. "You've done well."

"You have what you need, Your Majesty?"

The elf-queen nodded. "Having this to point the finger, we'll have no need to contemplate my husband's soft-hearted offers of clemency."

"Then our agreement—"

"After we burn this world, Grünwald is yours." She glanced up and saw us. Our eyes met and she said, "And do what you wish to that troublesome mortal."

She gestured, took a step, and, somehow, she was gone in a brief haze of shimmering air.

Having this to point the finger . . .

I didn't have a chance to ponder her words. Dudley strode across the room to bend over us. His sneering face suddenly filled our field of vision. I cringed and suddenly felt the horrible bruises where the blunted bolts had slammed into our body.

"Ha!" Dudley spat in our face. "Wakey wakey!"

He slapped our face on the side that had been clubbed by a blunted crossbow bolt. It was enough to send the room spinning.

He edged around us, his expression half sneer, half manic smile. In his left hand he held a black obsidian ceremonial dagger. I struggled with our bonds, but I think I might have mentioned sometime before that my skills were more of the picking pockets than the escape artist variety. Not to mention I seemed to be operating with only one hand under my control, and the cords pulled our arms too taut for any sort of maneuvering beyond twisting our hands at the end of our wrists.

Dudley slapped us again, and I spit some blood from a busted lip. It dribbled along my cheek to drip on the altar beneath my head. I focused blurry eyes on our captor.

"Yes," he hissed through clenched teeth. "Look at me."

"Where's Krys?" I muttered.

"What does the boy matter? He bleeds where he fell." He leaned toward us. "*This* is what's important." He pointed the dagger so it pricked our exposed breast. "You"—he gestured back at himself with the hilt—"and me."

If Krys wasn't any worse off than I was, and Dudley just left her in the alley, she might be able to make it back to The Talking Eye herself. I felt relieved that we didn't have to worry about her. Our imminent sacrifice was enough to concern us.

"I appreciate your interest," I said. "But I don't think

we make a good couple. Besides, I'm married to a dragon—"

"A dragon that will not save you this time," Dudley said.

It was hard to argue that point.

From beyond the bonfire, I caught sight of black-robed figures entering the chamber, alternately filing to the left and right. From their size I guessed that these were all the armored footmen that had captured us. I counted a dozen in all.

Even if I could free my arms, we'd have a bit of a problem getting out of this room intact.

"I am going to enjoy this," Dudley said.

"No, you aren't." I'm not sure why I said that, other than just a knee-jerk contrary impulse.

"What?"

"We've been through this before. How do you think this ends?"

His hand shook, gripping the obsidian knife until his knuckles whitened and cracked. "You took my mother, you took my church, you upended my kingdom so my own people drove me into the wilderness. You are marked by the Dark Lord and I am about to render your soul unto him. With the power he grants, and an ally in the Summer Queen Theora, I will sweep my vengeance across this land—"

I shook my head weakly. "Ain't going to happen."

"How dare you!"

"I don't know if it's fate or your own incompetence, but you'll screw this up like you always do. You'll make some arrogant bone-stupid mistake that—"

"DIE!" he screamed and plunged the dagger down toward the hollow between our breasts. I tensed and stopped breathing, but his thrust stopped with the tip of the blade half a finger's breadth through the skin over our sternum.

Silence filled the chamber for nearly a minute while blood welled up around the tip of Dudley's blade. I glanced up at his snarling face and wide eyes.

He laughed.

No mere chuckle, but a guffaw, a belly laugh that left him gasping for breath and trembling so badly that I worried that the blade might finish its mortal plunge by accident. It was a laugh that wheezed and strained against the prison of sanity and I was, for several moments, wondering if he was trying to force his way out of that prison, or break back in.

Dudley took several deep breaths, calmed himself, and took the knife away.

"Well played," he said.

Huh?

"But you aren't going to goad me into killing you out of turn. The forms of the Dark Lord will be followed. You will not deny me this prize on a technicality."

To be honest, I had just been a smartass.

Dudley set the blade down between our legs, raised his arms, and started chanting. Knives and chanting, never a good combination.

Four of the robed men came up and stripped Dudley's armor, anointed him with foul-smelling oils, and draped his naked form with a hooded black robe.

I spat another glob of blood onto the altar and said,

"You don't want to do this. It's a bad idea." Everything related to the Dark Lord Nâtlac was a bad idea.

No one listened to me.

The other figures withdrew, leaving the oily form of Dudley at our feet, still chanting, clad only in a black robe that hung distressingly open. He picked up the knife from between our legs and held it up toward the ceiling, still chanting. The stone on which we were tied was not high enough to spare us the sight of the fact that Dudley was enjoying himself way too much.

Our left hand struggled against our bonds by itself, and I joined in with the other. Not that we did much good.

I spat in Dudley's direction, but while I managed a surprisingly robust arc, our angle was not great and the glob of bloody phlegm splatted between our bound feet. Dudley had his eyes closed in some sort of spiritual ecstasy and didn't seem to notice.

His words reached a crescendo with our struggles and his grip shifted on the black knife. He approached the altar and rose upon an unseen step in line with our feet. He towered over us, arms and robe spread wide, and I turned away because that was *not* the last thing I wanted to see.

I stared into the flames of the central fire as Dudley completed his chant to the Dark Lord.

In the moment that followed, a sound from the fire broke the silence. As I watched a shadow twist into the flames from somewhere else, I realized what I heard.

Clapping.

The shadow resolved into a familiar figure draped in a grotesque leather cloak. A sense of dread preceded him, as if every step he took rasped something unpleasant on my exposed skin. When he stepped completely out of the fire, the flames shrank behind him as if he dragged darkness along with him.

The robed figures surrounding us knelt and genuflected, and I heard Dudley gasp, "M-My Lord?"

I felt something thud painfully into our left ankle and I glanced down and saw the black blade between our feet. It had fortunately struck hilt-first when Dudley dropped the thing. It was still close enough to my foot that, even as tight as the cords were on my leg, I was able to twist my heel to drag the hilt closer.

Dudley was preoccupied, watching the visitor approach with a dumbfounded expression.

"You expected someone else?" The Dark Lord's voice dragged through our brain like the branches of a burning thorn tree infested with wasps.

"But the sacrifice? The ceremony?"

The Dark Lord stood next to the altar. If I hadn't been bound, I could have reached out and touched the pained faces on his black leather cloak. The thought made me shudder.

The Dark Lord Nâtlac placed a gloved hand on the surface of the altar, fingers touching the blood that had come from my split lip, almost touching my face.

"Do you think that is all that may call me?"

I frantically moved my foot, trying to drag the cords binding it against the sharp blade of the knife. It seemed I cut as much of my own skin as my bonds. Dudley's Dark Lord slowly walked toward him, fingers smearing a trail of my blood along the stone of the altar, parallel to my body.

"Uh . . ."

"What is it that you want?" he asked Dudley as my foot came free. I frantically pushed the knife over toward my other leg, my heel sliding along the stone in a slick of my own blood.

Fortunately Dudley and the Dark Lord were focused on each other, rather than me.

Dudley stepped down and knelt like his robed minions. "I wish your favor, My Lord. I wish to be anointed with your dark power and be given the strength to crush my enemies. I wish to give this virginal sacrifice to you, a gift of royal blood flowing from the heart of one who wronged you."

"You wish my favor?"

My feet slid around so badly that I almost kicked the knife into the side of Dudley's face. Not that I found that outcome particularly objectionable, but it would have been awkward, especially since it would have hit with much less than lethal force.

"Yes, My Lord."

"And you believe that favor is bought with blood, like any other dark god?"

I was too focused on slicing more of my bonds than my own feet to focus on Dudley and his god. Besides, the Dark Lord Nâtlac was actually painful to listen to, and Dudley was terminally annoying. But as my other foot came free, I realized a few things . . .

Despite appearances, our visitor spoke nothing like the Dark Lord I had the misfortune to know. The voice burrowed in and laid its eggs in your mind like the Nâtlac I knew and loathed, but what he said? That wasn't the Dark Lord.

But it was very like the false Nâtlac from my dream.

It also sank in that this temple was *not* dedicated to Nâtlac. The Dark Lord's worshippers had a history of desecrating temples and rededicating them in his name. Dudley was arrogant enough—and stupid enough—to simply appropriate a space for his god and go ahead with his ceremony, regardless of whose temple he might be stealing.

I knew from experience that such acts didn't take very well, and typically left a deity pissed off at you for wrecking their stuff. Given my last real meeting with the Dark Lord Nâtlac, this place would almost certainly not be consecrated in his name until the sacrifice was made. That technicality was the whole reason I didn't eat Dudley's half brother when I had the chance—but that's another story.

This panicked chain of thought led to the faux-Nâtlac's comment, *favor is bought with blood, like any other dark god . . .*

I stared at the stone by my head, where a pair of the fake Nâtlac's fingers had dipped into the blood I had spit on the stone.

Oh crap.

I used my free legs to push my whole body, sliding back on the altar, away from Dudley and the unknown impersonator, adding slack to the cords binding my arms. I could feel the bindings loosen enough that I could yank my hand through them, abrading the skin on my wrist and nearly dislocating my thumb.

Of course, the arrival of their deity, however dubious, was not *that* much of a distraction. At my sudden movement, the hooded figures stood, drawing weapons. Dudley turned and looked at me, his expression turning from awe to anger. He grabbed the already blood-soaked dagger and shouted, "Now, My Lord, you will see our devotion!"

My other wrist tried to pull itself free without help from me, but seemed to lack the leverage and momentum. Not that it would have made much difference as a pair of Dudley's minions grabbed us by the shoulders, holding us in place on the blood-streaked altar.

Dudley approached with the knife and said, "I am afraid we'll skip right to the main event. I don't wish to keep the Dark One waiting."

Just like him to cut corners.

The minions held our arms straight out, aiming our naked chest at Dudley. I kicked and scrambled against the stone of the altar, but he easily walked around my thrashing legs.

I glanced at the bloody altar, then up at pseudo-Nâtlac.

What have I got to lose?

I looked at him and it felt as if molten sand tore into the flesh of my eyes.

I yelled at him.

"Do I have your favor?"

CHAPTER 17

That gave everyone pause. Even Dudley halted his approach to stare at me blankly, as if I has suddenly spouted a string of obscenities in a dead language.

Fake Nâtlac continued staring at me.

"Come on!" I shouted. "These guys come in and try and wreck the place, steal it from you. I gave you my own blood. I spilled it on your altar before these idiots could take it from you."

I think realization dawned in Dudley's eyes. I saw them widen.

Yeah, told you you'd screw this up, didn't I?

Dudley screamed "No!" at the top of his lungs and lunged at me, plunging the dagger into my chest.

I know, because I watched him do it. I watched myself, black blade plunging into my heart, my naked body collapsing to the ground, Dudley kneeling on my hips as he used both hands to pull the blade down my sternum.

This was rather startling to me, since I still sat on the altar, one minion holding my arm, watching Dudley laugh as he sliced up Lucille's naked body.

I glanced down at myself, and I still wore the same body I came here with. "What?"

I heard an echo of my own voice, and it wasn't just

someone else repeating my startled eloquence. It was someone using my voice.

Using Lucille's voice.

Using *our* voice.

I turned and looked at the minion that had been holding my bound arm. He was no longer a huge Grünwald warrior in armor and a black cloak. Instead, gripping my arm was someone wearing the naked body of a Lendowyn princess. My twin still watched Dudley's misplaced violence with an expression of shock. So I did the obvious.

I decked her.

I might have little hope overpowering a thug with a five stone weight advantage and a foot of height and reach over me. But a petite naked princess? I could take her with one arm tied behind my back.

Which was good, since that was literally my situation.

My fist hit her between her jaw and her temple. I'm no brawler, never was even before the whole princess thing, but I made up for it in pure terror and confusion. I hit hard enough to send shivers of pain up my arm, and I heard and felt something crack with the impact. The pain of the collision masked whether it was something breaking in my hand, or in my doppelgänger's skull.

She dropped, and my arm struggled to free itself from the last binding. I reached over with my other hand, the one I controlled, and tried to help Lucille with fingers still numb with impact. Just as I helped fumble the last loop of cord off my wrist, I jumped myself.

I turned, just in time to see another naked me rush the altar and attempt a flying tackle. She must have intended to pin me to the altar, but she wasn't wearing the same body as she had a moment ago. She fumbled her attack, failing to completely clear the altar. She struck me off center, rolling us both off the altar and onto the floor of the chamber.

We tumbled into a trio of other naked princesses, knocking them down.

Some strange, deviant part of me had the idle thought that this all would have been rather interesting if they weren't all trying to kill me.

I swung for the face of the Lucille trying to strangle me, and the real Lucille must have had the same thought, as both my fists came up and struck both her cheekbones simultaneously. Her head snapped back and she tumbled off of me as two other princesses grabbed for me. I was badly outnumbered, but I had two advantages. First, aside from Dudley—whom I couldn't see anymore, but whom I heard yelling obscenities past all the other Lucilles—all my opponents had been disarmed by assuming my naked likeness.

More important, I had spent a year getting used to moving in our body. These guys had less than twenty seconds. They didn't know where their feet were, where their arms ended, or where their center of gravity was. They tried to dodge, and didn't move their heads enough. They tried to block, and came up short. They reached for me and missed. Shove them a little, they overcompensated, wobbled, and fell on their unreasonably padded backsides. I punched one of them in the boob and she actually screamed, stumbling back, clutching a wounded nipple.

Dudley bellowed, "Back away from her! Back off so I can get her!"

Reasonable tactic.

They tried to disengage and I grabbed one of them by the arm and started turning, spinning us both on an axis round our clasped hands. Lucille reached up and grabbed our captive's wrist as I spun us both round and round while the others backed away from us.

One thing I remember from my own body transitions. It left you with one whopper of a headache.

I let go and stumble-hopped back to the retreating circle of Lucilles, and my victim spun twice more, unaccompanied, before falling to her knees and retching.

"Ha!" Dudley shouted as the wall of naked Lucilles parted to let him see the one on her knees. He ran toward her, ignoring the raised hand and the half moaned, "Wait!"

A few of the other minions, who had seen and understood what happened, rushed to restrain him before he sacrificed another minion. A few turned in my direction, trying to discern which one of the four Lucilles in this end of the chamber was really me.

I had less than a second, so I decided to retain the initiative. I kicked sideways, taking my neighbor's leg out from under her. I grabbed her shoulder and guided her fall into the two Lucilles slightly in front of me so all three of them collapsed on Dudley.

I now had a clear path, so I ran.

And slammed right into the chest of the Dark Lord Nâtlac.

I don't care if he was the actual Dark Lord, or just an

elaborate fraud, but touching him with my naked body felt like diving headfirst into a pit filled with salt, broken glass, and writhing maggots; one brush against that macabre leather cloak and I wanted to claw off my own skin.

I bounced off of him and looked up into a smile that had all the warmth of a shark biting a bloated shipwreck victim in half. I felt his hands touch my shoulders and the world went white.

I know things usually go black at this point, but this was *white*; a serious blinding white glare that burned my watering eyes and had me attempting to blink splotches of red out of my vision. A few more blinks and I realized that it was only the noonday sun, though it was a sun that seemed heavier and closer than I was used to. It hung in a painfully blue, cloudless sky almost directly above my head.

I looked away from the blazing sun and down to see an emerald green meadow at my feet.

And boots.

I wore boots, and they were farther away than they should have been.

No, that was wrong. Actually, they were *exactly* as far away as they should have been.

"What just happened?"

I spun around and saw a familiar scaly black form shimmering in the bright sunlight. The Dragon Lucille looked around, blinking her double lids, shaking her massive head and stretching her wings to the point they blotted out the sun from above me.

"I think someone brought us home to visit," I said.

The ground vibrated as Lucille jumped back, startled,

as if she didn't know I was there. She probably hadn't. I had spent a short stint in the dragon's body, and one thing I remembered was that it was easy to overlook people-size objects when you were that large.

"Who are you?"

I almost felt hurt, but I realized that Lucille last saw the original me over a year ago, and then only briefly. The last time she saw me as a man, I was in a completely different body.

"It's me," I said, "Frank."

She lowered her massive head to peer at me, her nostrils at eye level. Her breath was a moist brimstone-flavored breeze against my face. **"That does sound like the voice in your head."**

"That's probably just what it is."

"But that body . . ."

"This is what I looked like before Elhared—"

Her eyes widened. **"Oh."**

She drew her head back up, but her snout remained pointed at me. It was the kind of pose that would have been intimidating if I didn't know her. **"I'm sorry I didn't recognize you at first."**

"It's okay. The old me is just worm food anyway."

"But you're standing right there . . ."

I shook my head.

". . . and I'm a dragon." She sighed and flopped her head down on her forelimbs with a massive thud. **"This isn't happening, is it?"**

"It's happening," I said. "But our appearance here has little to do with our current appearance in the mortal world."

"Why are you talking like you know what's going on here?"

"Because I think I do." I walked up next to her head and placed my hand on her cheek. It was surprisingly warm for hide that looked so thick and armored. I found the touch surprisingly comforting. "I've run into the Dark Lord more than once. In *his* domain I don't wear my physical body, whatever it is at the time. I look like this." I gestured down at myself. "I suppose this is how my soul looks."

She rolled her head slightly so one eye peered at me quizzically. **"So my soul looks like a dragon?"**

I laughed. "Did you doubt it?"

Her head rolled back and stared at the rolling meadow before us. **"This doesn't look like the Underworld."**

"It's not."

"You said the Dark Lord—"

"That wasn't him."

"It wasn't?"

"No. And I'm beginning to have some idea who it actually was."

"Who?"

From behind me a high-pitched voice asked, "Yes, who?" It repeated, "Who?" with a sound that was almost a yip. I spun around to face the newcomer, the ground rumbling as a startled Lucille did likewise.

A bright red fox perched on an old stump that I was sure had not been there a moment ago. Also, regardless of the stump's status, the copse of trees behind the fox definitely had *not* been there the last time I looked in that direction.

"Who?" the fox yipped behind an impish grin.

"Like the Royal Court of Grünwald, the resident Thieves' Guild has their own patron deity. Lord of deception and mischief, illusion and masks. Just the type to go about impersonating someone else's god."

The fox chuffed a few times, and I realized it was snickering. "Can you think of a better response to men attempting to desecrate your temple?"

"Probably not," I said.

"And did you forget change and transformation?" the fox said, twisting its head around until it was nearly upside down as it looked at us. I was quite sure a real fox's neck couldn't do that.

"No." I shook my head. "I also remember the part where you're supposed to speak only in riddles."

"You prefer that to rhetorical questions?"

"No, that's quite all right."

The fox sighed, as if in relief, as it rotated its head back. "Do you have any idea how taxing it is to come up with appropriate riddles for such mundane communication?"

"I can imagine."

"So are you going to introduce us, Frank?"

I looked back at Lucille, who stared down at the talking fox with her jaws slightly agape.

"Dragon Prince Lucille," I said, gesturing toward the fox, "may I present Lothan, Father Fox, Patron of Thieves and Lord of Illusion."

CHAPTER 18

Lothan the fox jumped off his stump and started walking in a circle around us. As he did, I noticed that the copse of woods had become a full-blown forest and the rolling meadow had become little more than a clearing in the trees. Lothan looked at Lucille with an amused canine smile and I realized that the red fox hair was now a shaggy gray, and his muzzle was larger, more blunted.

Lothan the wolf asked, "Prince or princess?"

Lucille looked down at herself, and it was Lucille's body she looked down at, the original one. I didn't see the change. One moment she was the Dragon Prince, the next she was the human princess. **"What did you do?"** she asked in the dragon's voice, which felt very strange. I also noted that her eyes still resembled the dragon's: yellow, slitted, and double-lidded.

"What makes you think I did anything?" asked the wolf.

Lucille looked at me in confusion. I smiled at her, reached over, and took her hand. "What we are here is what we see of ourselves. You became a dragon, but you didn't abandon the princess completely."

"Father would disagree."

"Really? You've been ravaging the countryside? You

flew off to a cave to nest on your hoard? I hadn't noticed."

"Frank, I'm not going to abandon my kingdom, or my father, or you, just because I'm a dragon."

I lifted her chin because for once the height difference between us was in my favor. I looked into her golden dragon eyes. "No, you aren't, because the most important part of you is still the princess I tried to save a year ago."

She leaned in toward me. **"Frank?"** she whispered, and her breath was warm on my cheek, still carrying a hint of brimstone. I didn't care.

"That's the part of you I fell in—"

"Can we move it along, please?" interrupted an annoyed-looking elk.

I spun around burning with anger that I only restrained by reminding myself that pissing off yet another deity was probably not in our best interest.

The elk cocked its massive antlered head, framed by the mountainous horizon. Those mountains weren't there before.

Lucille spun on the elk and was suddenly the dragon again. **"Move *what* along?"**

The elk nodded its head at me. "What is it you want?"

"What?" Lucille asked.

"Oh," I said in growing realization.

Her massive head turned toward me. **"'Oh,' what?"**

"I summoned Lothan," I said. "He accepted my sacrifice. He's waiting for me to request a boon of him."

"More than saving us from Dudley the Inept?"

"Actually, that was a boon I granted *him*. Dudley was

about to claim Lothan's ritual space in Nâtlac's name. Judging by the Goddess Lysea's reaction to more or less the same thing, I suspect Lothan was happy for the opportunity to disrupt Dudley's efforts."

"Just because you spilled blood on the altar before Dudley did?"

"If it wasn't for happy accidents, I don't think any of my plans would ever pan out."

"You had a plan?"

"Still working on it."

"Was it an accident?" Lothan asked. He was now a bear wading through a rushing stream whose rocky shore ended near Dragon Lucille's forelimbs.

Was it? The questions were getting on my nerves. Before I could pursue the thought any further, Lucille — the human one — grabbed my shoulders and shook me.

"Frank! You know what this means!" She looked at me with an expression of what I could only call ecstatic realization.

"What?" I asked. For a moment I thought she must have figured out how to stop the impending war with the elves.

"You can have your body back!"

"Yes, if we do that we can stop — Wait, what?"

"Your body, Frank! You saw what he did to all of Dudley's guards. Their bodies changed! He can change you!"

"Uh, yeah. I guess he could." I hadn't even thought about that. She was right. Lothan's domain wasn't just illusion, deception, and chaos. As he had made a point to mention, he also dealt with transformation. You'd just have to ask the screech owl who stared at us impatiently from a dead tree that leaned a little to the left of where the bear had been wading.

"Did you think otherwise?" the owl contributed. "Can we speed this up?"

"Frank? What's the matter?"

I took a step out of her arms and turned away from her. "Thank you," I said. "That . . . it means a lot that you said that."

"Frank?"

"But you know we can't do that now."

"What do you mean? You deserve this. If we can—"

"But we *can't*, Lucille." I kicked a rock so it skipped across the sandy desert that surrounded us. "Sure I could ask that, and Lothan would be happy to grant me that one boon. But it's not just my body now, it's *ours*. And that's the problem."

"I don't mind having a—"

"And you've forgotten the part where our souls cease to exist?"

"That's not what Crumley said."

"No, but that's what it amounts to."

She bit her lip and looked down. **"Maybe it would be easier."**

"What? Are you seriously thinking . . ." I trailed off, because I knew she was. And I think I knew why.

"If I didn't want to be—*need* to be—the dragon . . . If you weren't in a body you were never intended to be in . . . We'd both get to start over at the same time. We could fit."

"Or we'd end up twice as screwed up."

"I've felt it. So have you. Would it be so bad?

Gradually thinking the same thoughts until there weren't any others?"

"We wouldn't be us anymore."

"But we'd be together."

Lucille was crying, and I took her into my arms.

"No," I whispered into her ear as I embraced her. "That isn't going to happen. I'm not abandoning you."

"You realize you *can't* abandon me right now?"

"You know what I mean."

It wasn't the dragon's voice that answered. "Yes, I do."

"You realize I'm still here?" A mule asked us as it scratched its rear against an old stone wall that bordered some farmer's fields.

We broke apart and faced Lothan.

"Can you prevent this? Split us back into our own bodies?"

The beaver set down his branch and asked me, "You would like both your separate spirits to own your own body, to control as they will?"

"Yes, that's the idea."

King Alfred the Strident, my father-in-law, straightened his crown and arched a shaggy white brow while wearing a half-grin that was alien to his normally dour face. He stepped off his throne, smoothing his robes, and walked across the throne room, toward a chest in one corner by the fresh timbers waiting their role in the castle reconstruction.

I swallowed, because I was reminded of the damage to the castle, and to the Northern Palace, and the dead and injured left in my wake. I wondered if I had made the right decision. Was this just me being selfish again?

I looked over at Lucille who stared, gaping as her father rummaged in the chest.

"How can he ..." She spoke as if she hadn't noticed Lothan's many forms up to now. I guess her father was different.

"Illusion and transformation," I said, reaching over and squeezing her hand, because I could.

I decided that I wasn't completely selfish.

King Alfred found what he had been rummaging for and lifted it up out of the chest. Only now he was King Dudley and we all stood in a wrecked temple lit by the remains of a dying bonfire. Dudley handed Lucille a metal flask, and I reached out and took it with her hand. Our hand. I stared at the dull gray metal flask, stoppered by an elaborate black wax seal. I looked up and we both said in Lucille's voice. "What do we do with this?"

Lothan/Dudley winked at us and said, "Why don't you read the instructions?"

We glanced down and there were engraved words on the metal surface. Unfortunately, the light was too dim in here for us to make out what it said.

Not that we'd get more chances to read it, since we stood, naked again, in Dudley's commandeered temple. It appeared that no more than a few seconds had passed since our departure. Dudley stood inside a ring of Lucille doppelgängers. Four of them, victims of Dudley's confusion or my brief fight, sprawled on the floor dead or unconscious. That left eight angry naked princesses, at least half of whom had managed to find some improvised weapon.

Maybe I should have asked for a discreet exit from this situation.

We gripped the flask and ran.

Lucille dove out the door, Lucilles in pursuit. We ran down a damp stone hallway partly lit by a few sconces holding burning torches. I realized now that she had wrested control of our body again. I hadn't actually realized it until she stopped just long **enough** at one of the rusty sconces to pull the torch from it. The torch was fresh, probably brought by Dudley's men.

I wanted to shout, "Stopping? Bad idea!" at her. However, one of those men, trapped in the body of a young princess, made the argument more eloquently for me.

He—she—swung at us with a long dagger.

Unclothed fighting is never a great idea in the best circumstances. However, if it is unavoidable, there are some weapons that you still just never, *ever*, want to face with naked skin. Near the top of those would be a burning torch wielded like a club.

Lucille was considerably more brutal with her twin than I would have been. And I felt relieved when our dagger-wielding opponent retreated, broiled but still living. However, the short confrontation gave Dudley's princess brigade a chance to catch up with us. They were too close for us to turn and run now; we were forced to back away, swinging the torch to keep the other Lucilles at bay.

It was a standoff in the relatively narrow corridor, but not one that could last. We were outnumbered, and all they needed was one lucky shot.

The corridor made a sharp turn behind us, and from that direction I heard running feet. My heart sank as I thought that Dudley's people had found a way to circle behind us.

I realized that the feet in question were clearly booted, and my heart sank further. Dudley must have left some guards at the entrance to this place, guards unaffected by Lothan's transformations, and we had just reached the point where they had heard the commotion.

We had to hope that the multiple Lucilles might confuse them enough to give us one shot with the torch. However, I heard two sets of boots. Any hesitation wasn't going to be enough. Lucille might disable one of the armored guards with a lucky surprise blow with the flaming torch. It was unlikely, but conceivable. Doing it twice in whatever window of surprise we had? That wouldn't happen.

But I felt Lucille's muscles tense on the arm that held the torch. Hopeless, but she would try anyway. I hefted the flask. I still had control of that arm. The metal might make a decent missile. If she went at one guy with the torch, I could throw the flask.

Still hopeless, but I could tilt the odds just slightly away from the completely impossible. Besides, if we died here, we weren't going to need Lothan's boon anyway.

We reached the bend in the corridor as the booted feet converged on us. Lucille spun, raising the torch as I lifted the heavy flask. We were going to need a miracle.

We got one.

Rounding the corner came Rabbit and Krys, fully armored, swords drawn.

Somehow, tense as we were, Lucille managed to keep the torch from slamming into Krys's face. My arm followed through on the throw, but I kept the presence of mind not to let the flask go. Where I had aimed, it probably would have sailed over Rabbit's head anyway.

Lucille hadn't expected my aborted throw. Her stance had already been thrown off balance by the sudden halt of her own swing. As my swing continued into the follow-through, we toppled forward at Krys's feet and the torch tumbled into the corridor behind all of us. Before our face planted at Krys's boots, I saw the wide-eyed expression of confusion on her face.

Of course, she had been looking past us toward all the other Lucilles.

Everyone hesitated several moments to take stock of the situation. Then, as Lucille lifted our face from the floor, we saw Krys's boot stepping over us. As Lucille pushed ourselves up, with my help, Rabbit leaped over our legs to join the battle.

Battle was a kind word.

When evenly matched, skin to skin, even with their disorientation, the other Lucilles had Lucille and me hopelessly outnumbered. Twelve on one, eight on one, it didn't matter that they were as naked as we were.

Facing two of my armored handmaidens, members of the only warrior order of the Goddess Lysea, trainees of the mostly insane but scarily competent Sir Forsythe the Good . . . not so much. Even though Rabbit and Krys opted to use sword pommels, boots, and gauntleted fists rather than their blades, Dudley's princesses still took a cruel beating.

By the time Lucille got us upright, Krys and Rabbit had the Lucilles pushed back all the way to the temple. As we watched, Dudley managed to rally the remaining princess guard to close the entry door in Krys's face. I heard a thud as a bar fell into place on the other side of the door. Rabbit pounded on the door a few times with her sword, but stopped when she saw how heavy it was.

Krys turned toward us, sparing a glance at the three unconscious and moaning Lucilles scattering the floor of the corridor between us. Most of the light came from the torch Lucille had been waving like a club, half out and guttering by our feet.

"This is not what I expected," Krys said.

This is awkward, I thought.

CHAPTER 19

"So the obvious question is which one is the real princess," Lucille said.

Krys looked down at the other Lucilles and nodded.

"Would it help to tell you that I'm Lucille, not Frank?"

Krys answered, "Maybe, but you were with them a while before we found you. They could have found out you're back in the princess's body."

I felt Lucille's shoulders sag as she realized that Krys was right. Theoretically nothing she could tell Krys was beyond the ken of anyone with a hot poker, a strong stomach, and some time. Throw in magic, which was obviously at play here with the multiple Lucilles, and they had little reason to trust us. Especially since our first act had been to level an attack in their direction, one that—given our face-plant—could have been simply incompetent rather than quickly aborted.

Rabbit touched Krys's shoulder. She had sheathed her weapon and held her finger up in a wait-a-moment gesture. Then she rummaged in her belt pouch and pulled out a small bundle of leaves. I felt Lucille wince in sympathetic disgust as Rabbit plopped it in her tongueless mouth.

The sight made me queasy as well, I remembered

what that stuff had tasted like when it was diluted into some tea. I couldn't imagine chewing the raw leaves. Then again, Rabbit was probably used to it, and I realized that she probably couldn't taste it anyway.

Yeah, but she could still smell. I recalled unpleasant memories of flatulent slime mold.

Frank? Spoke a mental voice that still sounded much older than her years.

Yes! I said. *Good thinking!*

So it is you and Lucille, there at the end of the hall?

Yes, it's us. I lifted the hand I still controlled and waved, still gripping Lothan's flask.

Good, just let me know one thing ... What's my name?

I almost thought *Rabbit* at her. Then I stopped and realized that she had just combined a healthy, and justified, bit of paranoia with her quick thinking.

Rose, I responded.

Rabbit smiled.

We found Lucille's clothes, along with the elf-king's pendant, in an antechamber along with a pair of Dudley's guardsmen. The guardsmen had received a surprise visit from Krys and Rabbit, and they weren't going to bother us, or anyone else in this world, ever again. At this point I thought it was unfair to be surprised at that. All my "handmaidens" had toughed it out on their own a long time before they fell in with me. Any one of them could be scary in a fight before, and now they had half a year of real training under their belts.

Besides, when the stabby end of a blade is plunging into you, it really doesn't make much difference if the other end is held by a burly warrior or a mute teenage girl. If I wanted to intimidate someone, I'd bring Brock, who was a walking mountain. If I wanted to kill someone, I'd be much better off with Rabbit or Krys, even if they weren't the most martial of the Goddess's warrior order.

I got dressed as Rabbit and Krys shut the doors to the temple corridor. The heavy oak door had no built-in way to bar it from this side, but the two girls managed to quickly improvise a barricade, wedging the gaps between wood and stone with daggers from the dead guards' belts, and taking a free-standing iron candelabra and hooking it through a massive ring that would have been used to pull the door closed.

Given that Dudley and his princesses would have to pull the door open from the other side, they would be working to escape for a long time. Once we were dressed and the door barred, Lucille asked, "How did you find us?"

I felt inordinately gratified by her use of the plural pronoun. When I was trapped behind her eyes, it was nice to have the recognition I still existed.

I didn't need to listen to the answer. As we dressed I had been "talking" to Rabbit.

How did you find us? I'd asked, about five minutes before Lucille had.

Krys faked being knocked out. She'd wanted to jump them by surprise wherever they were taking you . . .

And they didn't bother taking her.

No. That came with a mental snicker. *That pissed her off something good. Though that was for the best—I don't think she has the best grip of tactics. What exactly was she going to do if they'd taken her too? Conscious or not?*

She followed us?

As much as she could.

Krys had followed the rather obvious group of armored thugs through the streets of Fell Green into a district filled with temples, churches, and other structures dedicated to various gods. She lost them when Dudley's group went underground. That was when she returned for Rabbit, who had much better tracking skills than anyone else I had ever seen.

Rabbit was somewhat dismissive of her contribution. *A dozen large men tramping through a little-used underground corridor? I could have followed that trail if I was blind as well as mute. I don't know how Krys couldn't just follow the smell of their sweat.*

She asked me why there were a dozen copies of Lucille running around, and I told her. Her laugh that time had been more than mental, and drew stares from Lucille and Krys. She'd responded with a shrug that said, "If I could, I'd tell you."

Rabbit had the same thought about changing my misgendered body that Lucille had, and I had to explain the more urgent issue that faced us. She had responded with appropriate horror, and affirmed my decision to use Lothan's boon to try and fix it. Especially since Elhared wasn't around to reverse the problem.

Maybe. Maybe not. I thought as I picked up the dangling thought I had right before Dudley's attack.

What do you mean, "Maybe not"?

I think Crumley explained everything, and if I'm right, we have to do something about the elf-queen.

The elf-queen? What does she—

I'm going to need to talk to our half-elf guest.

Uh . . .

Rabbit?

Yeah, Robin . . .

Is there a problem?

About him . . .

Given the embarrassment dripping from her words, I knew that the dashing Robin Longfellow had managed to escape several paragraphs before she actually got around to stating it.

All he did was talk! Rabbit thought at me in frustration. *I watched him, and he talked. That was it! Then Krys was there, he was gone, and I had no idea what happened!*

I'm sorry. I felt for her.

Krys thinks I fell asleep.

Did you?

No! her mental voice snapped. Then, after a moment she added, meekly, *I don't know.*

You don't know?

One moment I was looking at him, the next Krys was shaking my shoulders. I still stood where I remembered, but he was gone.

I don't think it was your fault.

I didn't.

Robin had been a suspicious character since the moment we had picked him up. He'd been much too sanguine about being captured and restrained, as if he had wanted to come to Fell Green with us. The bastard— again literal, I thought idly—was admittedly at least half elvish. That meant he probably had twice as many tricks up his sleeve as a human con artist.

Blame Rabbit or not, the missing Robin pissed me off. The captive elf had been our best guide into the realm under the hill, and I had questions about the Summer Queen and what she might want with her late prince's scroll.

Worse, if my thoughts about the late Elhared the Unwise were close to accurate, we would need to pay the elves a visit.

"So what do we do now?" Krys asked when we returned to our rooms at The Talking Eye. Lucille spared a glare at the empty chair where Robin Longfellow had been tied. Then she took the metal flask that held our gift from Lothan from the belt pouch where I had placed it.

Inscribed in the metal were the words, "Consume while naked, standing at a crossroads, under the light of the moon."

It was early evening, edging toward suppertime. At least a few hours before moonlight entered the picture. I wondered if Lucille intended to strip here in town. Fell Green probably had a higher tolerance for oddity than most places, but a naked princess would probably still draw some unwanted attention.

That made me think of Dudley and his entourage.

I chuckled.

Lucille chuckled.

We froze for a moment, and I realized that she had not been thinking of anything remotely funny. To her, the small laugh came out of nowhere. I felt her hand tighten its grip on the flask. I reached up with her other hand and touched it gently in what I hoped was a reassuring gesture. She flinched a little in surprise, but didn't pull her hand away.

I felt her bite our lip and watched as her vision of the flask blurred. "I hope this works," she whispered.

Me too.

She nodded as if she heard me.

"Your Highness?" Krys asked, a note of concern in her voice.

Lucille closed her eyes and said, "Get a fire going in the stove."

"A fire?" I heard the incredulity in her voice. I understood. It was summer, and it was anything but cold.

"A small one." Lucille elaborated.

"Oh . . ." I heard the realization in her voice.

Lucille nodded. "Brew up some tea from Crumley's herbs. You'll have to pass Frank's words on to me." She looked at the pendant. "We don't have much time."

Evening light streamed into our room in The Talking Eye as we formed our war council. The shaman's flower tea was powerful enough that Krys and Rabbit only had to sip from a shared cup. From the smell, I think the essence of the slimy fungus nature of Brock's tea must have come from other ingredients; possibly *actual* slime and fungus.

We sat on the chair that had held our one-time prisoner and Krys and Rabbit shared space on the bed. Krys spoke for everyone when she asked, "What do we do now?"

Lucille hefted Lothan's flask in her hand. "We have a solution to our body issues . . . at least according to a trickster deity known for illusion and deception. We have to wait for moonrise though."

"What about Timoras?" Krys asked.

Lucille raised the pendant and looked at the sand. She shook her head. "I was hoping knowing the origin of the scroll might . . ." She shook her head. "This whole trip has been useless."

"No," Krys said. "You found Frank and we're going to get him back now."

Lucille glanced at the flask as if she didn't quite believe it. "What does Frank think?"

Frank? asked the voice of a young man in my head.

Elhared, I thought, my mind almost gagging on the name.

"Elhared?" Krys said aloud.

"What do we want with a dead wizard?" Lucille asked.

He's not dead, I thought.

"What?" Krys snapped, echoed by Rabbit's voice in my head.

"'What,' what?" Lucille repeated.

Krys relayed my assertion.

"What does he mean 'not dead'?" Lucille asked.

Krys repeated me, point by point. However, everything she said boiled down to a single chain of logic: the dragon had been resident in Elhared's body ever since the original spell misfired; the scroll, according to Crumley, had been authored by Elhared in order to reverse the original spell; if the scroll had reversed the effects of the spell—placing Lucille in her original body, the dragon in his original body, and only skipping me because my original body was gone—it left a single very relevant question.

Who now inhabited Elhared's body?

Lucille argued, and I argued back with Krys as a proxy. She asked why didn't the dragon's absence just leave Elhared's body a dead empty shell without any animating spirit? I doubted it. Given the logic this particular brand of magic seemed to follow, if nothing had claimed Elhared's body I'd have expected my displaced persona to take up residence. I strongly suspected that the scroll did its job, as much as possible, returning the original spirits to the original bodies.

Yes, Elhared might be dead, but that probably didn't mean that he was out of reach of the spell, since he was probably suffering eternal torment in Nâtlac's realm of the dead, and the spell was an invocation of Nâtlac's power.

Eventually Lucille ran out of objections.

"Not that we need Elhared. As long as Lothan's cure works out." Lucille hefted the flask and looked out the unshuttered window at the evening light. Rabbit followed her gaze.

"Actually we do," Krys relayed for me.

"Why? Even if he's rotting in elvish captivity instead of the dragon now—I still feel no desire to rescue him."

"The queen," Krys passed on for me.

What would Queen Theora, ruler of the Summer Court of the elves, want with Elhared's scroll? When she talked to Dudley, it sounded as if she was much more keen on the coming war than Timoras—if we were to believe Robin's assessment of his uncle. She had said, more or less, that using the scroll would preempt us from fulfilling the elf-king's ultimatum.

"How would . . ." Lucille trailed off and I knew she got my point.

So did Krys. "By her logic, Elhared is the one responsible for her son's death."

Right. And if that's the case, forget any other logic, it's her definition that matters to Timoras, since it's her—or her followers—he needs to appease to prevent a war. We have to give him Elhared.

Krys passed that on, and Lucille responded with an impressive string of curses.

"That means we *have* to try and save the bastard," Lucille said. "Only so we can give him back." She rubbed her temple with the hand she still controlled. "I hate dealing with elves."

Rabbit had gotten up from the bed and walked to the window.

"We don't know where he is," Krys said.

"And at this point I don't think the elf-king would be too willing to let us come by for a visit."

"Yeah."

"So how does Frank think this will work? Does he have some sort of plan?"

"I don't kn— What is it?" Krys turned to look at Rabbit, who was gesturing wildly at the window. I heard Rabbit's mental voice, *You need to see this.*

Lucille stood and looked over at Rabbit as Krys walked up next to her. Krys stared out the window with wide eyes.

What the . . . I heard her young man's voice trail off blankly in my head.

I felt uneasy, remembering a few months ago looking out the window of a rented room, and seeing an angry dragon waiting for me. However, when Lucille walked up next to the other two, there was nothing outside the window but the cobbled street outside The *Talking Eye,* washed by a ruddy evening light.

"What are we looking at?" Lucille asked.

You don't see it? Rabbit asked me.

See what? I responded.

"Crap. I think you may need some tea," Krys said.

CHAPTER 20

Lucille had been initially reluctant to take the tea—no question I was as well—but Crumley's admonishment about possible side effects were somewhat ameliorated by the weight of Lothan's flask in our hand. So at Krys's and Rabbit's urging I picked up the cup and held it up to Lucille's face. I waited until she moved her lips to meet the cup before I tilted it. She took a mouthful of the tea and I took the cup away.

She swallowed and the power of Crumley's herb hit full force, like we'd been stripped naked and tossed screaming into a near-frozen lake. We took a deep breath and staggered back a moment. If anything, the absence of the other foul components from this blend made it worse. Maybe Brock had added the slime mold and fungus to tone things down.

Wow! The dragon's voice exploded through my skull like a crossbow bolt through a rotten cabbage.

Don't yell! I yelled back at her.

Our hands went to our temple to press at the throbbing pulse there. Our hands? My hands?

"Lucille?" I whispered, and my voice came out of our mouth.

Still here . . . that was a jolt.

I know.

I think you're in charge right now . . .

Am I?

I lifted our head and lowered one hand from my temples. The left one hesitated a moment, then lowered on its own accord.

Almost in charge . . .

That thought was in a weird echoey hybrid of my voice and the dragon's. I shuddered, and Lucille's arm hugged me. I imitated her, wrapping my own arm around, over hers.

"Are you all right?" Krys asked.

"Fine," I whispered. "We just weren't expecting—"

I finally looked out the window so we could see what had captured the two girls' attention. The voice dried up in my throat.

Through the window to our room, I no longer saw the evening sky we'd been watching with half an eye ever since reading the inscription on Lothan's flask. Instead, I saw moon *and* sun near their zenith occupying the same too-purple sky, almost touching.

That was the sky I had seen under the hill.

Inside my head I heard Lucille's voice echoing my own thoughts, but fortunately not exactly.

"It tears down the walls between your self and reality."

Fell Green was a wizard town, it had been built between worlds, and it seemed as if it was closer to the land of the elves than any place in the world of men. The barriers between here and there were thinner, and under the herb's influence, we now all saw parts of elfland bleeding through, nestled in the cracks between this city and itself.

I know that doesn't make much sense, but I can't really describe it accurately to anyone who isn't under the influence of a magical hallucinogenic herb. What had before been a normal static city-scape, seemed to breathe or pulse, expanding without changing size or position, to reveal glimpses of a shining other place just around a corner that otherwise didn't seem to exist.

Sometimes the universe hands you an answer so obvious that you just have to take advantage of it, no matter how insane it might be.

Of course we had to test the theory.

We brewed a batch of the powerful herbs and poured it into a waterskin that Rabbit had been carrying. Then we left The Talking Eye and walked into the shifting almost-there landscape. We had barely gone a dozen paces before it became obvious that we all saw the same thing, not just a close approximation due to a shared hallucination. We saw something that was actually there in the real world.

Of course, "real world" had become a somewhat fuzzy concept by then.

As we approached a wall that had been a row of shops across the street from the inn, it seemed to fold inward until we stood at the mouth of an alley that had not existed when we stood across the street. Rabbit walked into the alley, where there should have been only a blank wall.

We followed.

Yes, it's very strange.

Lucille was obviously responding to someone. Since Krys had been responding to mental conversation aloud, I guessed she was talking to Rabbit. Apparently the tradeoff for the tea giving me control of the body—most of it, anyway—was the loss of my ability to "hear" anyone aside from Lucille. I suppose there was some sort of logic to it, but I found it annoying.

We walked through a space that seemed to pass between two buildings that seemed almost there, and through another that almost wasn't. The buildings we passed between were made from the elaborate white crystal I had seen the last time I'd passed under the hill.

When we reached the other end of the alley, it folded out into a city that was *not* Fell Green. On this side of the passage, it seemed the wizard town was the one that pulsed and tried to push itself through the cracks in this world.

"Welcome to elfland," Krys said quietly.

I don't believe it either, Lucille responded to the unheard Rabbit.

"Now we just need to find Elhared," I said.

When I say it like that . . .

. . . It sounds so simple.

"What's the plan?" Krys asked both of us.

I felt Lucille's hand go to the pendant around our neck. I glanced down and she turned the pendant so we both could see it. The sand was visibly moving faster. The side trip with Dudley had cost us; it looked as if we'd lost almost half the sand we'd had left when we'd visited the Wizard Crumley.

That confirms it. We're here, and running out of time. I involuntarily finished her thought. It left uneasy echoes in our skull.

We were running out of time in more than one sense. Maybe four hours in the glass, much less than that in our own head.

Plan. I was supposed to have a plan, wasn't I?

Below us, in the city that was almost here, I saw elves almost moving. I looked at them and said, improvising aloud, "We need to find Elhared, wherever he is."

"Yes," Krys said. Her tone reminded me that I was stating the obvious.

Are you making this up as you go along?

It's worked so far.

No it hasn't.

"Let me think." I paused, staring down into what might have been a city square, although there was nothing square about it. The roads below were laid out in a geometry that I think might have inspired a severe headache if I had thought about it too much. I could almost feel the accelerating sand in the hourglass through the surface of the pendant Lucille still gripped in our hand.

"Frank?" Krys asked.

"The trial," I said, thinking about the last time I had been here.

"What?" Krys said.

"The arena . . ." I remembered the place of the trial where the elves had convicted Lucille in her dragon skin, and the dragon in his Elhared skin. It had been hollowed into a mound on the outskirts of this city; a mound that—I realized now—the Goddess Lysea had shown me in a vision.

If that had really been the goddess.

Dream-Lysea's identity aside, anyone who wanted to write that dream off as coincidence had never dealt with prophetic visions before. "We need to find the arena where they held the trial for me, Lucille, and the dragon."

Is going there a good idea?

Is going anywhere here a "good idea"? I thought at Lucille. *But what **choice do we have?***

I shuddered when she answered for me, even though I was certain it had been my thought.

Deep down, I understood that she felt exactly the same way. And that was the problem, wasn't it?

I hefted the flask and glanced up at the elvish sky, sun and moon in the same sky, almost touching. That should count per Lothan's instructions.

Wouldn't it?

Wait, Frank.

Why?

We should take care of Elhared first. We don't know if that "cure" will have any side effects.

I almost thought, "Like what?" But I knew better. The only certainty with this kind of magic, especially the kind with a god involved, was that something unexpected would happen. I didn't know what, but given that Lothan was known for deception, trickery, and an unfortunate sense of humor, I accepted that Lucille was probably right. We should wait until solving our personal problem wouldn't interfere with solving the larger issues. We probably had a little time before the "cure" became urgent.

Rushing into things was always my biggest fault.

So instead of testing Lothan's flask, we rushed into the depths of the elf city.

Finding the arena wasn't quite as easy as it sounded. We were navigating a city whose geography was flexible in the best of times, and we did so while suspended halfway between it and Fell Green. Moment to moment the relationship between the two cities seemed to renegotiate itself, stretching, rotating, squeezing itself between the mortal structures that seemed to surround and engulf the elf city one moment, and be surrounded and engulfed in turn the next moment.

I knew it to be on the outskirts, so we moved in the direction of Fell Green's city wall, assuming some form of congruence between one world and the other. However, I think logic may have had less to do with us finding the place than our intent. The land of the elves worked like that.

Either way, while we found the place, a distressing amount of sand passed through the elf-king's pendant in the process.

The road became a twisting path of gold set in silver sand that glittered in the combined light of sun and moon. The tall spun-sugar towers of the elves peeled away from us as we climbed a hill that, somehow, occupied the same spot as the main gate of Fell Green.

As we approached, the signs of the mortal city seemed to fold away into the spaces between everything else.

"Is it always this empty?" Krys asked as we climbed the hill.

"I don't know," I whispered. We had been avoiding the natives as much as possible. The inhabitants of both places seemed insubstantial and ghostly. The elves moved way too slowly, the natives of Fell Green moved way too fast—all statues and blurs. Even so, there seemed too few elves for the size of their city, and the height of their towers.

I didn't like that.

However, that was just one item on a lengthening list.

Another thing I didn't like was the low resonating sound that filled the air as we closed on the arena. It was a rumble so low that it was more a rattle in the teeth and a humming in the bowels than a sound. I literally could not imagine a scenario where that would have been a good thing.

I didn't like the dark wood coming into view on the other side of the hill. Last time I'd been here, I had focused on the city and I had been facing away from the twisted forest that formed a brutal echo of the delicate city towers on the opposing side of the arena.

Mostly, I didn't like the sudden limp I had developed. I wasn't in control of my left foot anymore. *Lucille?*

I know, I'm trying to keep our balance.

It's progressing . . .

Elhared. We need him.

Elhared. We need him. I agreed at the same time.

Not just the foot, but the whole leg. I had the strange sensation of being stitched to someone else down the center of my body. I still felt sensations, heard and saw, but it was someone else's touch I felt, someone else's ear I heard through, and my eyes couldn't focus right. The left one didn't quite match what the right looked at, throwing the world into a painful blur.

Lucille must have realized that at the same time I did, because my left eye screwed itself shut. The right shot back into focus.

Being here . . .

. . . is accelerating the effects of the tea.

"Frank?" Krys said, stopping and looking back at us. Rabbit faced us as well. Distantly I could sense her too-adult voice.

Are you all right?

"Go on," I shouted at them, waving them ahead with Lucille's hand. My voice came out slurred. Lucille had tried to say the same thing at the same time, but she wasn't quite matched in tempo or volume. However, she managed a mental shout that, from the wincing, I saw everyone heard.

Move! We can't stop now.

We managed a limping run up the remainder of the hillside so we reached the edge of the bowl-like arena just a moment after Krys and Rabbit. They had stopped at the edge overlooking the arena, and when we saw what they saw, we drew to a stop as well.

We saw now the source of that low resonant sound, a vibration so intense that it felt as if our teeth were shaking loose.

It was the sound of tens of thousands of elves cheering.

CHAPTER 21

"It never goes wrong in the way you expect," Lucille and I spoke through our single mouth in perfect coordination. The sentiment came out whispered without a hint of a slur.

"Oh boy," Krys said.

The arena was filled to capacity—beyond capacity. If anything, the arena seemed much bigger than it had the first time I had seen it. The tall forms of the elves were wrapped in engraved armor of silver and gold. They held aloft silken banners covered by embroidery too complex for mortal eyes. Ranks of them stood, filling the arena, down to the floor below where a stage stood centered on the floor. On the stage stood Timoras, the elf-king himself, bearing the same icy armor he'd worn when he had issued his ultimatum. He had his arms raised in a gesture of martial incitement.

Or maybe he was trying to swat a bug; with the pose nearly frozen it was hard to tell.

Next to him on the stage was Queen Theora, just as I had seen her with Dudley; as tall as Timoras, her skin as brown as his was pale white, her leather armor bearing patterns as elaborate as any engraved in the silver and gold immediately surrounding us. Her forest-green hair flowed behind her like a cape. In her hands she held aloft a familiar piece of curling parchment.

Past her I saw the half of the arena closer to the forest populated by elves of a different character than the ones nearer us. *Her* elves had the same leather armor, and the same dark skin.

Lysea's vision—or Lothan's, I suspected now—had shown me these two elven armies converging here. I had the strong suspicion that this convergence of Summer and Winter, Queen and King, was unique.

That did not make me feel better.

"This isn't good," Krys said. "We need to get out of here before—"

"Shh," came sloppily out of Lucille's side of our mouth. "Loosh." She had meant "look," but she had seen it before I had, and our speech wasn't coordinated.

Despite that, when Lucille pointed Krys and Rabbit got her message. So did I.

On the stage, along with the elven sovereigns Timoras and Theora, was a golden cage surrounded by an honor guard of elves, half dark, half light. Inside the cage was an old man. He was tall, white-haired, and had skin the sickly white of an underground denizen. He wore the same robes I had last seen him in.

Elhared.

Krys shook her head. Rabbit looked back at us with wide, incredulous eyes.

The bailiff and judge from our prior captivity stood on the stage, flanking the wizard's cage. As we watched through one open eye, I saw the bailiff's massive staff slowly land on the surface of the stage at his feet. I saw the eruption of sparks as it struck, blue flashes that hung too long in the air. Moments after, the sound of the impact washed across us like a slow avalanche.

I realized that, aside from the king, queen, and bailiff, everyone on that stage faced Elhared. All of those, aside from the judge, bore crossbows that were loaded and cocked and already halfway up to point at the wizard.

"We can't—" Krys started.

They mean to execute him! Lucille tried to use our mouth, but the words came out slurred and incomprehensible. Fortunately her mental shout seemed audible to everyone thanks to the shaman's flower. Around us the impact of the bailiff's staff still resonated like a passing stampede. On the stage his staff had already rebounded upward.

Everything seemed to be picking up speed.

Of course it would start wearing off now.

Lucille gave up on our voice. *Get him out of there while we still have surprise on our side. Run!*

I had seen the doubt on both Krys's and Rabbit's faces, but Lucille managed the voice of command, and neither of them hesitated, rushing down the aisle between the no-longer-quite-paralyzed elves toward the stage.

Give him some of the tea! Lucille thought.

Then we tried to run after them.

That had not been a good idea on either of our parts. With control of our body split evenly between us, navigating the stepped descent would have been a difficult process at a normal pace. At a run it was suicidal. We managed three consecutive steps before we fell, and then only if you counted my frantic attempt to prevent the tumble as an actual "step."

We rolled down the steps, lucky that both of us had the same idea of tucking ourselves into a ball to minimize the damage. The bruising descent seemed to last forever.

The good news—we rolled out onto the arena floor much sooner than we could have managed under our own control.

We opened our unfocused eyes in time to see another flash of blue light from the bailiff's staff. Blue sparks slowly arced across the sky like a shower of comets above us, cutting across the face of the too-large elvish moon.

The sound of the crashing staff came quicker this time.

Around us, the ranks of elves had visibly moved, turning in our direction. I could almost see them moving.

I remembered Crumley's words, "If you can see something, it can see you."

Not good!

Tell me about it.

You have a plan yet?

I thought this was your plan? "Get him out of there."

I tried to push us upright, and Lucille's arm belatedly scrambled to help me.

Not much time, we both thought at the same time.

At the same time we both thought that, with all the paths leading to this arena, from the city and the woods, it probably counted as a crossroads. If that wasn't enough, we were still barely standing at the intersection of elfland and Fell Green. With our eyes unfocused, we could still just make out the wide cobbled road that separated the city from the woods—though that image faded almost as we watched.

We glanced up, at the elf sun and the elf moon.

Only one part of the instructions left.

We wouldn't be able to tell you who thought that. We were no longer thinking simultaneously, because that implied two voices in our head. A single voice now spoke our thoughts. Panic gripped us, because, if it wasn't too late already, we knew that point was only moments away. Not only with our merging personalities, but with the elves that turned toward us. Soon we would be a prisoner, and whoever was that prisoner, it would no longer be us.

We tore at our clothes.

Our clumsiness faded as our limbs began working in concert again. That was no comfort, just another sign of the acceleration of our merging. As we tore the armor off our body, kicked off boots, and shed the chemise underneath, sparks flew from the bailiff's staff a third time, the sound quick upon it. Around us, the elves moved, visibly accelerating as they faced us, blocking our view of the arena. It was hard to tell, were they moving at a quarter speed now? A third?

We held Lothan's flask in one hand, Timoras's pendant dangling from its chain in the other. In the pendant sand had begun racing through the glass.

Naked, standing in the crossroads of that arena, under the moon, we broke the seal with our teeth and drank.

We tasted blood.

I should have known what was coming.

The flask was a boon from Lothan after all, god of

deception, lies, masks, metamorphosis, and transformation. He was not a cruel deity, but he was known for a
juvenile sense of humor, often at the expense of those he
favored. That wasn't an aspect you wanted to dwell on
when you were relying on divine intervention, but that
was probably why, even after millennia, Lothan's jokes
still caught people unawares.

People like the Dragon Lucille and the Princess Frank.

Which is not to say he didn't grant us exactly what we
asked for, or even what we needed; like I said, he was not
cruel.

But it wasn't quite what we were expecting.

Even though the Wizard Crumley had explicitly told
us exactly what it would take to solve our two-minds-
one-body problem.

Even though the instructions about being naked under the moon had been a really big clue.

We drank, gagging at the taste of blood in our mouth. The
unpleasantness didn't deter us, and not only because we
had quaffed worse-tasting beverages in our lives—Brock's
fungus-laced medicinal tea came immediately to mind.
We drank because we knew it was our only chance to stop
the merging that had been accelerating along with the
movements of the elves. We were certain that if we had
hesitated until the elves' movements and ours were in
sync, it would be too late.

During the last swallow, as I felt something slightly clot-
ted slide down my throat, *I* realized that *I* was feeling the
nasty sensation of coagulated blood settle into *my* uneasy
stomach.

Lucille?

That was nasty.

I blinked my eyes and realized that I could focus on the circle of elves closing around us. I raised my hands, and they both obeyed me.

Okay, we're naked, unarmed, and an army of angry elves is surrounding us.

At least we're still an us.

Slight improvement, but beside the point right now.
Plan?

We have any of that shaman's flower?

Wouldn't that just undo what Lothan's flask did?
Wouldn't it?

That didn't feel right. He had promised us our own bodies, not just a return to the status quo.

That wasn't the only thing that didn't feel right.

I belched as my stomach roiled.

Ugh. Lucille's dragon voice filled my skull as my gut spasmed with rebellion against Lothan's boon. Everything lurched as I tried to vomit. That's what it felt like anyway.

I retched to bring up the swallowed blood, but instead of coming up my throat, the blood filling my gut slammed outward in directions it shouldn't have been able to go. I felt things twisting and pushing against my skin. I fell to my knees and, strangely, found my eye level did not drop. I threw my arms out to keep from falling forward and instead of my arms, I saw muscular forelimbs, covered by rippling red scales. I tensed the muscles in my jaw, and I felt the tension strain the length of much more neck than I should have. The elves fell back away from us, still at half the speed they should have been moving.

I felt our tail sweep out behind us as broad wings erupted from our back. We towered over the elves now, our head sweeping an arc a dozen feet above their heads.

Lucille glanced down and looked at herself. Her taloned hand lifted from the ground, the pendant dangling from its chain wrapped around a single long digit.

"Oh yes!" she hissed in a cloud of brimstone steam as she closed it in a massive fist.

I realized I'd been relegated to the back room of our skull again. I didn't mind, Lucille was the one with all the dragon experience. Hoping she could still hear me, I thought at her, *Get out before they speed up to normal. They could capture the other dragon, they'll manage this one.*

I don't know if she heard me, or had just thought the same thing, but she launched toward the moon above us at a gut-wrenching speed that I don't think the original dragon could have hoped to match. She glanced downward at the shrinking arena, and while my mental stomach churned with a queasy awareness of our velocity and distance from the ground, the golden cage on the stage below shot into focus. Elhared was gone.

"Yes!" Her triumphant scream came out in a ball of incendiary joy.

She turned and flew across the elf moon toward the shadow of Fell Green.

CHAPTER 22

I rode in Lucille's skull as she twisted, looped, and dove toward Fell River. As the sky regained its mortal night-time hue above us, lit by the full orb of the mortal moon, I saw her reflection falling up toward the surface of the river below in a clarity sharpened by the pure terror of her descent.

She was not the same dragon, not remotely. Where her old body had been thick and heavy, fifty feet of blunt object, her new crimson skin wrapped a body like a le-thal whip. When the old dragon dropped from the sky, it fell like a brick. This new body shot downward like a quarrel loosed from the deity of all crossbows, her nar-row skull a flaming arrowhead.

Just before we struck the water, and her own reflec-tion, she pulled up, sending a downdraft that blew spray against the moonlit walls of Fell Green.

Lucille can you hear me?

"Whoohoo!"

Lucille!

Frank?

She stopped rolling and dipping, for which I was grateful, and we continued at a considerable clip, bank-ing around the walls of the city below.

Focus!

Um, sorry. I could still feel her body, and I felt the lipless reptile mouth twitch in what I knew was a ghost of a grin. She wasn't sorry at all.

Not that I was angry at her. Far from it. I felt almost as much relief as she did. We had escaped something that wasn't quite death—but close enough for both of us. And trapped with the elves would have meant the real thing would have followed quickly along in any event.

And stop scaring the city guard.

Huh? She looked down and saw the guards rushing to reinforce the walls, leveling crossbows in her direction. She shook her head and called down, **"I'm not attacking! Haven't you ever seen a happy dragon before?"**

No one shot at us, so that was something. She banked another circuit around the city and came down to a landing on the road bisecting the island, in front of the city gate. As her feet clawed the blessedly solid ground she half thought, half vocalized, **"Frank? Where is your body?"**

I—I don't know, I replied.

That was the truth, since I hadn't had a spare moment to put two and two together yet.

She swung a taloned hand in front of her face, and I could see the elf-king's pendant dangling from one finger. She squinted, but in the moonlight we couldn't quite make out the state of the sand in the tiny hourglass. She sighed.

I guess the part about being naked makes sense now.

I felt her shudder. **"In armor? That would have been painful."**

At least. And if that thing would have been around our neck—

"Ack!" She made a choking sound and clutched her throat with a free hand.

Now I guess we need to find—

"Is that you, Your Highness?"

Lucille swung her head on its whiplike neck so fast that I felt as if I sloshed all the way to one side of her skull. I wasn't the only one taken aback. Krys scrambled backward from the sudden attention so quickly that she stumbled halfway back toward the woods and sprawled on her backside.

"Krys!" As a dragon, Lucille had managed, over time, to learn to modulate her voice. After several months of work, those who knew her were able to distinguish the difference in tone between, for instance, a hearty greeting and bowel-melting anger. I realized that this skill must have been due to her familiarizing herself with that one particular draconic incarnation.

Especially when Krys whispered, "Please don't eat me."

This body had a different voice, but it was no less intimidating. It also didn't carry the same nuance that Lucille managed in her mental discourse.

"No! Krys? I'm back to normal!"

Krys got unsteadily to her feet. "Normal?"

Lucille ignored that. **"Where's Rabbit ... And El-hared?"**

Krys frowned. "Where's Frank?"

"What? Ah." She reached up and tapped her skull with a talon. **"Still in here."**

"Still in there, huh?" Krys backed away, circling at a

distance, facing us and edging away from the woods at the same time.

"What's the matter?"

Krys gaped. "What's the matter? What's the matter? How can you— What do you— Do you— And Frank—" Whatever she tried to say accelerated to the point that only a word in three could make a sputtering escape from her mouth.

"Please, calm down."

"Calm down?" Krys repeated, the force of the words breaking the jumble of language that had snarled in her mouth. "Calm down!? You're a dragon!"

"Yes—"

"Where did a dragon come from!?" Krys yelled up at her. "There was just an extra dragon lying around somewhere?"

"I—I don't know."

"You don't know?"

"The tea was wearing off, the elves saw us. We drank Lothan's potion."

"Uh-huh. It was supposed to solve things for you *and* Frank."

"Yes—"

"And, again, where's Frank?"

Lucille sank back on her haunches. Her head retreated, and something shuddered inside her.

"How do I even know who you are? You don't look like the dragon I know."

"It's me. We drank, and we . . . changed."

I figured Lothan was busy laughing at us now, though I didn't know the extent of the joke yet.

"So the trickster's potion turned you both into a dragon."

"Yes."

Krys didn't look convinced.

"How can I persuade you?"

"I don't know. This is weird, even for you."

"Wait, here." Lucille reached out toward Krys. Krys stumbled back as Lucille opened the taloned hand that still held the pendant. **"Take it. It's too small for me to see the hourglass clearly."**

Krys edged up to Lucille's hand and gingerly took the pendant, as if she was afraid a too-sudden move might cause Lucille to clench the hand shut on her.

"How much is left?"

Krys backed away and held the pendant up in front of the full moon. After a moment, she said, "Maybe an eighth left? Less."

"All that time with the elves . . . Elhared better be worth it."

Krys stared at us incredulously.

"You still don't believe me?"

"Do you blame me?" Krys asked.

"But—"

Lucille? I whispered in her head, interrupting her.

"What?"

"'What,' what?"

Lucille held up a finger. **"Shh."**

Lucille listened and nodded as I gave her my suggestion.

"What?" Krys repeated.

"Frank says to tell Rose that she's the one adept at detecting the real Lucille."

*   *   *

That managed to convince Krys of who we were. Not that I blamed her for the paranoia. Given the events of the past year, and the habit of half the people around me to alter their identities at inconvenient times, I'd take the sudden appearance of a strange dragon claiming to be someone I knew with just a little bit of suspicion.

Lucille might have been a little annoyed, but she understood as well as I did. I think she'd only been taken aback because she hadn't yet realized that she was a *different* dragon. She had just been caught up with being a dragon again.

I understood how she felt. The last time I'd been a guy, I had taken over a body that wasn't my own. I had spent a few hours reveling in being male again before I started worrying about the other little details, like who the body had belonged to.

Fortunately I didn't think that would be an issue with Lucille's new body. Nâtlac's forte seemed to be the shipping of souls back and forth; Lothan seemed more at ease with changing the physical body. Disguise, transformation, and metamorphosis were among his spheres. So it only made sense that he had created this new dragon from the body of the princess.

Which was par for the course because, after a year, I had become resigned to thinking of it as *my* body.

Oh well, easy come, easy go.

Still, I couldn't be too angry about the loss. I was in no worse position than I'd been after the debacle at the banquet, and Lucille had been given something I didn't think was possible. She now wore her own body, in most of the senses I could think mattered. She had taken to the original dragon, but never quite perfectly, I thought now.

As much as she had filled the lumbering black monster Elhared had recruited, it had still been a stolen skin. It fit her better than the one she had left to me, but she grew herself to fit it and not vice versa.

This dragon *was* Lucille.

I had seen it as we'd descended toward the Fell River, and I still felt it in every serpentine movement. Her new red body was smaller, almost as long, but with far less bulk, and much more agile than its black-scaled predecessor. As she followed Krys into the woods, she moved with a lithe grace as if she had lived her whole life in this skin.

Also, I don't know if she had realized it quite yet, but unlike her prior dragon skin, this one was female. I wondered if that mattered to her. Given how much Lothan's work seemed to have captured Lucille's inner self, I suspected it probably did.

Good for you.

Frank?

Nothing, just thinking out loud.

Don't worry. We'll get you your own body again.

Yeah.

We have Elhared now . . .

I know. There was still something amiss about Lucille's perfect transformation. Hadn't Lothan promised us both our own bodies? He might be the deity of lies and deception along with everything else, but that didn't feel quite right. I realized I was missing something. *About that, don't you think it's odd—*

I didn't get to finish the thought because we broke through into a clearing where Rabbit and a still-bound Elhared sat by a campfire. The old wizard looked up, startled, and said, "Where'd you get *another* dragon?"

Lucille ignored him, focusing her attention on the third figure seated by the campfire.

"What is he doing here?"

"Good evening, Your Highness," answered Robin Longfellow, half-elf and sometime highwayman.

CHAPTER 23

"What is he doing here?" Lucille repeated.

Rabbit stared up at Lucille goggle-eyed until Krys ran up and told her who she was. Elhared shook his head as he watched the two girls. He didn't need to say anything. The expression he wore, one halfway between arrogant contempt and the sour disgust of a man who had just found half a worm in his apple, told me that the man in this skin was the same ass who had tried to kill Lucille a year ago.

Robin stood and dusted off his legs with some idle swipes from the backs of his hands. Unlike Rabbit, he didn't show any surprise at Lucille's transformation. I would have expected a little more concern facing an annoyed dragon's query. In his place I would have at least taken a step back at Lucille's tone, and I was married to her.

Though, with all the body swapping, I wondered if that was still the case. Technically, under Lendowyn law, whoever was in the body of the princess was married to whoever was in the skin of the dragon—the *other* dragon. What happened when the princess's body was gone?

Robin, verbose as usual, had been talking while my mind vanished down its own tangent. "I came to render what aid I could to the opponents of my less than beloved uncle."

"You escaped from the inn."

Robin shrugged. "Forgive my wandering soul. The young lady is a fine listener, but for conversation she has her faults. Boredom and I have never been boon companions. I decided to visit my uncle's realm, to see how sooth was your tale of imminent doom. Perhaps learn something of interest to my new companions."

"Really? You expect me to believe that?"

"Why should you not? Here I sit with all of you, unbound and of my own free will. And after assisting your squire and handmaid to rescue this grumpy sot."

"Watch your tongue, half-breed." Elhared snapped.

"Is this true?" Lucille asked Krys.

"Yes," Krys said. "We got to the cage, but there was no way to open it. Couldn't bend the bars or find a door. We drank two or three rounds of the tea—and it felt like we struggled for an hour before Robin showed up. I still don't know how he opened it."

"The doors to such a prison cannot be opened by mortal blood," Robin explained.

"But you weren't slowed down like the elves?"

"One advantage of my heritage. With one foot in the mortal realm, and one foot under the hill, I can traipse the edge between those worlds as I will. I could walk back there now with a single step. I stay simply because I hope you see me as an ally."

"Why?"

"To inconvenience my uncle, of course."

Lucille settled back on all fours and stretched to fill

nearly two-thirds of the clearing. She twisted her long neck so that her head was more or less level with Robin's body. Her new skull may have been smaller than the last dragon's, but her teeth were no less sharp, and I sensed her jaws still had the strength to bite a man in half. **"Then answer me this, Robin Longfellow. How did you know to address me as 'Your Highness'?"**

Everything fell silent. I think the half-elf would have suffered some unfortunate violence had he hesitated even a moment in answering Lucille's question. He didn't. He prattled on as if there wasn't any potential threat in giving a wrong answer. "Well, of course you're the Dragon Prince of Lendowyn, you're known far and wide, aren't you? Princess Frank told me some of what evil befell you, I assume that she found some magics in that musty wizard town to free you from what evil ensorcelment caused the death of Prince Daemonlas. Where is the princess? Back at the inn, I suppose?"

That actually made sense.

We had never let on to Robin that we'd been anything other than Princess Frank. Of course that meant he'd assume the Dragon Prince was still at large. If Krys led a dragon to meet him, who else would it be? It wasn't as if he had ever met Lucille in the other dragon's skin. He'd have no idea how different she looked now.

Elhared had made some comment about it, but Robin had probably missed it.

"Frank will be along later."

"Come on," Elhared snapped. "Can we dispense with the games?"

Lucille whipped her head around to look at Elhared.

"Trust me, my princess, you are not nearly as accomplished a liar as that black-clad fop."

"Are you accusing me of—"

"Forgive me, Your Highness. Being dead for over a year has frayed my diplomatic skills."

"You never had any," Lucille said.

"Perhaps. But it is very clear to me what has happened here."

"Care to enlighten us?"

"Care to release my bonds?" Elhared raised his wrists.

"We could give you back to the elves," Krys said.

Elhared tilted his head in Krys's direction and said, "The children are new. Is that what the Lendowyn treasury can afford now?"

"It's in your interest to talk to us."

He leaned back and said, "I know. And I know that it is not in *your* interest to return me to the elves, whatever ultimatum Timoras has given you."

Oh crap. He knows.

Shh. Let me deal with it.

"Elhared, I am losing patience with you." Lucille growled deep in her throat, and steam rolled from her nostrils. I felt a burning pressure building deep in her throat. Robin and Rabbit edged away from Elhared.

"You'd go to all this trouble to retrieve me, just to roast me in a fit of pique? That's not very good management of your limited resources. And what would you present the elf-king with?"

"Why would I free you?"

"You need my cooperation."

"We do?"

"If all you want is to appease Timoras, you can just hand me over now and worry about the other half of his demands yourself."

Sounds good to me.

"But who else is going to free Frank Blackthorne from that pretty skull of yours?"

Everyone was silent for the space of a half-dozen heartbeats. To my chagrin, Lucille seemed to actually consider it.

"Why would you help us?"

Lucille, this is not a good idea.

"I need you as well. The Summer Queen has cast me as the penultimate villain in her son's demise, despite the fact I was otherwise occupied at the time."

"That was apparent," Krys said.

"If we cooperate, and you deliver the dragon to Timoras, you can testify who is truly responsible for the prince's bad actions."

"Who?"

Elhared raised his bound wrists again.

"What will keep you from trying to escape?"

Elhared snorted. "The same thing keeping me from doing so now. The fae's misplaced desire for my blood."

I felt Lucille swallow a ball of fire. **"Fine."**

Don't trust this guy.

I know, Frank.

"Rabbit, free his wrists. Krys, ready your sword."

Elhared snorted and rubbed his wrists once Rabbit cut free his bonds. "You think a squire's blade is more intimidating than a motivated dragon?"

"Now, tell us what you know about what is happening."

Elhared nodded and looked up at the Dragon Lucille. "First, shall we consider the scales balanced at this point?"

"Are you kidding?"

"You and Frank killed me. I would think that was adequate payment for my political machinations. Given my rescue from elvish executioners, whatever your motive, *I'm* willing to forgive the dagger through the throat."

"Do you have any idea of the chaos you've caused?"

"How much of that can you lay at my feet? You certainly managed to survive the price on your head, and retain a peerage. Given your current state—one I imagine was an effort to attain—I can't imagine you find your status as a dragon that unpleasant."

"That's beside the point."

"Call the slate clean, and I'll be more than willing to reprise my role as Lendowyn court wizard, Your Highness."

I can't believe he—

"You think the elves can be convinced you aren't the one responsible for the prince's demise?"

"No question, once they understand the circumstances."

Wait? What? You're going along with— After what he did to us?

The man is a loathsome opportunist. But he's right.

What?

We need his cooperation.

That badly?

I want your body back, Frank.

I grumbled mentally as Lucille whipped out a taloned

hand so that the point of one finger stopped just touching Elhared's chest below the Adam's apple. I couldn't help but be gratified to see him wince.

"Wizard Elhared, the Crown of Lendowyn accepts your renewed pledge of service." Lucille snaked her neck so that her face was less than a foot away from Elhared's. Close enough that his wispy white hair fluttered in the brimstone breeze of her words. **"Do not disappoint us."**

If one knew only about the catastrophic results of the last master plan of Elhared the Unwise, it would be excusable to believe that the man was a fool and an idiot. That would be unfair, as the man was not an idiot. He had figured out most of the existing situation before anyone had talked to him. He had known that his year-old spell had been reversed the moment he was no longer dead. He had written that spell based on the one he had studied to do the initial damage. It had been an emergency measure, in case the spell went wrong. He knew the touch of his own magic instantly.

He also knew what that would have done to the surviving people affected. The original dragon would return to his own body, and Lucille would return to hers, and Frank wouldn't go anywhere, since his body had died along with Elhared.

"I'm impressed at the solution," Elhared said. "You obviously found life as a dragon gratifying. At some point you must give me the details on how you managed—"

"Never mind that. Who could have recovered that scroll?"

Elhared shook his head and chuckled. He gave Lucille a pitying look. "You don't know? Isn't it obvious?"

Something in his face made me sick to my stomach. I suddenly knew what was coming.

"Who?"

"Sebastian of course."

"Who in the Seven Hells is Sebastian?"

Elhared looked at her, and I swear his expression showed shock. I couldn't bear to hear the reproach in his voice. Not from an evil, scheming bastard like him. Especially since, in some sense, it was justified.

"After all you took from him, you don't even know his name?"

"Whose name?" Krys said.

Elhared waited for Lucille to make the connection herself. After a moment she started to say, **"Who . . ."**

She trailed off as it sank in. I knew when she understood, because I felt her stomach lurch, her heart accelerate, and her muscles clench.

Elhared's plan had been fairly simple. He hired a dragon to kidnap the princess of Lendowyn. Once the king offered said princess's hand in marriage, Elhared had hired a patsy from a dockside bar—yours truly—to suit up in armor to go "save" the princess. Once everyone had assembled in the same spot, he showed up to play round robin with everyone's souls. I had ended up as the princess, he had ended up as me, and the princess had ended up as the dragon. The plan had been to slay the dragon, now containing an inconvenient princess, so the newly minted hero Elhared would return with a newly compliant princess, and the head of a dragon. Instant peerage.

The dragon himself had always seemed the odd lizard out in that scenario.

The dragon had said that Elhared had bought his service with a promise to cover his marker for a gambling debt to the elves. Elves took those debts seriously. That promise seemed as fraudulent as everything else, given the state of the Lendowyn treasury. Even with the funds Elhared had been skimming from the crown, it seemed obvious in retrospect that he couldn't have possibly covered a gambling debt that had already consumed the whole of a dragon's hoard.

After Elhared's spell the dragon was no richer and he was stuck in Elhared's body. No prize that.

Lucille and I had always assumed that he'd been double-crossed as well as everyone else.

But what if he hadn't been?

What if that had been part of the plan? Had Elhared's plot gone as intended, the dragon who was in debt to the elves would be dead.

But what better way to cover that debt?

The dragon would be left in the body of Elhared the Unwise. Maybe not ideal, but free of any liens. He would have been established with a position, a title, and allies in the court to help enable the continuing fraud.

"The dragon's name is Sebastian," Lucille finally said.

"There you go," Elhared said. "After all that effort, and he still ends up in the hands of the elves. I suspect he was very annoyed."

"What? The dragon had your scroll?"

Elhared snorted and patted his robes. "No, *I* did. Just in case things went wrong. But Francis's interruption separated all of us, and I suspect Sebastian did not know whether to continue our plan or not. Besides, he didn't have the talent to invoke it."

So he had gone to the one place where it was certain that there would be someone who could, the wizard town of Fell Green. I felt sick. I remembered tackling him outside a gambling hall. I remember demanding to know the location of Elhared and the book, which he didn't know.

When I had been screaming in the faux Elhared's face, I hadn't known that, somewhere in his wizard's robes had been a scroll that could have reversed the whole mess.

If I had—

Something of the realization must have colored my thoughts, because Lucille interrupted them. ***No! Frank, it's not your fault!***

I could have stopped all this before it got so out of hand.

Don't you dare blame yourself.

I really didn't want to. I even tried to excuse it, explain it. After Elhared's spell misfired, I had only a few uninterrupted moments with the dragon—Sebastian—before the elves had shown up. After they had grabbed us, putting us on trial, Sebastian-as-Elhared had committed completely to the wizard fraud. Of course, in that context, he couldn't let on about the spell, much less the scroll that could reverse it. He didn't even let on who he really was until after sentence was passed.

My blame came later.

The elves had freed me, but had imprisoned the fake

Elhared and Lucille the dragon. I had made a deal with the elf-king to buy Lucille's freedom.

Just hers.

I could have bought Sebastian's freedom with the same act. It had been clear that the elves valued the dragon as a dragon more than Sebastian in his then-current state. In hindsight I could have freed him as well as Lucille without any extra cost on my part.

For reasons hard to justify in retrospect, I hadn't bothered. Sure, Lucille had been my priority, but at that point I'd believed the ex-dragon Sebastian had been as much a victim of Elhared's schemes as we'd been. Ignoring his plight had been, at best, petty vindictiveness on my part.

Worse, my pettiness had trumped logic that should have been clear to me at the time. Even though I had no idea of the scroll carried on his person, I should have realized that a former ally of Elhared might have been somewhat useful in tracking down the wizard.

Whatever Lucille may have thought, it *had* been my fault. I had abandoned Sebastian because I had been too blind to understand what I'd been doing. I had not only given up the undoing of Elhared's spell however unknowingly; I had also quite knowingly created an enemy when I could have created an ally.

It was *all* my fault.

CHAPTER 24

I think the chief problem in being a silent passenger in someone else's skull is how easy it makes it for you to disappear into your own thoughts, especially dark ones involving guilt and self-pity. For the past year or so, those latter ones had been a specialty of mine. Might-have-beens and self-recriminations can be even more addictive when you can't actually do anything physical.

I lost track of the conversation, huddling back in Lucille's skull and thinking quiet thoughts of my own uselessness. I tried to sulk in silence, because even long after the influence of the tea, Lucille still seemed to hear me. I didn't want her interrupting my depression telling me how she had come to terms with her life as a dragon, or how without me Grünwald would have conquered Lendowyn long before now. I'd heard her arguments before, and at better moments I could find them compelling.

But right now I couldn't help thinking of Sebastian the Dragon loosing his fury on an unsuspecting ballroom full of innocent people. Yes, I know, a bunch of nobles and diplomats, so they were really far from innocent. But they were innocent of the crime that fired Sebastian's wrath. Only one person in that room could claim credit for that. I didn't think Lucille could come up with a counter for my complicity in that.

Worse, now Sebastian was attacking villages with actual innocent people, pushing everything toward open war where even more would die. For all we knew, that war may have started already, the massed armies from my dream-vision marching for Lendowyn based on actions *I* had provoked.

I know Lucille would argue the point, and I didn't want to force her to. She had more important things to think about than inventing reasons to absolve me.

I should tell you that, at this point, it is perfectly acceptable to want to slap me. I share the sentiment. I know it's not all about me, but, then again, this is my story I'm telling, so, in a sense, it is, isn't it?

After Lucille's conversation with Elhared, there was a lot more back and forth as Lucille tried to form our group into something that might work as a team, and tried to craft something that might work as a plan. Too much time had been lost already, and they needed Sebastian the Dragon to fulfill the elf-king's ultimatum.

Elhared's rationale for working with us was, knowing what we did of where the scroll came from, that Sebastian would suffice as the one at root bearing responsibility for the death of the prince. Thanks to Elhared, we also had some clue to where he might have gone. Sebastian wasn't native to Lendowyn, and Elhared knew the mountain pass that his one-time coconspirator called home. It was back where we had come, a straight-line route that passed through the Northern Palace and kept going to the mountains beyond.

A few days ride at best. Given the state of the hourglass, we had little more than one mortal day left.

Fortunately we had alternate transportation now.

If there was any consolation to my status as an invisible rider in Lucille's skull, it was in that flight back to the Northern Palace. I had ridden via dragon before, and it would not be on any list I'd ever draft of fun things to do. Enough so that if it was a choice between escaping in the clutches of a friendly dragon and being immolated by an approaching forest fire, it would require at least a moment or two of thought on my part.

I had also, in my one prior episode in a dragon's skull, been used as a mount by a half-dozen teenage girls. That had been disconcerting in its own way. From a dragon's perspective, humans seem so tiny and fragile I couldn't help feeling that any wrong move would reduce them to a thin smear on my scaled backside.

Lucille being in control of the dragon freed me from both concerns.

Rabbit and Krys managed to quickly return to Fell Green and, in less than half an hour, trade the now-superfluous horses and return with a considerable amount of rope and leather. They used the supplies to knot together a rope harness around Lucille's chest and neck, giving the four humans something with which to anchor themselves.

Elhared was the only one to express any reluctance, but Robin said something to him and laughed. After that

Robin sprang up to straddle the dragon's neck. A grim-faced Elhared followed.

Krys and Rabbit sat forward, Rabbit in front.

Lucille launched herself into the moonlit night.

She was *fast*. I do not know what image that word conjures in your mind, but whatever it is, I can attest it is inadequate to convey the sheer velocity of her movement.

Wind tore by us as our passengers screamed.

Passenger, actually. I think it was Elhared. I'm not entirely sure, since Lucille did not move her head from the wire-straight path she followed. The ground blurred by below us, the hills and forest passing by so quickly that it almost seemed the earth undulated with our passage.

It must have been close to midnight when she'd launched from the island of Fell Green, the moon high in the sky. It was still night when we reached the Northern Palace, the moon low on the horizon and the dawn still hours away.

She circled the building, high up, and saw the guardsmen rallying.

"Krys, I'm going to land outside of longbow range. Run up and announce us."

"Yes, Your Highness!" Krys's shouted response was nearly inaudible over the rushing wind.

Less than a handful of minutes after we'd landed, Krys had returned with most of the Lysean guard; Mary, along with Laya and Thea, who had successfully made it away from Lendowyn Castle after our abrupt departure. Grace was evidently still hobbled by the injuries she had received during the banquet.

Krys had obviously filled them in, but it was clear they didn't know exactly what to make of Lucille.

"It *is* you?" Laya said nervously as she approached Lucille's crimson form.

"Who else would I be?"

Laya looked back at the Northern Palace nervously.

"There have been a lot of dragon attacks," Mary said.

"Sebastian is still attacking villages?"

"Who's Sebastian?"

Lucille explained and got more of the story from Mary.

Sebastian had been a busy dragon. He'd been torching farms and villages in a widening arc across Lendowyn's northern border and beyond. Places had been attacked three kingdoms away. It was obvious he was doing his best to incite as many nations against Lendowyn as he could.

"It's to the point that rumor has taken over," Mary said.

"Meaning?"

"It's impossible that one dragon could accomplish *all* the attacks we're hearing about. Three farms leveled at all points of the compass within a single day? Someone's making this stuff up."

It turned out that the Northern Palace was a garrison now, fortified with a hundred extra troops that Lendowyn couldn't afford. The only reason that no one had tried to shoot Lucille out of the sky was because none of the dragon attacks had so far focused on Lendowyn, and King Alfred had standing orders *not* to summarily attack the dragon that, as far as he knew, could still be his daughter.

Oh . . .

Lucille?

I never thought of . . . Letting Father think I was still the dragon, what if someone got killed because he ordered them not to attack?

No one has.

Yet. That we know of.

We'll stop Sebastian before it comes to that.

Yes. She didn't sound convinced.

Other news was predictable, but not reassuring. King Alfred was angry and conscripting every able-bodied man in the kingdom. Rumors of an anti-Lendowyn alliance had already reached the Northern Palace. And everyone seemed to realize that something was not quite right with the fae. No mortal had seen an elf for days, anywhere.

"We don't have any time," Lucille told them. **"We need to go after Sebastian immediately. We may have less than a day. Did you bring *Dracheslayer*?"**

"And the Tear of Nâtlac!" Thea said enthusiastically.

Oh great, I thought unenthusiastically.

"Back at the palace," Laya said.

"Fetch the sword. We'll head out at dawn."

Elhared looked up at Lucille. "Your Highness? What exactly is your plan here?"

"We take the dragon and return him to the elf-king, and hope that's enough for him to call off a war."

"Uh-huh. Do you have any specific ideas on how you're going to do this?"

"We have the sword and our own dragon. We'll bring him back."

Elhared nodded. "I thought not. You expect to coerce an unwilling dragon?"

"If necessary, we will kill him!" Lucile snapped. Everyone but Elhared stepped back from her.

"Might I make a suggestion?" I recognized the glint in his eye, and I didn't much like it.

Don't trust him, I thought at Lucille.

I know, Lucille thought back at me.

"What?"

"If I heard correctly, you have a Tear of Nâtlac?"

I didn't like where this was going. Using that artifact the last time ended in a disaster nearly as severe as the one we were embroiled in right now.

"So?"

"Your task would be considerably easier if Sebastian was easily restrained and the dragon had a more willing disposition."

"What are you suggesting?"

"The spells that placed you in Sebastian's skin, and returned him to it. They can swap him with a more . . . *cooperative* identity."

"You can do that without your spellbook, or that scroll?"

"Not usually. But with the Tear of Nâtlac as a focus, it would be trivial. That jewel is nothing but a solid manifestation of the same magics, distilled to their purest essence."

"Exchange Sebastian for an ally?"

"And return him when the elves have their dragon again."

I did *not* like the way Elhared smiled when he said that.

*   *   *

As the girls took our two guests back to the palace to equip for the trek into the mountains, I mentally yelled at Lucille, *You can't be thinking of going along with Elhared?*

Frank, he's right. We're on a deadline.

She spread her wings and lifted off to fly in the direction of the palace. *You can't trust him.*

Of course not. But I remember that dragon—even with Dracheslayer backing me up, I want every advantage available.

I don't feel good using Nâtlac's little trinket for anything. Not after last time.

She swooped around the top of the palace. The few guards gave us a salute as we passed. Better than an arrow in the eye, I guess.

You won't be using it.

But that kind of magical "gift" always has unintended—

I felt a queasy half-familiar sensation in Lucille's gut. *Our* gut. From the corner of our eye I saw that the moon was completely below the horizon. Everything fell into place as I had an instantaneous flash of perfect understanding.

"LAND!"

My panicked mental scream carried with such force that the word left Lucille's mouth in a small burst of sulfurous fire.

What?

Land now! Land now! Landnowlandnowlandnow . . .

We were too high up, way too high, and I could feel the cramps in our stomach radiating out to every part of our body. Lucille's flight became less controlled and we started tumbling down.

This wasn't going to be good.

I should have realized the risk much earlier, but I'd been distracted by Elhared's presence. Lothan had promised us each our own body, and he was, among other things, the patron of transformation. The potion he had provided was imbibed by moonlight, and the moon had been over our heads until this moment.

The *full* moon.

The Wizard Crumley had said that having dual personas in a single body would result in some sort of merging of our identities—except in certain cases of lycanthropy.

Lothan had an unfortunate sense of humor.

The potion hadn't turned us into a dragon. It had turned us into a *were*-dragon. Though not the solution I would have chosen, I probably would have admired its twisted elegance if the realization—and the transformation—hadn't hit me midflight.

Lucille did her best to retain some control over our flight as our body painfully shrank and twisted. Before our wings shrank to nothing, she managed to angle our decent away from a plummet straight down, toward the walls of the palace. As the massive window into the banquet hall rushed toward us, I noticed it had been boarded over since our departure.

Lucille closed our eyes.

We slammed into the boards midway into our transformation. That was probably for the best. The bone-breaking pain of impact was pretty much lost within the pain that already racked our body during the transition from dragon to princess. We still had mass and momentum on our side, so the boards gave way.

For a moment we tumbled in midair through the banquet hall. The sensation was almost as surreal as feeling our long neck withdraw into our torso, or our talons slide back into our shrinking fingers and toes.

Our back struck the flagstones and we bounced and rolled. I don't know how much of the boneless flopping of our limbs was from impact damage, or from the long bones breaking and reknitting as our body shrank from giant lizard to shorter-than-average princess.

We came to rest on our side against the far wall of the banquet hall.

I groaned.

I-It wore off. I heard the dragon's voice in my head, low and shaky.

"No," I muttered, amazed that my jaw still worked. During our descent it felt as if it had been broken—shattered, really—a dozen times from the impact with wood and stone. I reached up slowly and touched our face, half expecting to feel a squishy slab of bloody meat. Instead I felt the familiar contour of Lucille's face, skin and bones unbroken. "It didn't 'wear off.'"

But . . .

"The moon set." I pushed myself to a sitting position against the cold stone wall and blinked our eyes open.

The moon, what does that . . . She trailed off, because she wasn't stupid and had all the same information I did. *Oh. This complicates things.*

I got to my feet a little unsteadily. Part of that was due to the lingering strangeness I felt in limbs that my brain

felt should be little more than ragged stumps after the
punishment they'd just taken. The remainder of my
clumsiness was due to the fact that I could not take my
eyes off of the devastation.

An effort had been made to return the great hall to
some semblance of order. Our arrival had undone most
of that. The great window was again open to the night.
What planks hadn't exploded inward to shower debris
on the hall were dangling, barely attached to the edges
of the window. A trail of blood and splintered wood led
from a point about ten feet in from the window all the
way to where I stood. I hadn't felt it at the time, but four
long banquet tables had been broken or knocked aside
by our entrance.

Next to me I heard a familiar, tentative voice ask,
"Your Highness?"

I turned to face the voice, realizing that I was clothed
only in a sticky sheen of blood and adhering wood splinters. That didn't stop me from running forward and hugging as much of Brock as I could get my arms around.
"You're alive!" I shouted.

He grunted and said, "Brock still hurts."

I backed off and looked up at him.

He was obviously badly injured, his left arm wrapped
to the shoulder, and half his head and chest swathed in
bandages, but color had returned to the visible parts of
his skin.

Then I realized that, aside from the bandages and a
sheet hastily tied around his middle, he wasn't clothed
any better than I was.

This is awkward.

"Shouldn't you be in bed?" I asked him.

"Brock heard attack, and screams, and . . ." The sword he had held clumsily in his right hand clattered to the flagstone floor, and the exposed skin of his massive chest, neck, and face deepened its shade from healthy, to ruddy, to a half shade short of spontaneous combustion.

Then, showing more speed and dexterity than he had ever shown in combat, he tore off the sheet wrapped around his middle and wrapped it around my shoulders. Then it was my turn to flush.

Oh my, the dragon whispered in my skull before I had the presence of mind to turn away from the suddenly naked barbarian.

"What happened?" Brock asked.

"Unanticipated emergency landing."

"Brock doesn't understand."

"Brock is probably happier that way."

"Are you hurt?"

"No, I'm fine." Despite all the blood, and the way my recent memory ached with broken bones, it was the truth. I had—we had—come through the whole episode apparently unscathed. I glanced over my shoulder at Brock, keeping my gaze focused above his chest. "But you're still hurt. You should go back to bed and heal."

"Brock *is* healed," he protested. But now that the excitement had ended, I saw him sag, leaning against the wall. Other guardsmen ran up behind him now, and despite shaking his head in protest he didn't object when I told a couple of the newcomers to escort him back to his sickbed.

One bright spot, at least.

I still want to take apart that dragon.

Sebastian.

And not just for the elf-king.

I watched the reaction of the remaining two guards. They looked at the wreckage in the hall, and back at me covered in Brock's sheet.

"Gentlemen," I addressed them. "I am going to return to my chambers now and clean up. Can you have the able-bodied members of my personal guard assemble in the courtyard in an hour, along with our two guests?"

I didn't wait for their response before walking back to my rooms.

You were right.

About what?

About Elhared. We're going to need all the help we can get.

CHAPTER 25

My royal chambers were just as we had left them.

Once the door shut behind us, I let the sheet drop to the floor and retreated to the alcove with the water basin and began washing the blood and splinters off of us.

Were-dragon? Lucille thought as I washed off.

And apparently with the change we switch who's in charge.

At least we can communicate now.

I'm sorry. I should have seen that coming.

I was there, too. I should have, too.

I rinsed the cloth in the basin of now rust-colored water. *I guess this hasn't been the greatest anniversary.* I lifted my leg and began wiping it off. I had a brief flash of memory from shortly after I had first awakened in Lucille's body. That first night, after the immediate needs of survival had been met I had been so tentative dealing with the realities of cleaning myself.

Why was I thinking of that now?

It's not your fault.

My hand slowed on my thigh, and I realized that I was thinking about the past, because I was feeling that past right now. I felt, again, as if I was an embarrassed voyeur, looking at and touching things I had no right to.

I closed my eyes.

Lucille, it is my fault.

No.

Yes. Maybe not before I found Sebastian in Elhared's body. But after that—

You didn't know.

I should have. Even if I didn't, it was a mistake to abandon him.

Stop blaming yourself.

I know what I did. What I should have done.

Then you get to share.

What?

Who stole the dragon's body in the first place?

You didn't steal—

No? After you found Sebastian in Elhared's body? I have the same hindsight as you—and unlike you I had completely selfish motives not to see what we should have done.

That's not your fault.

As much mine as yours.

She had me there. I sighed and opened my eyes to resume cleaning off my leg. I looked at the curve of my own thigh and felt my face burn.

What's the matter, Frank?

What *was* the matter? I'd lived in this body for a year. That was long enough to get used to its existence. Even if it bore the shapes and curves that one-time thief Frank Blackthorne would have found very distracting back in his male heyday, repeated exposure had leached all the titillation from inhabiting it. I had thought those impulses had faded.

Apparently not, nor had the uneasy discomfort that they caused me.

F-Frank?

I realized that she felt what I did now. She could feel the flush of my skin, and the way parts of us became uncomfortably warm. And that realization made everything much warmer. I shuddered and closed my eyes again. *I'm sorry. I didn't mean—*

Does this always happen when you wash my—

No!

Frank?

Just—I—

What?

Because you're here, watching.

. . . oh.

I stood there, my breathing shallow, unable to think of anything but the touch of the wet cloth on my naked thigh and Lucille, right now, feeling every touch and tremor in my body.

Are you embarrassed?

Yes . . . no. I don't know.

Why are your eyes closed?

It's just too weird right now.

I heard the dragon chuckle in my head.

It's not funny!

Why worry about weird now? Open your eyes.

I blinked and stared at my hand and my thigh. The flush on my cheeks burned.

I've seen that leg a lot more than you ever have. Why are you so nervous?

I . . . I couldn't give her an answer.

Come on, Frank. Something different had leaked into her voice. Her dragon's voice had always been low and husky, but something smoothed it out now, turning it to dark velvet. *You have no reason to be nervous with me.*

I k-know.

But you still are.

I sighed and nodded. I put the cloth back into the basin and stared at the water.

I'm a lowborn thief. I've managed to screw up every responsibility I've ever been given. I've lost track of how many times I've hurt you. Our "marriage" is a political fiction that exists only to keep you in the royal family and provide Lendowyn a tourist attraction. There is no possible way you should want me the way I want you.

You forgot that you're an idiot.

What?

Look up.

I did as she asked, and faced the mirror above the basin. The naked princess Lucille stared back at me. I noticed the red eyes.

Had I been crying?

Is that why, when we were both human, you did nothing about it?

How could I? I'd betrayed you, and started a war—

And if you hadn't?

What? I was thinking that a lot.

If there hadn't been a coup, a war, or all those other excuses? If we had just both been human, for that moment?

Wha—

Her sigh interrupted my thought.

Step back.

I did and more of Lucille's nakedness appeared in the mirror. I bit my lower lip, and something in me had distanced from us enough to find the lost, pensive expression very attractive.

That was confusing.

I'm going to tell you a fantasy I have.

Uh . . .

And you're going to help me.

Lucille's fantasy involved me being a dragon, and that's all I'm going to say about that.

While my own armor rested on the floor of an elven arena, the princess of Lendowyn happened to have a half-dozen members of the only warrior order of the Goddess Lysea as her handmaidens. Grace was about my size. I had her fetched to my rooms.

She still hobbled on a crutch as she came in. She looked me up and down. I was free of blood and dressed in a clean chemise. "Your Highness?"

"Frank," I said.

She nodded. "I've heard that we have the Dragon Prince back?"

"More Dragon Princess now, I think?"

Grace arched an eyebrow.

"Complicated," I said.

"Where *is* Lucille?" she asked. "There was a commotion—"

"She's here," I said.

"Where?"

"Complicated, remember?"

Frank, just tell her.

I sighed. "And she thinks I'm being too coy with you."

"I don't understand."

I nodded. "Let's go to the armory and I can confuse you more along the way."

"Were-dragon?" Grace said incredulously as she wrapped her leather breastplate across my chest. I had to suck in my breath and hold it, since while Grace and I were well-matched in height and length of limb, I had inherited a body that, in at least two particulars, was far more developed than Grace's.

"Yes," I gasped.

"Then why not just wait until nightfall to confront the dragon?" Grace stepped back and admired her handiwork constraining me. "So you'd be more evenly matched."

"No time," I said. "The sand has almost run out of Timoras's pendant."

"But if you rely on that wizard . . ."

"It's a risk," I agreed.

"Risk?" Grace snapped. "I've heard the story enough. It's his fault all this happened in the first place."

"I know. But he's what we have."

What are you thinking about? Lucille asked as Grace accompanied us down to the courtyard.

What aren't I thinking? Our time's almost run out and we still have to reach this dragon without our fastest method of transportation. I'm worried about what happened with Sir Forsythe. I'm worried about what will happen with

Elhared. I grunted as we descended the steps. *And I think our boobs are being crushed.*

I think we'll make it.

Based on what?

We've made it this far. I have faith in you. In us.

We descended a few more flights. And I came to a decision.

Lucille?

What?

I regret things. I second-guess myself. It's what I do. I know you think some of that is self-pitying nonsense—

Some?

But there is one stupid decision that I will regret to my grave. It was my choice, it was wrong, and I am sorry.

What choice? I think I heard a note of worry in her dragon's voice.

When we were both human, alone facing each other in the woods . . . I didn't kiss you.

Frank? Her voice sounded very small and far away.

I should have kissed you, embraced you, and told you how much you meant to me.

After a long moment, she answered. *Agreed. That was a stupid decision.*

I'm sorry.

You say that a lot.

I know.

Well, do something about it.

I almost tripped on the stairs down to the courtyard.

Do something about it?

It wasn't as if I could kiss and embrace myself right now. Besides, we'd already passed that level of intimacy before we'd called Grace to our room. I wouldn't say our marriage had been officially consummated, and in this body I was still technically a virgin, but I'd say we'd come as close as was practicable.

Only took us a year.

We walked across the courtyard, to the cluster of people waiting for us. The red dawn light reflected off my handmaids' armor. Krys had collected mounts for all of us, replacing the horses she'd traded back in Fell Green. She gazed into the elf-king's pendant as we approached, then looked up in surprise, "Princess . . . Lucille?"

"Frank," I said.

Elhared snorted.

Laya asked, "Where is Lucille?"

It was too much to go into again. "She'll be along later. How much time do we have?"

Krys shook her head. "It's almost gone."

I spun back to Elhared. "You can show us to Sebastian's home turf?"

"I can lead you to the area. If you have *Dracheslayer*, its glow will lead you the rest of the way."

I looked across at Laya, who held the magic dragon-slaying sword in its scabbard up so I could take it. I began reaching for it when a voice in my head said, *Were-dragon, remember?*

Even as Lucille reminded me of that, I realized that I felt an unearthly heat radiating from the direction of the sword. A heat no one else here seemed able to sense.

Yeah, anti-dragon enchantments wielded by a were-dragon? That idea couldn't be any worse if the blade was pure silver and packed in wolfsbane . . . or was there something called dragonsbane? That was a question for Brock.

"Ah," I said, "give that to Krys. You're better with the ranged weapons anyway."

"Your Highness." She complied with an arched eyebrow.

"What about him?" Krys nodded toward Robin the half-elf.

I sighed and shook my head. "After the last time I left some royal bastard behind me in my travels, things did not turn out so well. He's coming with us."

CHAPTER 26

"Has there been any word from Sir Forsythe?" I asked Laya, as we made our way deeper into the mountains.

We rode next to each other, behind Krys and Elhared who were leading the way. She shook her head. "He disappeared after the dragon, and that was the last anyone's heard of him."

Do you think he's . . .

What else would stop him?

There were plenty of stories about lone knights going off to slay dragons. But the reality generally did not bode well for the knight. My experience with dragon-slaying had only gone as well as it had because it had all been a scam in the first place.

The thought left a sick feeling in my stomach.

Sir Forsythe and I had not gotten off on the right foot to begin with, and I'd become convinced the man was a complete nut. But over time, I'd grown to understand him, and appreciate exactly *why* he was insane. There was a deep pain in the man, and a loyalty to rival Brock.

If Sebastian the Dragon had killed him, I was going to make him pay.

Actually Lucille would make him pay, because if Sir

Forsythe couldn't take on the beast, Princess Frank wasn't going to have much of a chance.

Elhared led us up into a mountain pass that was just big enough to ride two horses abreast. I slowed my horse until I rode next to Robin Longfellow. "What's your game?"

"My game?"

"Why are you here?"

"Didn't I tell you that I desire to make the life of my dear Uncle Timoras more difficult? Or was that your better half?"

"That can't be all of it?"

"That is not enough?"

I cocked my head at him. "You're answering all my questions with another question."

"Then, Your Highness, perhaps you're asking the wrong questions."

His statement relieved me more than it should have. "What is the right question?"

"That one might do for a start," he said. "But here's another. How did a scroll possessed by Sebastian, prisoner of my dear uncle, end up in the hands of the late prince?"

"I would assume, as part of his plot to escape, Sebastian must have given it to the prince."

"That is, of course, the least complicated answer. But that leads to another question, doesn't it?

"Which is?"

"What compelled Prince Daemonlas to actually use that scroll?"

He has a point.

"So what did?"

Robin shrugged and said, "Now *there* you have a question."

Yes, we do.

You talked a lot about elf politics with Robin earlier, any clues there?

You weren't paying attention?

There were other things going on.

Well, you can guess why the Summer Queen was on-stage with the king, right?

Mother and Father I presume?

Summer and Winter have always been at odds. The prince was all they shared between them.

So they both want war?

Maybe not the same one . . .

What do you mean?

The ultimatum was from the king, just the king. He is looking for a way to back out.

I got the idea. *But he can't. It's a choice between war with us, or with the queen.* I might not be an elf, but I knew what every other male monarch would have decided given that scenario.

And the "one responsible" is to appease her and her followers.

And she knows that. Elhared's right. The queen is angry enough that she was going to kill him, not because of any actual "responsibility," it was just to cut off that avenue, for us and Timoras.

She has some anger at the mortal world that has existed long before the prince's death.

As I said before, about knowing the noble mind: the

disaster we'd suffered at the banquet would likely just serve as a pretext for some campaign that had already been planned. To be honest, I couldn't be too unhappy that I hadn't been quite cynical enough to imagine Prince Daemonlas's own mother thinking of his death in those terms.

But why was she so at odds with the mortal world that she seemed more interested in prosecuting a war than identifying the true responsibility behind her son's death?

Had the Elf-King Timoras been *restraining* the queen until now?

It made me wonder how strained things were between the king and queen of elfdom. From what little I knew, I imagined things were not terribly warm between them at the best of times. I mean, separate bedrooms was the norm among monarchs, most all such marriages being political in nature. But separate kingdoms? That was a whole other level.

And thinking about their marriage made me suddenly think about an odd detail of my last dealing with the elf-king, before the current mess.

In my deal to free Lucille from the elves, I had bargained with a ring I had stolen from the Nâtlac-worshipping Queen Fiona of Grünwald. And for all that the elf-king wanted it, Queen Fiona had not seemed too concerned about keeping it. *That* ring anyway.

According to the late Queen Fiona, it had been an *engagement* ring.

She had never specified *whose* engagement. None of the potential options seemed to bode well for the relationship between the king and queen of the elves.

It seemed unlikely that King Timoras would pledge himself to Queen Fiona. He already had one queen he seemed to have difficulty with. It also didn't seem likely that he'd hand his queen's ring out as a token to a mistress. That seemed spectacularly ill-advised no matter how difficult the relationship between him and the Summer Queen had become.

Though well-planned acts rarely conclude with having a thief steal back your engagement ring . . .

But who said it was the king's engagement ring?

What if it was someone else's?

Robin had said something that made me think, what if—

"Look out!" yelled Thea, her words rising to a painful shriek.

I snapped out of my thoughts just long enough to see a large shadow pass over us, then Laya tackled me out of the saddle.

"What the—"

Dragon!

We landed painfully on my back and I saw what had cast the shadow across us. A massive ceiling of black-scaled muscle blotted out the sky, close enough to touch. Close enough that if Laya hadn't tackled me, I probably would have been in reach of tooth or claw, if a wall of dragon didn't just collide with me.

Our horses, being sane creatures, screamed, bucked, and ran. Thea pressed herself against the wall of the pass as the panicked animals galloped a hand's-breadth past her. The horses showed no concern for Elhared's and Krys's mounts. They stampeded Elhared's animal as it reared and the wizard tumbled off. Krys barely had control of her horse as the small stampede passed her.

I glanced behind us, and watched the dragon continue to swoop by, above the small pass that trapped us. Robin had been thrown or had jumped from the saddle. He crouched on the floor of the pass, staring up at the dragon. Rabbit had somehow retained control of her mount and leaned forward, hugging its neck as the flying lizard passed overhead. As I watched, the dragon's tail whipped by Rabbit's head, striking the rock wall of the pass, and knocking a shower of gravel down on her.

"Everyone all right?" Krys yelled as she got her spinning mount under control, barely avoiding trampling the downed Elhared.

Everyone yelled back, except Elhared who only managed a weak groan as he rolled to a sitting position with his back to the stone wall of the pass.

I pushed Laya off me and got to my feet. Krys drew *Dracheslayer* and yelled, "Get over here! The blade protects against dragon fire, but only for about ten feet or so."

We all started running toward Krys's side, but the shadow swooped down on us again.

Why hasn't he blasted us already?

That is what you're worrying about?

This is the perfect trap, a confined trench in the stone, limited visibility—

A horse's scream interrupted me. I looked back and saw Rabbit's mount galloping away, riderless as a dragon lifted up and away. That wasn't the most troubling thing. Even seeing Rabbit grasped in a set of dragon's talons being carried up into the sky wasn't the most troubling thing.

The most troubling thing was the fact that the dragon that carried her away had scales colored a deep cobalt blue.

Oh crap!

"There's more than one dragon!" I yelled as I sprinted toward Krys.

At this point my warning was redundant. While Krys faced the blue-scaled lizard that had taken Rabbit, a green-scaled forearm reached down from the sky behind her and caught her completely off-guard. The new dragon darted back up, its wings creating a downdraft so powerful it blew Thea back into my arms. It was all I could do to stay upright.

I saw the black blade of *Dracheslayer* tumble from the sky, its glowing red runes carving a spiraling arc in the air as it fell.

I was mesmerized by dread for a moment, and then Laya pushed us out of the way right before the sword tip gouged a shower of red sparks out of the stone where I'd been standing holding Thea. The sky was now nothing but a chaotic swirl of scales and wings, talons and teeth. That sword was our only defense, so I dove to grab it.

Frank, no!

Yeah, bad idea.

I knew that, but I had a full head of panic, at least three dragons descending on us, and I wore gloves . . .

AAAAAAAAAAAAAAAA!

The leather under my gauntlets was nowhere near thick enough. I grabbed the hilt of *Dracheslayer* and it was as if I'd grabbed a branding iron from the wrong end. In the brief moment I touched the sword, my gauntlets smoked, and every muscle in my body twisted in agony. I didn't let go nearly quick enough, and I landed on my back with no memory of falling. It felt as if my consciousness tumbled into a deep well. Even Lucille's screams of pain seemed to recede into the distance.

Aaaaaaaaaaaaa ...

Through a dim tunnel I saw a hazy circle of reality. In it, I saw Laya's face screaming something at me. Then she started floating upward.

Or was I falling?

Or rising?

I rolled to my side, or someone rolled me, and all I saw was sky.

Then nothing.

CHAPTER 27

I dreamed again.

I stood in the depths of King Timoras's throne room, surrounded by walls of crystalline ice, facing a giant mirror. I stood alone on the frozen floor, fine drifts of snow blowing across my feet as I stared into a reflection that showed not only me, but Elhared, and behind us, two dragons locked in battle, one red, one black.

Lucille and Sebastian.

A frost-coated scepter swung around and smashed the mirror.

I spun to face the attacker and the Elf-King Timoras shook the scepter in my face. "You think you can challenge me?"

I took a step back. The light in Timoras's eyes was not quite right. "I don't think—"

"You don't think, do you?" He swung the scepter and I ducked the blow. "Do you see the big picture yet?"

"I don't know what you're talking about."

"Why would you?" He sneered and swung again. I ducked as the scepter—which at this distance seemed more like a foofy mace—took out a chunk of wall with a cloud of frost and a shower of ice chips. "Why would you ever ponder the consequences of your actions?"

I held up my hands in what I hoped was a mollifying gesture. "Look, I know I've made a few mistakes."

That seemed to infuriate the king. "You think you are the only person here guilty of error? Could you be more arrogant?"

He swung again, and this time I wasn't able to duck in time and the icy weight of the scepter crunched against the side of my skull.

I opened my eyes to a painfully cold blue sky and groaned.

The pain in my skull was genuine.

Frank? You're awake?

Yeah.

Good! What the hell were you thinking?!

I winced. *Ack. Think quieter!*

I rubbed my temples and I heard Krys's voice call out, "Frank? Are you all right?"

"Yeah," I grumbled and pushed myself upright. I winced again, because my hands still hurt from where they had gripped *Dracheslayer*.

Wind whipped by me and I looked out at the peaks that had been our destination. I watched the horizon as the winds tore clouds across the distant mountain. It wasn't quite as distant as it had been before.

Why aren't we dead?

Again, that's what you decide to worry about?

I'm sorry I went for the sword, I panicked.

Yeah.

"Hey, watch your step." Krys grabbed my arm.

"What?" I responded. Then I looked down.

And down.

And down.

I felt my stomach try to beat its way up my throat so it could run away from the scene. My foot was a half step from a drop down a sheer cliff. The wall below was worse than vertical, the cliff undercutting where I stood enough that I seemed to stand on a stone island floating a thousand feet above a pile of gravel.

Then I realized that the gravel I saw was made of boulders the size of small houses. I backpedaled quickly into Krys's arms.

"Where?" I gasped, staring at the small area of stone by my feet to calm the vertigo.

"The dragons dropped us all on these ledges."

"Ledges?" I blinked and forced myself to look around.

The cliff that descended below where I'd stood continued up almost as far. Krys and I stood on a flat outcrop that jutted out about ten paces or so from a sheer wall of stone. It wasn't the only such shelf of rock. I saw dozens, all various sizes, randomly dotting the cliffside.

I saw Rabbit wave to us from a small jutting wedge of rock about sixty feet away and another thirty feet up the cliff. As I watched Laya and Thea emerged from behind her and waved. They all appeared unharmed. I looked over to the other side of our ledge, and about a dozen feet from us in the other direction, a small ledge held Elhared sitting alone on a rock about ten foot square.

"Hey!" I called out, waving.

"Don't bother," Krys said. "He hasn't moved or responded to anyone."

Some help he turned out to be.

You can say that again.

"My Liege!" called a familiar voice from behind us.

I spun around. "Sir Forsythe!"

He's alive!

"You're alive!" Before I thought about what I was doing, I ran up and hugged him.

He stiffened a bit and said, "Yes, Your Highness, indeed I am."

I let him go and looked him up and down. He was still immaculate, his long blond hair shining in the painfully cold sunlight. "How did you get here?"

"From there." He gestured up the cliff. Above us, maybe another hundred feet up, there was another ledge.

"You climbed down from . . ."

"I have been lulling the monsters into a false sense of security, awaiting my chance to strike."

I heard Lucille's derisive snort in my head.

Now now.

"I don't think anyone would expect you to take on multiple dragons all by yourself."

"Of course not," Sir Forsythe said. "That would be suicidal."

I wondered if some spark of sanity might have ignited in Sir Forsythe's brain.

"Of course," he continued, "one must attack them one at a time."

A spark that flickered and died a lonely death. "Of course," I answered.

"But now that they have taken you, Your Highness,

our first priority is escape. I've scouted the rock face and our best path—"

"No," I said, surprised at how the sudden command reached my voice.

Sir Forsythe stepped back, nonplussed. "Your Highness?"

"Escape is not the problem." I glanced at the sky and saw the sun lower in the sky than I expected. "By nightfall that problem should sort itself out."

"Then we stand and fight!" Sir Forsythe said with way too much enthusiasm. "Say that you brought us *Dracheslayer.*"

I sighed.

I think I'm glad he's on our side.

"No, the sword is on the floor of a mountain pass somewhere down there." I gestured back over the edge of our stone shelf.

Sir Forsythe's excited smile turned to a grim line as he drew a dagger from his belt. "Then we will make do with what we have."

"We're not fighting our way out of this."

"It will be glorious."

"No glory," I said. "Diplomacy."

"Diplomacy?"

Diplomacy?

"We're all still alive," I said. "That means there's a chance we can reach some sort of accommodation."

You think you can talk us out of this?

I've done it in worse situations.

Well, you have until moonrise.

I know.

Sir Forsythe sheathed his blade and gave me a small bow. "As always, I am at your service."

I patted him on the arm, "I know."

Thinking about broken mirrors, I began to have a glimmer of a plan. "Where's Robin?"

"Robin?" Sir Forsythe asked.

"I don't know," Krys said.

"Crap," I whispered. Of course if I was right about him, he could be long gone by now, and who would blame him?

Frank? Are you improvising?

No, I have a plan.

Care to share?

Once I figure out—

"Looking for me?" A voice came out of the shadows near the cliff wall. Sir Forsythe spun with a start, hand going to the dagger at his belt. Robin Longfellow stepped out of an impossibly narrow shadow. At some point he had replaced his hat.

"My Liege." Sir Forsythe interposed himself. "This man was not here before—"

"It's okay," I said. "He's a friend." I leaned over so I could look at Robin past the tall bulk of Sir Forsythe. "Isn't he?"

"Would I be here otherwise?"

The way he said that reminded me uncomfortably of my nightmare about the elf-king. I supposed there was a family resemblance.

"So what you said about freely walking between this world and the elves', you can do that anywhere?"

"Every spot in the mortal world touches upon the fae

world somewhere. It's all a matter of understanding where you want to go."

Just as I'd hoped. Better than I hoped.

"So you can lead people out of here?"

"Mortals? They must meet me halfway by taking the preparations you—"

I spun around and called up to Rabbit. "Do you still have the shaman's flower?"

She nodded and gave me a thumbs-up.

We could do this.

"You three, take some!" I called up to them. "Then have Laya toss down a package!"

The distance had me worried. I could have had our teleporting half-elf go up and get it, but I felt the press of time. There was no telling when the dragon—dragons—would return for us. When Robin left for those two, I wanted him to have company.

In a few moments I saw Laya back up, then run forward. She had rigged her belt into a sling, and she swung it up and forward with a snap, sending a small bundle tumbling into the air. It arced up and started falling toward us. Krys ran up as the package bounced off the cliff wall about ten feet above her and perilously close to the near edge of our ledge.

She plucked it out of the air before it tumbled back out over the thousand-foot drop.

Okay. What's the plan after we escape?

We're not escaping, Lucille. They are.

You better explain that.

Just listen as I tell Robin what I want him to do.

*   *   *

To her credit, Lucille didn't start calling me insane until I told Robin what to do after leading Sir Forsythe to where *Dracheslayer* had fallen, and the girls back to Lendowyn Castle.

That can't possibly—

Events prevented me from elaborating on our dearth of options. I heard Laya yell, somewhat slow and distant, "They're coming back!"

I glanced back and saw a trio of large shadows cross the front of the mountain. Looking up, the three dragons were just dots in a cloudless blue sky.

Oh crap.

"Move now!" I called as I turned back. Robin had anticipated me. He was already gone. Krys and Sir Forsythe held hands and looked past me with somewhat dazed and unfocused expressions. Krys reached toward me, and her hand shimmered and passed right through my body. I saw her eyes widen as she took a step toward me and vanished.

I spun around to look at the ledge where Laya, Thea, and Rabbit had been, and they were already gone.

I didn't realize I'd been holding my breath until I exhaled in relief.

I looked to the other side, and saw Elhared standing on his ledge, the odd man out, along with me and Lucille.

I followed Elhared's gaze with my own and watched the dragon trio descend. In a few moments Sebastian would be here and all four of us would be together for the first time since that cave over a year ago.

Princess. Thief. Dragon. Wizard.

I lifted the elf-king's pendant and gazed into the tiny hourglass. As I watched, the final few grains of sand started to tumble from one side to the other.

You better be right about this.

I know.

CHAPTER 28

A trio of dragons descended from the sky, the familiar blocky black form of Sebastian, flanked by two smaller companions, the left one green, the right one cobalt blue. As they closed on our section of the cliff, I could see Sebastian's blocky head swing back and forth. I saw Sebastian's eyes widen at what he saw.

Actually, I suppose, what he didn't see: the missing prisoners.

He looks angry.

Yeah.

Sebastian the Dragon bellowed. Even from a hundred feet away, I felt the hot brimstone wind from his breath and the sound was enough to knock me back on my heels. The sound was filled with roars and painful screeches and I initially thought it was an expression of inarticulate rage. But then his companions screeched in kind, and I realized that I was listening to dragons' native speech.

It was the kind of language that would have made an idle comment about the weather sound like a battle cry from the depths of all the Seven Hells. I leave it to the imagination what actual anger sounded like.

After a midair brain-melting exchange consisting of

syllables sounding as if they'd been manufactured by the torture of molten granite, Sebastian's two companions flew away. The green one flew up, over the top of the cliff. The blue one flew down, to follow the cliff's base.

Looking for escapees?

That'd be my guess.

Remind me why we're not one of them?

Remember the plan.

I had to stumble back all the way to the cliff wall, as Sebastian chose my ledge to make his landing. The downdraft from his massive wings pressed me against the stone. Then a wall of black scales and muscle blotted out the sky, the distant mountain, and every other thing in the world.

Sebastian landed offset to my right, toward the ledge where Rabbit and Laya had been. He lowered his massive head, snaking his neck in front of me to look at me from my left, blocking my view of Elhared.

"Hello, Francis."

I hate it when people use that name.

How long is it until nightfall?

Diplomacy, remember?

It took a moment to find my voice. "Hello, Sebastian."

"And how was your year?"

I opened my mouth, then I closed it.

"You transformed from a useless, lowly thief into a noble hero."

"That's not quite—"

Sebastian slammed a scaled hand down in front of me, the taloned fingers just missing me, peppering my legs with gravel as they dug into the stone at my feet.

"You stole my life!" Sebastian screamed into my face with marrow-boiling rage. **"Abandoned me to the tender mercies of the elf-king!"**

"I don't think—"

"You don't think?" He lifted his massive head and screamed into the heavens in a jet of crimson fire. My skin burned from the proximity, and I felt dozens of pin-prick burns from the resulting shower of ash blowing from the superheated rock above.

Diplomacy, he said.

Bad timing, Lucille.

"Can we talk about this?" I don't think I could have made Lucille's voice sound more like a little girl.

"Talk?" Another belch of flame came perilously close, and I think the dragon was laughing at me. **"Talk then, Francis. Explain yourself."**

"I'm sorry about the elves. Really. I should have done that different. But I was concentrating on Lucille . . ."

"Of course."

"I had more leverage than I realized. I didn't think I could get more than I did."

Sebastian shook his head. **"No."** He raised a taloned finger from near my feet and tapped the point of it on my chest hard enough to push me back against the stone wall. **"You knew exactly what you had. You chose to leave me bound there. You *chose.*"**

I nodded. "Okay, I chose. I've been known for bad decisions. But there are other things going on now. The elf-king is going to war as we speak."

"Should I care?"

"Your debt—"

The talon fell from my chest and Sebastian laughed at the sky.

"—is funny?"

"The debt was the service of this body, Francis. You absolved that debt to free your dear Lucille. There are no liens on me now, nor will there be."

"I see . . ."

"Do you?" He withdrew his head and leaned back on his haunches so he towered above me. **"Why did you and your entourage come to my domain?"**

I straightened up, now that I wasn't being backed into the wall. "Do you have any idea how many people you killed and injured at my banquet? In the villages you and your companions have attacked? In the war that might result?"

"I am a dragon. What else do you expect? Death, mayhem, screams of terror, that's what we do."

"And you didn't expect anyone to come after you?"

"Oh, the knight was expected. You? You're here for different reasons."

I nodded. "I'm trying to prevent—"

"I know what you're trying to prevent. Again, why should I care? I have no love for you and yours, and even less for the arrogant posturing of Timoras. I will have them *all* burn."

I stared up at him, gaping.

"You think this was all unplanned? If the knight had not saved me the trouble, I would have ended the prince myself once he served his purpose."

"Why?"

"To see the elves fall. To see Lendowyn fall under the weight of its arrogance. To see all my enemies burn."

"So you wouldn't consider surrendering to Timoras to avoid a pointless war?"

"Still trying to avoid the consequences of your own decisions, Francis?"

I shook my head. "This is your doing now."

"You inspired me. And I wasn't the only one."

"What?"

"You think you and Timoras destroyed just one life with your deal? You think I was the only . . ."

A voice interrupted us. "Are you just going to babble on forever?"

Sebastian snorted a cloud of steam and turned to look in Elhared's direction. The wizard stood impatiently on the ledge, staring at both of us.

"I was enjoying our chat."

"Yes, I know, but if you want this done, it should be quick. Before moonrise, and before the escapees return with reinforcements."

"My harem will find them."

"Across trails in the fae realms? I think not."

"Want what done?" I asked. They ignored me.

"Did you get it?" Elhared asked the dragon.

"Yes, yes." Sebastian jumped backward with a powerful rush of air from his wings. He flew sideways just enough to face the ledge with Elhared. He extended a taloned fist toward the wizard, not the one that had struck grooves in the stone by my feet. He uncurled his fingers, and in the huge palm rested a small carved box.

I recognized it.

That's the Tear of Nâtlac!

Yeah.

What do they want with that?

Elhared retrieved the box and opened it. His wrinkled face turned up in a cadaverous grin.

"Please tell me you're still going with our plan," I whispered to Elhared.

You were right about not trusting him.

That doesn't make me feel any better.

The dragon retreated from Elhared's ledge, flew past us, and landed on the far side above us, where Laya and Rabbit had been. Gravel rustled down the cliff as his talons gripped the stone ledge.

"What do you think you're doing?"

Sebastian cocked his head, **"Watching you squirm."**

I spun around and called to Elhared. "You're still the royal wizard of Lendowyn, right?"

He ignored me. Instead he was using the tip of the jewel to scratch arcane runes in the stone of the ledge.

"You owe us something for getting you away from Timoras!"

Elhared kept working.

"You have an annoying habit of not expounding on your diabolical plans when you have everyone at a disadvantage!"

"Allow me."

I spun around and looked up at Sebastian. He should have been too far away to loom over us, but somehow his size made up for it.

"You see, after I got myself free—thanks to you,

despite your best efforts—I simply planned to destroy you. Simple. Flaying, gutting . . . maybe let you watch your kingdom burn and your friends die first."

Thanks to me? What does he mean by—

You were going to negotiate with this monster?

Wait a minute. He said earlier, that my deal with Timoras destroyed more than one life.

How close is moonrise? You better be ready to strip that armor.

Queen Fiona.

I'm going to burn that smug expression off his ugly face.

That used to be your face.

I have a prettier one now.

Sebastian continued, oblivious to my own internal dialogue. **"But Elhared's back. That means we can finally fix the original plan."**

"The original plan?"

"The one you disrupted, in a cave, a year ago."

"But you said . . . Your debt was cleared when I freed Lucille."

"Yes."

"Why go on with this then?"

"That was only part of it." Sebastian stroked his scaly torso. **"After all, it was inevitable that the odds would shift in my favor. But he offered more for my body than a canceled debt."**

"What?"

"You were never supposed to be the princess, Francis, and I was never supposed to be the wizard."

Oh crap.

What?

Now I see what Elhared's doing.

I stepped toward the center of the ledge and kicked around, my boot scuffing the stone.

"It should have been Elhared and I who married a year ago."

Oh . . . that just sounds . . . weird.

We're in no position to criticize.

I'm still burning his face off.

My foot found a good-size rock.

"Control of one kingdom would have been the step to much greater things. And thanks to you, we can pick up where we left off, and I get to keep my body this time."

I grabbed the rock and hurled it toward Elhared. It arced up and sailed toward his ledge, falling down into the gap between the ledges, bouncing off the cliff on its journey a thousand feet down.

"We don't even need a ceremony. By Lendowyn law, this body is already the prince."

"Elhared! You bastard! You were already planning this back at the palace!" I grabbed another rock and threw. This one barely made it two-thirds the distance.

I spun back to look at Sebastian. "What's the point? The elves are going to raze the kingdom. If not them, there's the dozen other kingdoms, duchies, and principalities that you've incited to war against Lendowyn! They've probably already begun. There'll be nothing left to rule!"

"But the Dragon Prince and his harem will swoop

down to save the day. Immolating elves and any other invaders. Meanwhile, Timoras's army will attack other kingdoms, destroying them as he destroys himself. Our Lendowyn will survive to absorb what pieces remain."

In my head Lucille's words burned with brimstone and frustration. *Where's the moon? My moon should be here by now!*

I hurled another rock, and it fell far short. It was obvious at this point that I did not have the upper body strength to reprise the last time I'd disrupted Elhared's spellcasting.

Okay, were-dragon, right?

Right?

I drew a dagger from my belt, shook off my left gauntlet, and slashed myself across the palm.

Ahhhh! That hurt! What are you doing?

The blade's not silver.

As I watched, the lips of the wound in my hand sealed themselves shut, leaving just a smear of blood behind. I started backing away from Elhared's ledge.

Sebastian echoed Lucille's words. **"What are you doing?"**

Incongruously I realized that Sebastian and Lucille now seemed to have distinct voices.

Frank?

We survived that impact into the palace.

Oh no, you're not—

Got to stop him, right? Before moonrise.

I unbuckled the straps of our armor as I backed away. I dropped the leather to lighten my load, to the relief of

our boobs. I reached the end of the ledge farthest from
Elhared, then I sprinted right toward him.

This is insane!

Got a better plan?

I was fast. My legs had much more strength than my
upper body. I was under no illusions of my chances in
clearing the distance. But I figured I could get close
enough for the dagger to count. As for after . . .

Like I said, we had survived slamming into the palace.
This fall was about ten times greater, but the same prin-
ciple should hold.

I hoped.

I sprang up from the ledge, leaping with all the
strength my legs could muster. I lined up my aim and, at
the top of my arc, I let fly with the dagger. It sailed true,
right toward the wizard's head.

I glanced down at the thousand feet of nothing below
my feet.

YOUR PLANS ARE STUPID! Lucille screamed in
my head as we began falling.

A huge, scaly black hand plucked us out of the air with
a neck-straining jerk. It pulled us back from the drop and
up onto our ledge, suspending us over the space between
our ledge and Elhared's.

I was deeply disappointed when I saw the wizard
standing there, blotting a bloody cheek with the sleeve
of his robe. "Sebastian, you dolt! After what happened
last time, you didn't restrain her while I worked?"

"I wasn't expecting her to jump."

"Just hold her."

"If you—" I started to say.

"Hold her, cover her mouth, and make damn sure her arms aren't free to throw anything else." He pressed his sleeve to his cheek and winced, muttering, "At least this time I wasn't in the middle of the spell."

He wasn't? Lucille thought at me as the dragon's massive fingers covered our face and arms. Then Sebastian brought up his other hand and wrapped it around us as well. Held so tightly, the only parts of our body I could move were our eyebrows and the toe of our left boot.

Elhared sighed and resumed scratching runes into the stone.

I guess he's writing down the spell, not casting it.

Maybe you caused him to misspell something.

I can hope.

"**I'm sorry about—**" Sebastian began saying.

"Please. Just be quiet until I'm done here."

I heard a massive sigh rumble behind us.

That was a stupid risk.

I know. But I think I ran out of smart risks.

Like stalling them till moonrise?

I have to work with what we have.

What about the others?

If Elhared pulls this off, it might be better if those plans don't work out. I'd been planning on reinforcements, but if Elhared was in the princess's body, I didn't want to think about how many complications that would cause, especially if he and Sebastian planned to impersonate me and Lucille.

And one thing made the potential so much worse: were-dragon.

Elhared in a dragon's body, even temporarily, was a thought to give anyone pause.

Maybe he'll take so long the moon will come up.

Yeah. That's a good thought.

But too soon, Elhared stopped writing and began chanting.

CHAPTER 29

Elhared chanted words that were not designed for a human throat. The incantations that drifted from his position on the ledge sounded as if some demonic imp with a lisp had attempted to gargle with hot coals while being repeatedly kneed in the groin: strangled, high-pitched, and as painful as a cinder in the eye. I couldn't move this time so I could do nothing but watch the wizard and hope for something to go wrong.

He held up the jewel on its chain, and stared at it as he chanted. By his feet the runes he had scratched in the stone began to glow. They pulsed red in time to the kind-of-words he spoke to the Tear of Nâtlac. The glow intensified as all the light around him, and around us, seemed to darken. It wasn't just the setting sun. Something in what Elhared was doing, calling on the Dark Lord's magic, using the jewel, prompting the fiery glow from the twisted runes around him, it banished more healthy light. The darkness crept into the world, pushing away everything but Elhared, the jewel, and the glowing runes.

I felt the presence of the Dark Lord Nâtlac. I felt it as a thousand tiny insects crawling across my skin. I felt it in a thousand tiny splinters biting the flesh of my eyes, carving painful sigils that echoed the glowing alien script.

I felt it as needles in my ears, and a feeling that I breathed air filled with broken glass.

Frank! It hurts! It hurts . . .

I couldn't move, but I felt a rushing sensation, as if I flew away at great speed. My eyes involuntarily focused on the gem dangling from Elhared's hand. In it I saw the burning sigils reflected, twisted, inverted in a million different facets as it became the whole of my field of vision, then the whole of my universe.

"Oh crap!"

I no longer felt Sebastian's grip holding me. I could talk, and move, for all the good it did me. I floated in space, Nâtlac's hellish script reflected and refracted through an infinite number of facets surrounding me.

"Lucille!"

I no longer heard her voice.

I looked down and I could see myself; my old self, my original, long-dead self. I no longer wore the body of a virgin princess. My heart sank as I knew—not guessed, *knew*—that I no longer inhabited that body.

I could feel Nâtlac's laughter like a knife slicing into my soul. A knife coated with acid, salt, and children's screams.

I was back in Nâtlac's realm, bodiless. I knew it by how the heavy warm air carried the smell of decay, and how the omnipresent red light never carried far enough to illuminate a wall or ceiling. Through the sigil reflections I could see pillars, and below a plain made from living cobblestones, cobblestones that stared, that screamed, that wriggled tongues and fingers at me.

And I understood.

The gem, the Tear of Nâtlac, was created, according to legend, by a soul escaping from Nâtlac's grasp. This one in particular had apparently been formed in the wake of my own escape from the Dark Lord's clutches. The gem had properties, when worn, to swap souls between two bodies.

Again, legend had it that death would end such a transfer.

But legend was somewhat vague as to how.

"Oh you bastard!" I shouted into the ruddy darkness. "You unholy evil bucket of ogre spit!"

This gem wasn't a gift, or a reward. It was a trap.

This thing had been sitting around waiting for me to die, just so it could suck up my soul like a goblin shucking an oyster. Even if I never used it, I suspected—no, again I *knew*—the moment that something other than the gem itself separated my soul from my body, I would have ended up here.

I didn't think I had much chance negotiating with the Dark Lord this time. I didn't have another Queen Fiona to negotiate with.

I felt despair descend over me, a fatal realization that it was over.

Wasn't it?

Something itched in the back of my brain, and it wasn't just the ambiance of the Dark Lord's domain.

He'd never been shy about terrorizing me every time I set foot anywhere near his realm. Why wasn't he already facing me, expounding upon my eternal doom? It seemed like something he'd do.

Why was I still floating between the reflected sigils of

Elhared's spell? What exactly was the droning rumble that seemed to slowly oscillate as the alien runes dimmed and brightened? It wasn't the unnerving insect-like buzzing I associated with this place.

It reminded me of the elves, partly frozen around us, but not really frozen. They'd just been moving very slowly.

Because time ran differently there.

Time ran differently *here.*

Under the hill time seemed so slow, minutes there could be hours or days in the realm of mortals.

Here, where the Dark Lord dwelled—wherever the gods dwelled, in fact—hours could be mere seconds in the mortal realm.

It *wasn't* over. Elhared still chanted. That was the drone I heard. It was why I still saw the flickering sigils of his spell. The spell was still proceeding. I floated somewhere between the mortal realm on that mountainside, and the realm of the Dark Lord. I still had a chance to do something.

Yeah, just like when I was trapped in Lucille's skull.

Even if I had another dagger, or a broken sword hilt, I didn't have anywhere to throw it. Elhared's rumbling chant was everywhere around me. I also wore my old body, and the real physical body of Frank Blackthorne was buried and rotted to bones by now.

I remembered the dream I had, Elhared—or the Dragon Sebastian-as-Elhared—digging up my skull, Frank Blackthorne's skull.

"The gang's all here."

Yes, they were.

"Digging up a wedding present."

Not an anniversary present, a *wedding* present. The gem, the Tear of Nâtlac, had been a "wedding" present from the Dark Lord.

Why was I thinking of this?

"I don't think this is going to work," as he tosses me the skull, "I think it's broken."

Why does that seem relevant?

My dreams had seemed odd for a while, at least the vivid ones. More like visions. The one about Timoras and the shattered mirror had inspired my plans with Robin, our half-elven camp follower. Not just to lead my people to escape the mountainside, and not just to lead Sir Forsythe to *Dracheslayer*.

When I had made my deal with Timoras for Lucille's freedom, I had also extracted a promise from Timoras. A promise and a mirror.

I think I had understood that dream.

Could the dream about faux-Elhared digging up my skull, could that have been about this? The "wedding present" that would not work? Because I was dead? Because Elhared was dead?

Because we both were?

The idea clicked in my mind as the consequence of a series of unsupported and tenuous assumptions that had solidified in my mind as unambiguous fact. Either I had tapped into a stream of deeper understanding, or I had just declared the world of the Dark Lord my home and as my first step in making myself comfortable, I had gone insane.

But if I was right that the Tear of Nâtlac was a trap for

souls that had escaped the Dark Lord's clutches, then it had to be as much a trap for Elhared as it was for me — more so, since Elhared had been unquestionably deceased, dead, and gone, absent from the mortal coil for over a year. As far as I could tell, my own person never counted as actually dead, or if so, my current trapped situation was as close as I'd come.

So if I'd shown up here — in this faceted prison wrapped by the burning sigils of Elhared's spell — then it was only a matter of time before —

Several things happened.

The rumble of Elhared's slow-motion chanting ceased.

The reflection of the burning runes all around me flared red, obscuring the details of the disturbing alien lines until all was just a flat red glow.

All except a white crack that formed between some of the facets just ahead of me.

The white expanded, pushing the glowing red facets aside until it seemed the mouth of a tunnel.

A shadow, human-size, floated in the tunnel drifting toward me and picking up speed.

I had nothing to push against, as if I floated in an endless ocean that buoyed me but gave no purchase with which to swim. I spread my arms. Despite the knowledge that the body I wore wasn't physical, I hoped that it might still act as if it was a physical body in a physical world. I prayed to every god aside from the Dark Lord Nâtlac that the newcomer's path would intersect the point where I floated.

The newcomer kept accelerating, as if he fell toward me from a great height. His body language began showing the distress from falling, flailing arms and legs, cloak flapping in winds I didn't feel. At the speed he fell, I only had a moment to read his expression. For only the briefest fraction of a second, he was close enough for me to see his face in detail.

I saw wide-eyed confusion.

I grabbed for his arm as he passed me. That pulled me backward, but also started us spinning around the point where I had grabbed him.

His back struck the faceted wall opposite the white tunnel. I let go of his arm and slammed both feet into his chest, springing off of his body—

Okay, *not* his body.

His *body* still stood on a mountain ledge back in the mortal world.

Where *I* was, my soul, cloaked in the form of the one and only original Frank Blackthorne, placed both booted feet into the apparent chest of Elhared's spirit hard enough to crack nonexistent ribs and send his undoubtedly spiritual form into a wall of nonphysical semiprecious stone only symbolically solid enough to stop his imaginary descent and break his nonliteral neck while I rebounded into the whiteness from which he'd come.

My last sight of him was as a tiny ragged form lit by a fading ruby light as I fell upward, away, into the light.

CHAPTER 30

I blinked my eyes and focused. I held up the Tear of Nât-lac at the end of its chain, suspended in front of my face. As I watched the gem flared red and faded to a dull black that reflected no light. A bit of foul smoke curled up from it.

My hand shook and the chain slid from my fingers, the dead black gem falling to my feet.

Elhared's feet.

I fell to my knees and felt old bones creak. I shook my head, unable to take my eyes off the horrible alien runes that the wizard had scratched into the stone. They no longer glowed, but the scorched stone still steamed slightly. I felt the throbbing disorientation and headache that always seemed to come after the transition of bodies.

Despite the sense I had taken the sacrament of the God of Hangovers, what sickened me and made me tremble was the sense of age, six or seven decades plowing into me in less than a second. I felt like Nâtlac's evil jewel, burned out and smoldering.

I stared several seconds at my wrinkled, bony fingers, and gathered what was left of my will.

Not completely unexpected.

There were still things that needed to be dealt with, and Sebastian was one of them.

I turned and saw the black dragon watching me with his head cocked. I was—Lucille was—wrapped in a double fist before him, feet dangling over the stone ledge.

You're smart, I thought at her, even if she couldn't hear me. *Follow my lead.*

"Elhared!" I yelled, even though it made my head throb. "What have you done?" I pointed an accusing finger at Sebastian's fists.

Lucille's mouth was covered, but I still heard something like muffled curses. Sebastian glanced down and uncurled one finger from in front of her face.

"Sebastian, you dolt! Put me down."

I held back a grin as I said, "You are going to pay for this, you misbegotten—"

"Elhared?" Sebastian said, glancing from Lucille, back toward me.

"Who else? What do you think the point of this exercise was?"

Sebastian set her down on the ledge before him. She gave a very masculine "harrumph!" and made a show of brushing dust off her chemise.

"So it worked?"

"Obviously! And it would have worked the first time if you had kept that annoying thief restrained."

The grin I held back vanished of its own accord. I watched her straighten up and look at the dragon next to her with thinly veiled contempt, and I wondered, what if Elhared's spell had worked? What if everything I had just experienced had been some sort of meaningless dream?

It had felt real at the time, but the longer I looked out Elhared's eyes, the less real it felt.

"So now I can kill him?"

"Why bother? He's irrelevant now."

"Irrelevant? After what he did? He deserves far more than—"

"Leave it. You're a prince now and we have a kingdom to take over."

"Leave it? You aren't sounding like Elhared."

"Priorities, Sebastian."

"Yes, yes." Sebastian the Dragon turned his head and lifted it so he looked almost straight down at her. My doubts about successfully defeating Elhared were fading, but it didn't make me feel any better to see Lucille's deception slipping. **"There are more important things than punishing the man who left me to rot with the elves."**

"Yes, we—"

"After all, that was only the whole point to giving that addled prince your scroll."

"But the bigger picture—"

"And you said he killed you."

"What's important now is—"

Sebastian swept his forearm back and swatted her toward the stone wall of the cliff. I saw her petite body rise up and slam into the stone with bone-breaking impact. She dropped to the ledge like a rag doll that had lost half its stuffing.

"You aren't Elhared."

Oh crap.

I fought the disorientation and sprang to my feet. As I did I felt like something literally jolted loose from my knee. "Wait! Sebastian! We still need her!" I tried to sound like the evil wizard I knew, but all I got was a sidelong glance from the dragon.

"Enough second chances," he grumbled through a roll of brimstone steam. **"I don't care if you're Elhared or the thief. You I finish next."**

"No!" I called out. "Stick to our plans!"

Sebastian didn't listen to me. He turned his head to face the fallen Lucille.

But she wasn't fallen anymore.

Sebastian did a double take when she wasn't where she had fallen. He swept his head around and finally caught sight of her. I squinted and saw her standing on the far end of the ledge, facing the dragon. She wiped blood from her lip with the back of her hand and spat at the ground. "You have to do better than that."

"How?"

The answer came to mind unbidden: *were-dragon.*

"You're pathetic," Lucille said to Sebastian.

"What?"

I think both Sebastian and I were equally stunned by Lucille's bravado. Yes, I'd berated an angry dragon before—but that was when the dragon was Lucille and I was pretty sure I wouldn't be roasted.

"You heard me," Lucille continued. "You have the gall to be angry when this was *all* your doing?"

"Francis Blackthorne—"

"—should have put you out of everyone's misery. You

indebted yourself to the elves, which was incalculably stupid to begin with. But instead of dealing with the consequences, you conspire with Elhared? An unstable wizard? Are you insane?"

"That had been a good plan." Sebastian actually sounded slightly cowed.

"It was an idiotic plan. You'd give up everything you are, all that power, and hide from the scary elves as a princess for the rest of your life? Married to *Elhared?"*

"He would have found me a new body afterward."

"And you believed that treacherous ass?"

Why was she taunting him like that? Did she want him to attack her? I saw an amber glow leak from between Sebastian's teeth, and his next words came in a cloud of steam. **"You're making me angry!"**

Lucille laughed. "The only thing making you angry is that I was ten times the dragon you ever were."

Sebastian reared and vomited a stream of flame.

"Lucille! No!" I screamed impotently from the ledge where I stood.

I watched the jet of flame tear through the air to saturate the half of the stone ledge where Lucille had been standing. I felt a blast of hot wind by my face, despite the distance. My heart sank. I couldn't see Lucille through the flames, but whatever capacity for healing Lothan's gift gave her, I couldn't imagine it would save her from being reduced to ash.

After ten or fifteen interminable seconds Sebastian stopped and the flames subsided, revealing nothing but cracked and blackened rock and the shimmer of heat in the air.

I called up to him, past caring. "She was right! I should have slit your throat when you wore this body!"

The dragon turned to face me. I could see steam and flickers of flames dancing around the edges of his mouth.

"Whatever the elves planned for you is too kind!"

"Big talk for someone so flammable."

"She *was* a better dragon than you. *I* was a better dragon than you."

"Nice try, but you aren't going to go as quickly. You, I'm going to make last."

From behind Sebastian, someone grunted. I saw the dragon's eyes widen as he turned his head back around. I ran to the side to see around the dragon's bulk, and yelled at what I saw.

"Lucille!"

"I said . . ." Lucille's voice was hoarse and raspy as she pulled herself up over the ledge. Even at this distance, I heard the skin sizzle as it touched the still-hot stone. She was nearly bald now, her blonde hair little more than sooty streaks across a blistered scalp—a scalp that healed and regained its normal color as I watched. ". . . you have to do better than that."

Lucille stood facing the dragon again. Her upper body had been burned, and badly. She didn't heal as quickly from that, but those wounds still faded as I watched. She stood now, her clothes charred rags, looking up at Sebastian with a scary smile.

"No. You can't . . . That's just not possible . . ."

It wasn't, I thought. But she hadn't borne the brunt of the dragon fire. She must have jumped and dangled from the ledge as Sebastian attacked.

"You're also a cad," she continued as if she hadn't been interrupted.

"W-What?" Sebastian's voice was filled with complete confusion now.

"Your 'harem'? Green and Blue fruitlessly searching for my friends right now? Do they know why you abandoned them?"

"I did not abandon—"

"You left them to become Elhared's princess."

Sebastian let loose with the fire again, but now I saw Lucille move. It took close to a second for Sebastian to aim, open his mouth, and let loose, but Lucille had been watching him, and seemed to know when the flame was coming before Sebastian did.

She rolled and dodged, and only got splashed by the edge of the fire. The dragon, in theory, could have swept the fire to follow her, but she had rolled right into a blind spot where Sebastian couldn't see her through his own flame.

I couldn't believe it.

No, actually, it made perfect sense. She had *been* this dragon. She knew what it was to belch fire, and what she could see when she did. Lucille had had over a year to grow familiar with how the dragon moved and reacted. In that same year I'd been doing what I could to train her old body so it was probably in better shape now than when I had first gotten it. The healing provided by Lothan's gift was an edge, but it might not have been the decisive one.

She dodged and tumbled away from the dragon's flame a couple more times, yelling taunts and insults to keep him focused.

She's stalling.

I looked at the deep purple sky. The moon should be here any moment. She was tiring him, making him use up his reserves of flame before she changed again. She was right. She made a much better dragon than he did.

Come on, I urged her. *You just keep it going for a little longer and then—*

I heard a horrible screech from above. I looked up and saw a giant green lizard diving out of the twilit sky.

CHAPTER 31

It all seemed to slow down as I watched.

The green dragon fell on the battle between Lucille and Sebastian. She opened her mouth to add her fire to Sebastian's.

Lucille saw her coming and dove underneath Sebastian, between his legs.

The entire ledge blossomed with fire.

As the green dragon cleared the top of the cliff above us, I saw a glint of metal and heard a cry.

Sir Forsythe.

The knight—*my* knight—leaped from the top of the cliff above us as the green dragon dove past his position. He arced into the air holding the black sword *Dracheslayer* in both hands, point aimed downward. The runes etched in its blade glowed like hot coals as he landed on the green dragon's neck. *Dracheslayer* plunged in, just behind the base of her skull before the dragon knew what hit her.

The green dragon slammed into Sebastian's ledge face-first, shattering the heat-weakened stone and continuing downward in a shower of gravel, leaving Sebastian perched on a rocky outcrop barely big enough to hold him.

At some point in the descent, Sir Forsythe had leaped aside and landed on the upper ledge where Rabbit and Laya had been. He still held *Dracheslayer*. He pointed the weapon at the black dragon.

"As I said to my liege, 'One at a time.'"

Sebastian howled in fury and sprayed fire up at Sir Forsythe. I wasn't worried much. Now that Sir Forsythe held the sword *Dracheslayer*, dragon fire could do nothing to harm him. Sebastian made a furious effort, producing a massive jet that splashed up toward the ledge Sir Forsythe stood upon. For the space of nearly a minute, Sebastian's flame turned night into day.

The fire subsided and Sir Forsythe stood astride his rock. Everywhere around him the cliffside was stained jet black with soot, except for a sharp circle centered on Sir Forsythe and *Dracheslayer* that remained free of any sign of damage.

"Now foul beast," Sir Forsythe said, "Prepare to face the wrath of—"

Sir Forsythe's words were cut off as a giant foot with blue scales and talons the length of my forearm scooped him off the ledge. *Dracheslayer* tumbled from the knight's hands as the other dragon lifted him off into the sky. I yelled something in frustration as the blade tumbled and struck the side of the mountain.

To my horror the glowing blade broke as it hit five hundred feet below. The halves of the blade flared red, then went dull as they tumbled the rest of the way to disappear into the cloud of dust that was just settling around the green dragon's body.

Sebastian howled. It was a sound to make my ears

bleed and tear the bowels free from my body. Gravel tumbled down the cliffside as his wail shook the stones loose. Looking up, I saw the beast spasming, muscles locking. He leaped upward, frantically beating his wings. As he lifted off the stone in a panic, I saw Lucille crouched between his legs, all her hair and clothes burned away, showing some wounds that were still struggling to heal.

Not *all* her clothes. I saw the end of her belt in her hands. The other end of the belt I couldn't see, but it rose with Sebastian. She held on to the belt, and her arms rose with it to give a final jerk, tightening it around something as it dangled from beneath Sebastian.

Sebastian's wail of pain rose so many octaves it became inaudible despite its volume.

I winced. Dragon or not, there are some places you never want a tourniquet.

Sebastian cried and tumbled in the air, tearing at himself with his talons so desperately that I winced again. He almost fell down next to the green dragon before he threw a broken strip of leather away so hard that it cracked like a whip. He wheezed as he beat his wings to bring him back up to Lucille's level.

"I. Will. Kill. You." He panted as he hung between the cliffside and the distant mountain.

Lucille stood on the broken shelf of rock, naked, unarmed, nowhere left to dodge. She stood straight and looked Sebastian in the eye. "No," she said with a silver glint in her own eye. "You won't."

Sebastian tried to immolate her, but his breath came out in a cough and little more than a roil of smoke. He had exhausted his flames.

"I can still crush you to a pulp!" he screamed as he dove at her.

Lucille smiled.

I realized that the mountain behind Sebastian was to our east, because the silver glint in Lucille's eye was a reflection from the bright sliver of moon peeking just over the mountain's shoulder.

If I didn't know what was coming, I would have thought Lucille had started to cower just before Sebastian's hand slammed her into the cliffside, pinning her with such force that the remaining ledge crumbled away.

But I knew that what I'd seen hadn't been her ducking her head and raising her arms.

Her back and shoulders had been growing.

Sebastian didn't notice—or just ignored—the second set of arm-like growths springing from her back, or the lengthening limbs and torso. In his fury he just forced his own head over hers and snapped his jaws shut.

Or tried to.

His jaws didn't close completely. His teeth bit into the flesh of Lucille's neck, flesh that was red, scaled, and rippling with muscle. That neck kept growing as her torso swelled, pushing Sebastian's hand away from the cliffside.

I stared in horrid fascination as the black dragon's monstrous jaws were slowly pushed apart by the growth of Lucille's own skull. Then a white-hot glow erupted inside Sebastian's mouth, so bright I saw the light through the skin of his cheeks. Flame shot through his nostrils and his head popped off of Lucille like a cork flying off of some overfermented wine. He fell off her, hand going to his face.

"My noth! My noth!"

Lucille pushed gracefully off the cliff, launching herself into the air almost as if she was swimming. As she
did, she spat out a leathery flap of flesh. **"Hurts when the
backwash hits the sinuses?"**

Sebastian shook his head. **"Thith ithn't happening!"**

She dove suddenly, striking quicker than I could follow. A blur, then she swam through the air on the other
side of the dragon and Sebastian bled from a half dozen
parallel slashes across his face and neck. He didn't seem
to notice. He flew upward, away from her, **"You're not
the printheth!"**

"I AM PRINCESS LUCILLE OF LENDOWYN!"
she screamed, in a fury that would make the Dark Lord
Nâtlac shy away. She looped, became a blur again,
streaking toward him. She slammed him into the cliff
above me, raking another series of gashes along his back.
He tried to push off, but Lucille fell on his back and her
head dove at his shoulders like a giant snake snapping at
a rat in a hole. In this case the rat was the joint where
Sebastian's right wing met his shoulder.

He screamed as her jaw clamped on the base of his
wing and twisted.

He tried to turn his head to bite at her, but he was too
slow and she sprang off into the air and his jaws clamped
on nothing. She spiraled around above us, looking down.

She was a magnificent sight, red and lithe and grace-
ful. Sebastian, for all his size, seemed pathetic now. One
broken wing draped itself, twitching, across his back. His
wounds bled freely, spilling down the cliff, some pooling
on my ledge now. One eye was swollen shut, and a third

of the teeth in those massive jaws were broken and missing.

Lucille called down, **"Frank?"**

I waved up at her and called out, "I'm fine!" The shout made me cough and wheeze. I wasn't fine. I was half past ancient. But if I had to choose between decrepit and dead, I wasn't going to choose dead.

Sebastian's skull turned toward me. **"Francith? You're Franthith now?"**

"Funny how things work out," I said.

"Why I thould—"

I held up a hand and pointed at the sky, "You really want my husb—my wife to keep killing you?"

He glanced up at the orbiting Lucille and stopped moving.

Serves you right, I thought.

I sucked in a breath and called up, "Do you see what happened to Sir Forsythe or that blue dragon?"

"No sign of them."

I was about to call her down to grab me so we could look for them. Sebastian wasn't going anywhere. My thought was interrupted by a sound on the ledge behind me.

I spun around to face the Elf-King Timoras bringing his hands together in slow and deliberate applause. "I will say, Francis Blackthorne, you are never *boring*."

CHAPTER 32

Timoras clapped, and I saw the half-elf Robin Longfellow leaning against the rock wall a few steps away.

"I wouldn't worry overmuch about your knight," Robin said with a cryptic half-smile.

I collected myself. This was the·plan. There was an incipient war to deal with, and I had told him to try to bring someone from the Winter Court back.

That he did.

I gave the elf-king a bow and said, "I prefer Frank, Your Majesty."

"And I can't tell if you've become more or less insolent." He folded his arms and cocked his head. "And I have a war to manage, so make your parley quick."

I pointed up at the cliff wall, at Sebastian. "You wanted the dragon? Take him."

"Oh thit, wait a—"

The elf-king waved a hand and the dragon froze in place. Even his blood stopped dripping. "Thank you. I will."

"So we can stop this war now?"

"You know what else I asked?"

I sighed.

"Since you did not give me what I asked—"

"You have the one responsible already!" I snapped.

"What?"

"I'll start with a question for you. Did it ever occur to you, or Queen Theora, that the prince was acting on his own initiative?"

"What do you mean by that?"

"Another question," I asked him. "You remember that ring I stole for you?"

"Yes? What does that have to do with—"

"Was that *your* engagement ring?"

"Of course not," he snapped. "It was . . ." He trailed off.

"Prince Daemonlas gave it to Queen Fiona, didn't he?"

The elf-king stared at me. From the corner of my eye I saw Robin smile slightly. *Yes, I remembered what you said about the prince and mortal women.*

"You didn't approve, did you?" I asked. "And when I say you, I mean you and your queen."

And when I said "you and your queen" I meant "your queen."

"The woman was a power-hungry harlot who cared for little but her own twisted needs. Besides, she was human. Ending that engagement is the one thing the queen and I have agreed on this past century."

And I was ready to bet it bore no small part in the queen's hostility to the mortal realm. "And let me guess, you couldn't just order him to break it off."

"That ring was an inviolate pledge as long as she wore it—"

"You couldn't grab it, but I could." I shook my head. "It didn't occur to you that this might just piss him off?"

"Why? The game is ever played thus. Agreements are followed to the letter, are they not?" I caught something in his eyes, regret maybe?

"Yeah. I get that's a big thing with the elves, especially elf royalty. Did you or the queen ever think that the poor sot fell in love with that evil bitch?"

"Explain." He cocked his head slightly, urging me to elaborate. I had the feeling that our audience might consist of more than Robin, Lucille, and the frozen Sebastian.

"Love," I said. "Pledging yourself heart and soul to another. Give them your life, the stars, the moon. Roses, sonnets, L-O-V-E, love!"

Timoras shook his head. "I honestly don't think that ever occurred to the queen."

And I bet she's watching right now.

"The prince himself is the one responsible," I said. "You had me steal that ring and break the engagement. Then you dropped me off right in front of Queen Fiona and her army so I'd end up killing her."

"I'm still unsure exactly how you managed to do that."

"Which means that the prince was more than a little annoyed with both of us. You connived to break his engagement *and* helped me to murder his beloved."

"Now I didn't plan for you to kill her, did I?"

"I think it made little difference to Prince Daemonlas. He wanted to embarrass you and the Winter Court, and he wanted to punish me. He was an easy target for Sebastian here," I waved up at the frozen dragon. "He had a scroll to reverse the spell that had swapped us all originally. If the prince cast that spell at the banquet, he'd loose Sebastian the dragon to do all manner of havoc—ignite a war between Lendowyn and everyone else, probably killing me in the process. I don't think the prince required much convincing to go along."

Timoras nodded slowly. I think I was making his own arguments to the unseen Queen Theora. Just like an elf, make sure you convince someone else to do all the heavy lifting for you, and have them thank you for the privilege.

I looked up at Sebastian. "Unfortunately, Prince Daemonlas was too blinded by anger and vengeance to see that Sebastian never intended him to survive."

Timoras followed my gaze. "So this creature plotted the death of my son?"

"And the war you're about to start."

"I see."

"So there you have both the dragon *and* the one responsible for your son's death. Just as you demanded."

The elf-king sighed and seemed to deflate. "Thank you for telling me this." Sill looking at the dragon he said, "We will find some suitable punishment."

The tone of his voice chilled me so much that I almost felt sorry for Sebastian. Then he clenched his fists, and the Dragon Sebastian disappeared.

"If there is nothing else, Frank Blackthorne, I will make my leave."

"So you'll call off the war," I asked with some measure of relief.

"Of course not." His voice sounded weary.

"What?"

"The agreement was the dragon, and the one responsible, *in the time allotted you.* You are too late." He turned and I knew if he took a step he'd disappear. I grabbed his shoulder.

"You *dare* touch me!?"

"There's another agreement you have to honor."

He slapped my hand from his shoulder. "I am done with you. There is no agreement." His hand went to his side as he began to draw his sword.

"The one you made for the ring I gave you."

His hand stopped.

"What do you speak of? That pledge is fulfilled."

"Not quite," I said.

"How do you mean?" His voice was low. I had his attention now.

Again I acted on a series of tenuous assumptions, but I didn't have much left. I thought of the shattered mirror from my dream. "You remember, when I left you with Lucille, you gave me a mirror?"

"Of course. A mirror you saw fit to break before ever using it."

Because you dropped me in the middle of an enemy army, I thought. *Magic hand mirrors are generally not battlefield equipment.* "Do you remember why you gave it to me?"

"Yes."

"To contact you—"

"Yes, yes, I know."

"Once I had gathered us all in one place—Me, Lucille, and Elhared."

"What is your point? To restore your body? It doesn't exist anymore . . ."

"If I returned to you with all the principals, you promised to set things back to my liking. We have myself." I gestured up to the orbiting red dragon. "Lucille." I reached down and picked up the blackened Tear of Nâtlac. "And here is what remains of the Wizard Elhared."

He almost shied away from the blackened gem. "You expect this to suffice?"

I hoped that our earlier assessment of Timoras's motives were correct. He didn't *want* this war, he just found it politically impossible to do otherwise. He gave his ultimatum looking for a way out; a way to keep the queen from having her pretext for war.

The original ultimatum might have played out, but I hoped that the elf-king would see the straw I held and see just enough left to grab.

"You bargained for that ring on the queen's behalf," I said. "Should she not be willing to abide by the terms you set for it?"

"You are dealing with me," he said. I notice the pointed absence of any denial of my assertion.

"I have performed in good faith my side of the agreement, can you do less?"

"And do what?" he snapped in annoyance. "Restore your body? As I said, there is no body."

"And 'set things back to my liking,'" I responded.

He froze for a moment, staring at me. Then a smile slowly broke across his face. He actually chuckled.

Then he laughed.

I sagged with relief.

"I assume," he said, "that it would be to your liking if this war did not happen."

"Yes, Your Majesty."

He clapped his hands and said, "Done! Never let it be said that the Winter Court shies from its obligations. The queen shall be displeased, but at least I have a dragon for her to vent her frustrations upon."

He turned and took a step out into empty air. He paused a moment, then looked back over his shoulder and said, "Thank you."

Then he vanished completely.

The Tear of Nâtlac, still dangling from my hand, had ceased smoking. A slight wind rose up and carried away flecks of ash from the now flat black surface. In less than a second, the entire thing had lost cohesion and disintegrated into a stream of black motes that floated away in the direction of the distant mountain.

I dropped the chain.

"You did it!"

I looked up and saw Princess Lucille the red were-dragon perched on the cliff above. I smiled and waved at her. "You beat up a dragon, I just negotiated a cease-fire."

"You're wonderful!"

"Ahh, isn't that in my job description? Princess, diplomacy, negotiation?" Raising my voice caused me to cough again.

"I don't think you're the princess anymore."

I nodded. "It's all good! I'm a guy again!" I looked down at myself, and it sank in just *what* guy I was. I leaned against the cliff wall next to Robin and sighed. I felt every year of Elhared's age in my joints.

I heard a sad note in Lucille's voice, dragon or not. **"I'm so sorry, Frank."**

I dismissed it with a wave and a shake of my head. "You know I'm into destructive self-pity, don't encourage me!"

"Oh, Frank."

I felt a hand on my shoulder, and I looked up to see Robin's too-pretty face. I wanted to slug him. "Are you all right?" he asked.

I blinked a few times because his face kept going out of focus. "Of course. Didn't you just see? Won the day!" I coughed and my voice came out in a hoarse whisper. "I just had to be separated from the woman—the dragon—crap, the *person* I love."

"What?"

"She's right here, Frank," he said.

"And I'm right here."

Lucille flew down to the end of the ledge holding me and Robin. **"What are you talking about?"**

"Lendowyn law," I choked out. "We're no longer married. Your marriage is to that—"

"What does that matter? We'll annul the marriage."

"Then what, marry me?"

"Of course."

"Look at me! I'm a wreck. I don't even have Elhared's magic to compensate for it!" The excitement was getting to me and I started wheezing. "He was probably only alive because of some sort of magic."

"**Stop it! I don't care about some stupid law. You're my wife!**"

"You deserve better."

"**I deserve you.**"

"Why?"

"**Because I love you!**"

"I love you, too. But that's beside the point." I staggered a little and slid against the cliff wall.

"**Gods, Frank, did you inherit Elhared's senility?**"

"No," I gasped and clutched at my chest. "But I think I inherited his heart."

"**Frank?**"

I slid down to the ground and Robin's face became even more blurred above me as I gasped for breath.

"**Frank!**" The dragon screamed, so far away.

I closed my eyes and the darkness chased the pain away.

CHAPTER 33

I stood in the banquet hall in the Northern Palace. The stained glass was intact and there was no sign of a dragon rampage or crash-landing princesses. So I gathered that it wasn't *really* the banquet hall.

I turned around and wasn't surprised to see Robin Longfellow.

"You're not really Timoras's nephew, are you?"

"Lies and disguise are sort of my thing."

"And you aren't speaking in questions?"

"What kind of disguise would it be if a simple conversation could trip me up?" He was King Alfred again.

"That wasn't what tripped you up."

"Oh? You saw through me?"

I nodded, walked across the Lendowyn king's throne room. The chest was right where we had left it. I closed the lid so I could sit down. My old bones ached. "I guessed, anyway. You disappeared from the inn just in time to appear to Dudley and his minions. You reappeared just as conveniently. Good thing I was right."

"How so?"

"Leading the escape, returning with Timoras. Asking that of you was a long shot—since I doubted a real estranged half-elf nephew would have returned with him.

And if you had walked under the hill to get him, you would have taken days or months. You had to be moving between the mortal realm and here." I waved a hand at the world around me, which had become a wooded glen again.

Lothan stood on a fallen log, again a large and very regal-looking fox. "So you planned for me?"

"I improvise with what I have."

"Do you now?"

"And those dreams were all you?"

"Who else?"

"Why?"

"Do you know what the classical definition of a 'hero' is?"

"I—"

The fox held up a paw and sighed. Robin lowered his hand and used his hat to brush the dust from a stone that had fallen from the abandoned temple that now stood next to us. He sat down in front of me. "Forgive me, I tend to fall into the question thing. Force of habit. What was I saying?"

He slapped himself with his hat and said, "Stop it!"

He took in a breath and the wood creaked as the ship beneath us crested a wave. Salt spray glistened on his hair, which was longer and grayer, contrasting with the eyepatch he wore now.

"See, Frank, you are a 'hero' now." I could hear the emphasis on the word. "The gods have touched you, chosen you, and have pretty much used you as their plaything. Me included."

"But—"

"No buts," he said, replacing a broad-brimmed hat on his frizzy red hair. He leaned conspiratorially over the campfire between us and whispered, barely audible over the chirping insects. "You're mortal. We're gods. You just have to deal with it."

"Why me?"

He laughed, breath fogging in the winter air. Ice crystals danced in the air between us, catching the sunlight. "Don't get maudlin. You've just been caught on the edges of a battle between Nâtlac and Lysea. It didn't begin with doomed elven love, and it won't end with your own happily ever after. Me? I just took a liking to you."

I opened my mouth and Lothan pointed across the table with a tankard of ale. "You're going to ask why. I'm the patron of thieves, deception, and transformation, don't you *dare* ask why."

I shut my mouth and glanced at the hearth. We sat inside The Headless Earl, and Lothan now looked the part of one of its scruffier denizens. "Following you about was just as much fun as I'd hoped."

"I'm glad I could amuse you."

The depth of my sincerity must have shown, because blacksmith Lothan set down his tongs, walked around the anvil, and said, "No self-pity, remember?"

"I said that to Lucille."

Lothan nodded. "So you did."

"What now?"

"You have a choice. Your story can end now and you pass on beyond to where all heroes eventually go."

"Die, you mean."

The gravedigger gave me a gap-toothed smile as he

leaned on his shovel. "Or you can offer me something in return for another boon."

"What do I have left to give?"

Ex-King Dudley twirled the ceremonial dagger in his fingers, casting complex shadows across the altar I sat on. "What does any god ever want?"

The realization hit me. And, of course, if Lothan granted me the boon I wanted, I'd be in a position to grant it.

I gave him a promise.

In response he touched my shoulder and I fell against the grass. When he looked down at me, it was with Lucille's face. I closed my eyes. "No, that's just creepy."

"But you must receive your boon." Lothan kissed me with Lucille's lips.

"Ahh!" I screamed, batting him away. God or not, some things are just too much. I sat up spitting. "Blagh. Ack!"

"Frank?"

I shook my head and blinked. Lucille knelt on the grass next to me, wearing only a too-loose chemise.

"No. That's going too far. Mortal or not! God or not!"

"Frank?" she repeated and grabbed my shoulders. "Are you all right?"

"No!" I spat again. "You make yourself into—then you—what . . ." I trailed off because Lucille stayed Lucille, and the grassy hillside remained the grassy hillside.

After a few long moments, I said, "Lucille?"

She looked at me as if she was going to repeat the question about Elhared's senility.

"Wait," I said. "Last I saw, you were a dragon."

She pointed up at the dawn sun.

"Were-dragon," we said simultaneously.

I rubbed my head. "I was unconscious?"

"All night long."

I nodded, and realized my hands were tangled in actual hair, not the wisps that covered Elhared's bald pate. I pulled my hands away and stared at them. They weren't old and wrinkled, they weren't dainty and feminine, and they were still familiar.

"I-I'm me?"

Lucille smiled, "You're you."

I sprang to my feet and spun around. "This is some sort of vision again. Where is he? Where's the Dark Lord?"

Lucille got to her feet next to me. "Frank—"

I spun to face her and jabbed a finger in her direction. "You're Lothan!" I furrowed my brow. "Or Lysea? You're mad I sent Evelyn packing?"

"It's really me, Frank."

"No. Look. You have hair!"

"I have . . ." Her fingers brushed her unbound blonde tresses. They were a frizzy mess shimmering in the early morning light. "Oh, it came back this morning. When I changed back."

"And where'd that chemise come from?"

She rolled her eyes. "I had to take it. Poor Sir Forsythe would have died of embarrassment otherwise."

"Sir Forsythe?"

"My Liege! You've awakened!"

I spun at the new speaker, and saw . . . Well, I guessed it was Sir Forsythe. I'd never seen him so . . . unkempt.

His long blond hair had not grown back, either on his head or his face. He was naked from the waist up, and it was hard to tell where the streaks of soot ended on his torso and where the bruises began. His breeches had been torn in several places, burned in others. One boot seemed to have split open and was being held together by an improvised leather strap.

He stood up from the midst of a pile of dirty, dented armor. He had a rag in one hand, and a gauntlet in the other. Half of the small armor piece was dull and soot-covered, the other half gleamed.

"How are you still alive?" I blurted. "I saw that dragon carry you off."

"I have slain many monsters, My Liege. It's what I do."

"I saw you lose *Dracheslayer*."

"Lulling the beast into overconfidence," he said.

I shook my head.

"Believe him," Lucille said. "He would have finished me off, too." There was a hint of amusement in her voice.

Sir Forsythe's gaze dropped and his skin reddened. "Mistaken identity," he said quietly. "I did not know Your Highness was yet *another* dragon."

"Fortunately we worked things out. You should have seen the poor man's face when the moon set."

"This isn't a dream," I whispered.

"Frank?"

I patted my face, and my body, then my hands together. "I haven't been pulled into some vision quest. This is real." My voice rose. "It is real." I ran up and grabbed Sir Forsythe by his considerable biceps. "You're real!"

"My Liege?"

I ran back and grabbed Lucille's hands. "You're real. That dirty chemise is real."

"Yes."

I shook my head, openmouthed. After a moment I said, "How?"

"You were there for most of it."

"No," I said, "How am I ..."

Lucille's eyes were shiny as she said. "I thought you died. I think you did."

"Died?"

"You said something about Elhared's heart and clutched your chest."

I nodded. "I remember that. Things went dark."

"You collapsed and stopped moving. Robin even closed your eyes. I may have gotten a little hysterical."

I think I was glad I missed that.

"But Robin said he owed you something. He picked up your body—I mean Elhared's body—and disappeared. I think I died a little myself, I screamed at the world from that cliff most of the night."

"That made Your Highness easy enough to find," Sir Forsythe interjected.

She nodded at the knight. "If it wasn't for him snapping me out of it, I might not have stopped."

I looked down at myself, and the hillside. "Then when ..."

"After that unfortunate confusion," Sir Forsythe said, "it was my duty to accompany Her Highness out of the mountains and back to her kingdom."

"At least until I can fly again." Lucille shrugged and

the neck of the oversize chemise slid off one shoulder. I reached up and put it back.

"Just make sure you land before dawn," I said.

"Robin returned with you an hour or so ago." She smiled and shook her head. "I'm afraid I did all my screaming and jumping and hugging while you were still unconscious."

"I feel cheated."

"I'll make it up to you." She threw her arms around me and squeezed.

I hugged her back.

"It was Lothan," she whispered in my ear.

"Yeah."

"He remade you like all those guards he made copies of me."

"God of transformation," I replied.

"Then," she whispered, "just tell me her name."

I froze for a minute, caught off-guard by the question. Then it struck me. After everything she had no assurance that I was actually me. There had been so much body hopping and transformation in our short time together, how could she be certain I was who I said I was?

"Rose," I whispered back to her.

She kissed me and we tumbled back on the grassy hillside. I kissed her back and we rolled, hugging each other so hard that it seemed as if we were trying to inhabit the same body again.

Eventually we came back up for air, her on top of me, head resting on my chest. I noted from the corner of my eye that Sir Forsythe had returned to deliberately polishing the remains of his armor.

"You're you," she said.

"And you're you."

She nodded. "That I am."

"Are you okay?"

She lifted her head and looked down at me. "What?"

"This," I patted my thigh. "It's what I wanted all along. I was never comfortable being the princess."

"You have no idea how happy I am for you, Frank."

"But this," I patted her thigh and she squirmed a little. "You were so much happier as a dragon."

"You're sweet."

"Can you even be the princess again?"

She smiled evilly. "Frank, now I'm the princess *and* the dragon."

"Were-dragon. You only get to be the dragon a few times—"

She silenced me by placing her finger on my lips. "I might only get to fly and breathe fire a few times a month now." She leaned forward to whisper into my ear. "But I'm *always* going to be the dragon."

"I love you," I told her.

"Took long enough for you to say it."

"That's not how you're supposed to respond."

"As if you didn't know I love you."

I'd like to say we arrived back to a heroes' welcome, but life doesn't work like that. Avoiding a catastrophic war is almost never as well regarded as winning one, or even surviving one.

What was uppermost in everyone's mind, including the king's, upon our return to Lendowyn Castle, had been the absolute debacle of the anniversary banquet. And, absent marauding elves, Sebastian's reign of terror was the act of war that was most pressing. Fortunately no one had organized an attack yet, so Lendowyn was able to bring to the negotiation table the heads of two of the three hostile dragons.

That placed those kingdoms attacked by Blue or Green in our debt, banquet catastrophe aside. Those new allies and Lendowyn's recent history of victories on the battlefield was enough to keep other potential threats from developing past the saber-rattling stage.

Ironically enough, Lendowyn's staunchest ally proved to be the new crown of Grünwald. As luck would have it, the fact they'd snubbed our ill-fated anniversary banquet meant that it was the one nearby kingdom Lendowyn retained cordial relations with.

Also, despite all the headaches Sebastian's flaming tantrum had caused, it was surprisingly difficult for Lucille to convince her father and his advisors to annul her marriage to him. Legally it wasn't really an issue; the marriage had obviously never been consummated. But even though King Alfred was maybe inappropriately happy that his daughter was actually his daughter again, the Dragon Prince had been a major financial draw for Lendowyn and it was hard for anyone relying on the state of Lendowyn's finances to admit he was really gone.

I was impressed Lucille got them to see sense without directly threatening anyone with bodily harm. But, after all, a were-dragon was almost as good, and the Dragon *Princess* was royal by blood rather than marriage, so that should count for something. Also the accountants were somewhat mollified when they realized that they wouldn't have to pay to have the rampant dragon removed from all the kingdom's heraldry just a year after it had been added.

She only had to resort to threats *after* the annulment, when she announced her intentions for a new marriage.

Our second marriage was to each other again, and this time she wore the dress.

Unlike the first one, this wasn't a political spectacle. King Alfred seemed to want to downplay the ceremony and save money. It was just Lucille and me, the girls, Sir Forsythe and Brock, the king, and a handful of courtiers I really couldn't care less about.

We exchanged vows, attended a banquet I barely remember, and I took her up to *our* bedchamber. That night had been pointedly planned for the quarter moon, so that we could share our wedding night here.

We hugged and kissed as *man* and wife, or as man and conveniently shaped were-dragon spouse, and she said, "I love you, Frank Blackthorne."

"I love you, Princess Dragon."

She giggled and kissed me again. Then she leaned to my ear and said, "Remember that fantasy where we both were dragons?"

I nodded, feeling my face blush.

"Well," she said, "I have *another* fantasy."

And that's all I'm going to say about that.

So what does any god want?

Well, if you ever visit Lendowyn Castle, you might happen to notice that the walls between the great hall, the throne room, and the kitchens do not quite meet, leaving a gap in between all of them, a void inaccessible from anywhere inside the castle itself, It was surprisingly simple to doctor the plans of the reconstruction to add what I wanted.

It was harder to divert the funds for the statues, tapestries, braziers, and other paraphernalia, but it was really only appropriate to use embezzled funds.

Lucille is the only other member of the royal court to realize I'd built a full-blown temple to Lothan in the center of Lendowyn Castle. Her response was to laugh and simply require that miscreants who brave the tunnel complex leading to Lothan's house remember where their loyalties lie.

Have I mentioned that I love my wife?

And should Lendowyn ever be threatened again, every resident cutpurse and brigand will stand to defend her, or face Lothan's displeasure.

Happily ever after?

To be honest, I don't know yet. I'm still really uncomfortable with all this nobility stuff. I'm not prince material. But as long as I have Lucille, I think I'll have the "happily" part taken care of.

But . . .

I now have *three* gods who have an unhealthy interest in me. There are at least a dozen kingdoms that are probably an insult away from open war. I have a father-in-law who tolerates me only because a few times a month his daughter can literally bite him in half. King-Dudley-in-exile is still out there somewhere, and very unhappy with me. And, as I've always said, things never go wrong the way I expect.

So the Thief and the Princess—and the Dragon— lived happily . . .

. . . *after* is another story.

S. Andrew Swann

THE MOREAU QUARTET: VOL. 1 978-0-7564-1125-1
(*Forests of the Night, Fearful Symmetries*)
"As vivid as a cinema blockbuster loaded with high-budget
special effects." —*New York Review of Science Fiction*

THE MOREAU QUARTET: VOL. 2 978-0-7564-1126-8
(*Emperors of the Twilight, Specters of the Dawn*)
"An engaging, entertaining thriller with an exotic cast of charac-
ters, in an unfortunately all too plausible repressed future."
—*Science Fiction Chronicle*

HOSTILE TAKEOVER omnibus   978-0-7564-0249-5
(*Profiteer, Partisan & Revolutionary*)
"This is good old-fashioned military SF, full of action, colorful
characters, and plenty of hardware." —*Locus*

**DRAGONS AND DWARVES: NOVELS OF THE
CLEVELAND PORTAL**   978-0-7564-0566-3
(*Dragons of the Cuyahoga & Dwarves of Whiskey Island*)
"Skillfully done light adventure with more than a dash of
humor."—*Science Fiction Chronicle*

BROKEN CRESCENT   978-0-7564-0214-3
"A fast-paced, entertaining tale of the boundary between magic
and science." —*Booklist*

To Order Call: 1-800-788-6262
www.dawbooks.com

DAW 123